To Julie,
Jan 4 -
2017

very good !!!

# SHADOWS AND IMAGES

MERIOL TREVOR

# SHADOWS
# AND
# IMAGES

A Novel

*With a Foreword by*
*Leonie Caldecott*

IGNATIUS PRESS   SAN FRANCISCO

Originally published by
David McKay Company, Inc., New York
© 1960 by Meriol Trevor

Cover painting by Stephen Dudro

Cover design by John Herreid

Published in 2012 by Ignatius Press, San Francisco
With permission of the Meriol Trevor Estate
Foreword © 2012 by Ignatius Press
ISBN 978-1-58617-602-0
Library of Congress catalogue number 2011930699
Printed in the United States of America ∞

# CONTENTS

# FOREWORD

Meriol Trevor was one of the most prolific Catholic writers of the twentieth century. She wrote more than thirty novels, both for adults and children, and several major biographies. Best known for her comprehensive biography of John Henry Newman published in the early 1960s, she also wrote about St. Philip Neri, Blessed Pope John XXIII and King James II, among others.

Born in 1919, of Welsh descent, Meriol was the daughter of an Indian army officer, and was educated at the Perse School in Cambridge and St. Hugh's College, Oxford, where she read Greats (classics and philosophy). During the second world war she worked first in a day-nursery (she loved children, although she herself never married) and then on the cargo-barges on the Grand Union Canal between London and Birmingham. After the war, she volunteered for relief work and was sent to the Abruzzo. As a young woman she had had some early inklings of religious experience, yet until this point Meriol's spiritual life had been conducted against an intellectual, humanistic background. 'I suppose it was the spirit of our time, which had me, a slave to unrecognised ideas, in thrall ... I thought I already loved God, when I had barely got to know his presence in the world.' Now, through the people of this remote area of Italy, she came into contact with a deeply rooted Catholic culture. Attending Mass one feast-day with another relief-worker, a local man, Meriol was struck by the packed church and the 'entirely natural way of praying'.

During this period, Meriol had an experience which she later described as 'the piercing of myself'. This, she said, 'broke through all the veils of ideas to the real creature.... As I had suffered before my nothingness as an intellectual creature, so now I had to suffer it as a human being: body and heart and soul.' Like John Henry Newman before her, Meriol brought back from Italy an altered point of view which would prove decisive in her life. 'Out of it I have come to Christ.... He has drawn me through my life in the world and brought me to the point where I can begin to live in his Kingdom', she wrote at the beginning of 1950, the year she was received into the Church, in Oxford.

The writings of the leading light of the Oxford Movement, whose life-story forged such a compelling path into the 'one fold of the Redeemer' in the previous century, supplied both intellectual and spiritual ballast to Meriol's conversion process. Under the guidance of Father Stephen Dessain of the Birmingham Oratory, she now set out to write her comprehensive two-volume biography of Newman, *The Pillar of the Cloud* (covering the years up to his reception into the Catholic Church in 1845) and *Light in Winter* (covering the second half of his life, as a Catholic and an Oratorian priest). Published in 1962, it was awarded the James Tait Black Memorial Prize for biography.

One of the fascinating things about Meriol Trevor's work is her ability to combine extensive historical research with a lively element of human interest. Her development as a novelist flowed naturally out of her more academic work. Her novels about Ancient Rome and Roman Britain make ample use of her understanding of classical civilisation. But her biography of Newman went much further, in terms of detail, since the detail was there to be had. It was based on a close reading of his correspondence, at that time unpublished, which was kept at the Birmingham Oratory.

*Shadows and Images*, the novel which sprang, almost as a byproduct, out of that work, was published in 1960, two years before the biography, and was Meriol's response to living in such close proximity with the 'voice' of her subject. Yet instead of writing it from Newman's point of view, she chose to trace his life through the eyes of a fictional character: a woman whose life providentially shadowed his, from the early days of the Oxford Movement, on to Rome and thence to Birmingham, in the throes of the social and economic upheavals that accompanied the full flowering of the Industrial Revolution in the late nineteenth century.

A feminine point of view, or in the children's novels a child's point of view, revolving around a male character who has to come into his own through trial and tribulation, is an abiding theme in Meriol Trevor's fiction. I had a number of conversations with her about the character who recurs again and again in her novels—the hero whose 'unhealing wound' marks him out as a type of Christ. Meriol was fascinated with the relationship between personal tribulation and the fabric of society. Particularly in her children's novels, she explored how men who were rejected, misunderstood or maligned by the powers that be—often from within their own families—prevailed through patience and forbearance. *The Letzenstein Chronicles*, *The Rose Round*, *The Sparrow Child* and, significantly, the novel set in the Abruzzo, *Four Odd Ones*, all contain portraits of men who transform the lives around them by allowing the 'wounds' of Christ to be manifested in their own lives. Their primary supporters are women and children.

If the more serious adult novels (Meriol did write some historical romances too, a la Georgette Heyer) are not quite so tightly plotted, it is because they take place on a wider panorama in which things are not so straightforward. *Shadows and Images*, like her novel about the Rome of St. Philip and the early Oratory, *The City and the World*, had of necessity to be as faithful to the historical facts as possible, since it centres on an historical figure about whom a great deal is known. For Newman's own part of the fictional dialogues, she used as much of his actual correspondence as she could. The device of having his 'journey' interwoven with the story of a fictional married couple may have robbed her of a neatly 'eucatastrophic' plot-line, but then Newman's life was, in point of fact, a century-long chain of trials followed by resolutions followed by more trials. He once said he loved saints who had to endure into old age, and his own life followed this pattern. The love between Clem and Augustine Firle provides a nuptial counterpart to the love-affair between Newman and his God, which like their love came into focus and bore fruit over a great many years. It is the portrait of changing views and perspectives which form a slow organic development, marked out, to use a Newmanian term, by true 'chronic vigour'.

Meriol Trevor was a profoundly Christian artist at a time that did not favour or understand her point of view. Her great achievement is to have incarnated, empathetically, the Christian mystery into lives with whom the reader is able to identify. She knew, as Newman had foreseen, that she was living through a time when Christian civilisation was breaking down all around her. She knew that her vision of life was not shared by most establishment literary figures—even though she herself was elected a fellow of the Royal Society for Literature in 1967—and had to endure her share of mockery and derision from her peers. But, as she told me towards the end of her life, that is what being a Christian is all about. Meriol is at her strongest as a writer when she is engaging with this theme. So as you embark on the delights of the world according to Meriol Trevor, and her greatest mentor, I leave you with her own words, from an interview given a decade or so before she died in January 2000—just as the new millennium dawned. Here she touches on the truth which, I suspect, is at the heart of why Pope Benedict beatified John Henry Newman a decade later.

'I think what interests me most is how Christianity works through disasters and defeats. It actually does much better in adversity than it does when people are comfortable and settled. It is in fact a religion to cope with defeat. Christ the innocent man, was judicially murdered. Yet he rose again and so his followers are able to cope with disaster and defeat. Or should be able to.'

Leonie Caldecott
Literary Executor for Meriol Trevor
September 3, 2011

# PREFACE

In 1950 when I made up my mind to be a Catholic, I had read no Catholic books; the first one I picked up was *The Development of Christian Doctrine*, which Newman wrote at Littlemore (where I am now living) in 1845 just before his reception [into the Church]. Perhaps it is worth saying I am here in one of the cottages he converted from stables, for a semi-monastic retreat, in 1842. It is now comfortably modernized. Newman slept on a straw palliasse; I do not. His room is as it was, with uneven red brick floor and small window. The tiny chapel has been restored. Many visitors have begun to come, from Europe and America.

I meditated writing on the Tractarians for several years; for I find that period very interesting, and Newman understood the deep issue between Christianity and sceptical materialism that is working out in our own day. Also he seems to me as a person psychologically closer to us now than to most of his contemporaries, perhaps because his own life was more in our pattern, of search, anxiety, continual adjustment and tension within and without, forced against fundamental realities.

Meriol Trevor
From Author's Note in 1960 Edition

# I

# TWO VIEWS

# Brighton: 1827

The December day seemed all the brighter because it was so short and cold. The sun gilded the narrow curls of the sea unfolding along the strand under his eye, because in the south of England the sun is not over the land looking out, but over the sea looking in.

The Reverend Samuel Burnet walked the Brighton promenade with his sister-in-law Mrs. Scarvell, listening, or appearing to listen, to her complaint of her only son's recent imprudent marriage; his daughter, Clem, who was just seventeen and always wished she had not been christened Clemency, walked a little behind them and tried not to listen, because she had heard it all so many times. Besides, Lucy Pierce had been an older girl at her school, and Clem had admired her, a tall slender creature with a Raphael face and hair parted in the middle, smooth and dark. Clem herself was very small and rather chubby; her round face, however, was too shrewd to look babyish, as she feared it did. Why did Mrs. Scarvell disapprove of beautiful Lucy? Just because her father was in business in London and her friends were the daughters of bankers and that kind of person. Aunt Scarvell, the eldest daughter of a Dean and the widow of an Honourable grandson of an Earl, was particular about such things. Clem suspected that she had not approved her sister's marriage to a poor country parson who was plainly never going to get preferment, but it was

3

impossible even for her to convey disapproval to Samuel Burnet, an eccentric whose own opinions so possessed his mind that he was entirely unaware of other people's. He had been much older than his bride, yet he survived her. Clem was an only, and a lonely, child, lonely because she was sociable by nature.

It was fun to come out of their distant Cornish home and see so many people; Clem's quick brown eyes were on the watch for every trick and gesture of the fashionable ladies she saw, not to copy them, simply to notice. The gentlemen too were highly interesting, but she had to be careful how she looked at them; it would be improper to catch their eyes at all. Coming towards her now were a group of three girls and their mamma; evidently mamma found the wind trying, for she had a shawl tied over her bonnet. Although the day was bright a sharp salt breeze was blowing and the colour of the sea was thick and bitten with white. The girls' dresses ballooned out behind them and they ducked their heads, laughing, at the gusts, while mamma softly and anxiously moaned.

There was something familiar to Clem about the liveliest of the laughing girls, and as they came closer she cried out with delight, 'Mary! Why, it's Mary Newman!'

Mary heard her name and looked round and instantly ran to Clem and caught her hands, almost dancing her round in her excitement.

'Clem! Oh, you dear little Clem!'

Mrs. Scarvell stopped at once and raised her lorgnette for a haughty glare.

Clem hastened to introduce Mary; her explanations were a little confusing. Mary had not been at her school, but had often visited there while she had been at her aunt's little school at Strand-on-the-Green. Mrs. Scarvell stared suspiciously at Mrs. Newman, a gentle pale woman with rather a long nose. All the Newman girls had long noses too, soft full lips and ringlets. Mary was the youngest and Clem liked her best.

Mrs. Newman asked if Clem could spend the evening with them, at their house in Marine Square. Mr. Burnet said yes at once, in order to close the conversation, as Clem very well knew, for he disliked what he called females, especially in quantity. As they went on, Aunt Scarvell let him know her disapproval, but it was too late then. Clem's evening was safe.

Eager and a little chilly in her best muslin dress, she walked round to Marine Square in the company of her aunt's elderly maid. The minute she was inside the door the girls surrounded her, laughing and talking all at once.

'What do you think, Clem? John has come!'

'John?' she said, smiling and bewildered. 'Who's John?'

Mary laughed at her. 'John Henry is our brother', she said. 'He's the eldest. He's very grand now, for he's a fellow of Oriel College in Oxford and that's the cleverest college of the lot, don't you know! He's so great and learned we hardly dare open our mouths while he is here.'

Laughing, she dropped a deep curtsey as they went into the drawing-room, teasing her brother, who rose to meet them.

'I should have said that you never shut it, Mary', he remarked mildly.

He was tall, so that Clem could not get a look at him till they sat down; then she saw that like his sisters he had a long nose, bigger still, of course, and that he wore metal-rimmed spectacles, which convinced her at once of his learning and made her fear he would launch into some dull and incomprehensible lecture. But instead he sat and listened to

Mary's chatter, with his thumb in the book he had been reading.

His mother kept quietly fussing over him. 'John, had you not better drink a glass of wine? It is so strengthening. John, dear, why do you not put your feet up? That is so much more restful.'

The young man was evidently a little embarrassed by her attentions.

'Mamma, I assure you I am not ill any longer', he said at last. 'My visit to the Wilberforces quite set me up again.'

'You look so pale, my dear', said she tenderly. 'What is that book you have? I do not think you should study so much. Did not the doctor say your breakdown was due to overwork?'

'Overwork, yes, the examining and so on', he answered. 'Not reading. Did I tell you the Fathers had come?'

The fathers? Whose fathers? Clem wondered.

'Splendid folios and so cheap', John Newman said, and she realized that these Fathers were books and listened, awed, while John and his sisters talked about people called Chrysostom and Gregory and Origen: she had no idea who they were, but it seemed they had written a great many sermons, all in Greek too. Her own father, Mr. Burnet, was not interested in these other Fathers; what he liked was to classify birds and bones and shells and rocks; when he read, it was old Norse sagas, about brawny heroes fighting each other and halls being burnt down.

'They open up a new world to me', John was saying.

'It must have been a very different world from ours', his mother said.

John smiled, and when he did his serious, almost owlish face, looked mischievous, as Mary's did when people's misconceptions amused her.

'Perhaps not so very different, Mamma', he said. 'As members of the Church they had as much trouble with the State then as we do now.'

'Good gracious!' said Mrs. Newman. 'I hope our government knows better than to make martyrs of the bishops!'

The girls giggled and Harriett, the eldest, said, 'Why, Mamma, don't you know John thinks that is the best thing that could happen to them?'

'Harriett!' her brother remonstrated.

'If you did not say it then your precious Hurrell Froude did', Harriett retorted.

'Froude likes to say startling things', said John. 'It makes people stop and think.'

'Harriett, you are not to tease John to talk', said Mrs. Newman. 'He has come home to rest.'

But nothing could stop the young Newmans talking. Clem, who had been afraid John's learning would make him a bore, listened almost with excitement to his opinions. She could not make out his politics. He attacked many new liberal ideas as if he were a diehard Tory, and yet some of his remarks would have astonished the old Tory squire at home. He seemed to judge everything by how it affected the church, and yet the church itself came in for some hard knocks.

His sisters joined in; Harriett argued and sparred with him, Mary was eager and lively. Only Jemima was mostly silent; she sat brooding, her large heavy eyes dreaming perhaps of some quite other occasion.

In the drawing-room after dinner Mrs. Newman showed Clem a portrait of Frank, the third son, and she was much impressed with his beauty.

'What a fine face he has', she said, holding the miniature in her hand.

'Yes, is it not?' the proud mother agreed. 'And he is so clever! A double first! That was partly John's tuition, of course.'

'He did better than I in his schools', John said.

'That was because you overworked, my dear, as I fear you so often do', said Mrs. Newman. 'Frank owes you a great deal.'

It was a disappointment to hear that this paragon was away in Ireland.

'Have you not another son, ma'am?' Clem asked.

'Oh yes, poor Charles', said Mrs. Newman, and sighed. Clem suddenly remembered that there was something odd about Charles; he was unsatisfactory, perhaps even a little unbalanced. They seemed all such a sensitive family, emotion and intellect playing on each other, not very tough. Charles, Mary whispered to her in a corner, was physically the strongest and mentally the weakest of all of them. He went from job to job, with too many opinions and too little common sense.

'And your brother John has been ill?' Clem said, under cover of some lovely repartee from Harriett at the other end of the room.

Mary's face was grave. 'You know, it was not exactly a physical illness', she said. 'He has been doing far too much, not only at Oxford, but trying to manage my poor aunt's money affairs for her when her school failed. It was a kind of breakdown of the nerves. He told me that for a day or two he lay in his rooms with his mind racing uselessly, like a machine with a loose cog.'

Clem gazed at John's taut, concentrated face and murmured, 'He does look as if he thinks too hard.'

'Some people can think without feeling', said Mary. 'But not John.'

Harriett jumped to her feet.

'Now, we really must have some music! John, get out your fiddle.'

Mrs. Newman anxiously remonstrated, but her son rose at once.

'No, Mamma, I should like it', he said. 'And I always sleep better after music, if that is any comfort to you.'

Clem could not play or sing herself, but she liked to listen and watch. It somehow surprised her to see serious John Henry tuning his fiddle. He tucked it against his chest and played away, stiffly but with vigour. Clem watched his tensed face relax as the music absorbed him; talking, he seemed all mind, but now she saw he could feel too; yet his feeling seemed to her in some way sealed up, a spring with a stone over it, perhaps a force he had no use for, busy with his intellectual work, and yet which was there all the same and found itself a channel of expression in his fiddle-playing. Clem found herself wondering if he had ever fallen in love. But Frank, she felt, was the romantic one, the one she would like to fall in love with herself.

She was sorry when her father came to fetch her away. She saw him look with his usual critical glance at the young clergyman from Oxford.

'Oriel, eh?' he said. 'Whately.'

'I owe him much', said John Newman. 'He taught me to think.'

'Think!' said Mr. Burnet scornfully. 'I don't advise you to do much of that, Mr. Newman. People who think are never comfortable.'

John smiled uncertainly.

'No joke, young man', said Mr. Burnet testily. 'I had ideas myself once. That's why I'm left to moulder in Cornwall.

The great men don't like ideas. Sam Burnet's not sound, let
him stay in Cornwall, let him die and be buried there, it's a
long way off.'

His bitterness embarrassed everyone a little.

John murmured, 'If the opportunities are less, the service is the same.'

'Pooh!' snorted Mr. Burnet. 'The money is not the same,
let me tell you. And don't tell me you would like to spend
your Sundays droning out the Ten Commandments to dolts
who don't even know when they are breaking them! Clem,
come, put on your bonnet, girl.'

Outside was winter moonlight, colourless and cold. The
sea they could hear, sighing on the sands out of sight.

Mr. Burnet said crossly, 'These clever young men are all
the same. A good job and plenty of money: they can afford
ideals. I can't.'

'Mr. Newman seems to have many calls on him', Clem
said.

'Oh, ah, all those girls', said her father. 'He'd better find
husbands for them quickly, get them off his hands before
they turn ugly and particular.'

Clem ignored this. 'His brothers have to be helped too',
she said. 'One is clever, but the other doesn't seem able to
fend for himself; may be a little abnormal, I believe.'

'Ha!' said her father, pleased, as he always was, to hear of
someone evidently more of a failure than himself. 'Unsta-
ble! These clever families always produce a ninny. Shouldn't
be surprised if that young don didn't go off his head too.
Oriel! Logic! That's all they know at Oriel. I never knew a
logician yet who wasn't mad. Stands to reason, the world
being such an unreasonable place.'

Clem thought of Mary whispering anxiously about her
brother's recent breakdown. She stared up at the bare, pitted

moon, riding so high, and shivered. The world was so full of dangers, and nobody cared.

'I do hope nothing terrible will happen to him', she said earnestly.

Mr. Burnet snorted. 'Now don't treat me to your feminine enthusiasm', he said. 'You know I cannot abide it. Though it would be new for you to go swooning over such a learned young owl.'

'Mr. Newman plays the violin', said Clem demurely, to irritate him.

'That proves he is no gentleman', cried her father. 'A banker's son, who fancies he's somebody because he's quick at Greek.'

'Aunt Scarvell would agree', said Clem calmly, knowing how he hated to agree with his sister-in-law.

Mr. Burnet fizzled for a moment and then exploded. 'Mr. Newman is a fool!' he announced. 'All clever young men are fools. Mr. Newman is a clever young man, therefore Mr. Newman is a fool! There's logic for you.'

Clem looked from the moon to the wide brimming sea, folding and folding waves on the wet slant of the shore.

There was no answer to her father; there never was.

So they went back to Cornwall, where a thick white mist was blowing in from the sea, the great western ocean, so that there were no more hills or grey church tower or bent trees, only shadows in the sky, and the world was a circle of ground and people walked in cloud. Christmas came in the cold church, with Mr. Burnet declaiming that Christ was born of a pure virgin and Mr. Beer the clerk ponderously answering Amen from the three-decker pulpit, and fog went creeping along the damp slate floors, oozing through the skin of the slabs, turning them from grey to blue. In the huge empty dark vicarage Mr. Burnet shut himself in his study, brooding over his brown skeletal plants, his ranks of labelled stones and the fierce northern griefs of the Volsungas. Clem stared out of the blank windows and wondered what was going on in Marine Square, Brighton.

Late in January she received a letter from Jemima Newman.

'How can I tell our sad news? Dear Mary is gone.'

Mary had died after a sudden attack on Epiphany Eve. Clem could not believe it. Mary, with her bright intelligent eyes, her affectionate nonsense, Mary always so very much alive: how could she be dead, dead and buried in a churchyard and not yet twenty?

Clem walked restlessly about her room, flung down the letter, picked it up again. She went out of the house towards the church, but saw Mr. Beer in the porch and turned away, unwilling just now to hear his usual gossip.

She stood in the bare windy garden with the letter fluttering in her hand and her heart seemed to swell up inside its cage of bones like a well rising after heavy rains, but the fountain of feeling would not break. She did not know what it was she was feeling: sorrow, anger, fear? It was stifling but it was vague, and the vagueness also distressed her. It was like the grey sea thundering round her head.

'Mary!' she called into the January gale that whistled over the wild bare land.

'Mary!'

# Oxford: 1833

Mr. Samuel Burnet took it for granted that a daughter was a convenience assigned to him by Providence for the comfort of his old age. It never occurred to him that a girl might want something more from life than to see that his meals were ready on time and to make his tea in the evening. He was perfectly content, in his grumbling way, classifying his specimens and writing to other amateur scientists: why should not Clem be content too? Clem tried hard to be content with village sewing circles, kitchen talk and the old stiff books on her father's shelves, but she found it very dull indeed. After their sudden visit to Brighton they did not go anywhere for five years; not a long period to an old man, but to a girl growing up an eternity of wasted time. And then her schoolfriend Lucy, who had married her cousin Bertram Scarvell, wrote and asked her to stay in Oxford, where Bertram had recently been given a parish.

'Go to Oxford?' said her father, sniffing violently, so that his spectacles hopped on his large fleshy nose. 'And who will make my tea, pray?'

'Nancy knows how you like it, Papa', Clem pleaded. 'Do let me go.'

Mr. Burnet snorted and stirred his tea vigorously.

'You will certainly find that worldly life tiresome', he said.

'It can't be very worldly in a vicarage', said Clem, surprised.

'So you, in your innocence, imagine', said Mr. Burnet. 'The Scarvells would be worldly anywhere. You will be glad to get back to a rational life, I assure you.'

If life in her father's home were rational, Clem felt a strong desire to try the irrational, so she took this assertion as permission and packed her boxes.

'But take care not to fall in love with some ridiculous young curate', her father said, as he saw her off on the first stage of her journey, accompanied by old Eli Trewin, a gnarled and suspicious Cornishman who would see that no strangers spoke to her.

'I can't have you going off and marrying some bleating young jackanapes', said Mr. Burnet.

As the coach drove away Clem could not help thinking what fun it would be to get married and go right away from Cornwall. She felt a little guilty at this inward betrayal of her father, not knowing she was smiling as she gazed hopefully out of the narrow window.

'But not a curate', she said to herself. 'Nobody to do with the church at all.'

Perhaps it was rash for a girl who felt she had had enough of clerical life to expect to enjoy herself in Oxford, where every other man was in Holy Orders. Black clothes were everywhere, but then they looked suitable against the stone background of college walls and ancient gateways. June was beginning and the city was full of light and long shadows; the bells chimed as the coach came rattling in, bells from towers all round, and pigeons flew up, patterning the air.

A light carriage met her; Bertram's parish was on the edge of the city; in fact, it was a village just outside. There was only a servant to meet her, and so she sat silent, looking round eagerly. In all these colleges, she supposed, learned men were poring over old books and writing new ones: the thought of so many clever people was quite overpowering. But she saw crowds of young men in gowns walking about who did not look at all clever or learned, or indeed as if they ever would be. No doubt they were the future prime ministers, generals, bishops and judges who would be too busy ruling England to write learned books. And all these important people had to have wives; no one could be important without a wife, it was not done. It really was not necessary to marry a curate, Clem thought hopefully.

Then she arrived at the Scarvells' house, large beside the small church; it had been improved with rounded bay windows not long since, after Waterloo. The garden was full of lilac and wallflowers; rooks were cawing in the tall still trees. It all seemed very rich, tranquil, a deep place to Clem, after the bare cliffs of Cornwall, a place where winds did not blow and generations of men working at the soil had won the long battle with nature and could take their ease in peace.

Indoors, too, there was stillness, comfort, well-cared-for rooms. Bertram Scarvell, though barely thirty, was no penniless clergyman, but the only son of a reasonably wealthy father, long since deceased. Clem had never met this cousin and wondered what he would be like. But when she was shown into the drawing-room, he was not there.

Lucy was lying on a sofa by the window, and to Clem she looked very much the same, but more beautiful, her skin like living ivory, her blue eyes heavily lidded, giving her a languid look. Clem could still admire her and was delighted.

Lucy seemed very pleased to see her. 'Dear Clem', she said, holding out soft white arms and gently kissing her.

'How well you look! I wish I had health like yours. I'm so glad you were able to come. What talks we shall have!'

Clem remembered with a sudden qualm sitting on Lucy's bed at school, getting colder and colder while Lucy went over her troubles, her aches and pains, and her misunderstandings with the mistresses, so hard-hearted, and the other girls, spiteful creatures. As she presently unpacked and changed her dress Clem wondered whether her visit was going to be a disappointment. The window of her room looked across a lawn to the church, standing squat and grey among the trees. Even the graves, grass mounds golden in the evening sunlight, looked comfortable. It was impossible to think of skeletons underneath; fat people peacefully snoring were the appropriate inhabitants. Away across the fields she heard the Oxford bells tolling out the hour and her apprehension lifted. It was a new place, she would not look for trouble.

Mrs. Scarvell was in the drawing-room when she went down; she had made her home with her son as a matter of course. She asked Clem about her father, the servants, the village and the local gentry; Clem answered the inquisition as well as she could.

Presently the door opened.

'Bertram?' said his mother. 'Here is your cousin arrived.'

Bertram Scarvell advanced smiling towards her.

Clem's immediate feeling was that no clergyman should be as good-looking as Bertram. He was tall, and perhaps his clerical black made him look even taller than he was; he moved with a kind of careless grandeur, very much the master of his house. His eyes were blue, light and penetrating. Clem had never seen such a handsome man and the experience embarrassed her. Nature would have jumped up with a gasp of admiration, but nature had to be crushed, and polite conversation maintained.

Bertram made an enquiry about her journey which she managed to answer, and then, much to her relief, he began to talk of what was of interest to him.

'I've just ridden back from Iffley', he said.

'And are the Newmans safely settled in Rose Bank?' asked Lucy. 'Clem, do you recollect Harriett and Jemima Newman? They are all come to live at Iffley, to be near their adored John Henry. How they did boast of him! I was tired to death of his name, and now I declare, Bertram is just as bad.'

'They are worried because the last letter they had from him was dated in March', said Bertram. 'He had left the Froudes in Rome and was set on returning to Sicily alone. This letter was written in Naples, where he was waiting for a ship, and since then, silence!'

'How shocking!' cried Lucy, with gleaming eyes. 'Why, he may have been murdered by bandits for all we know.'

'How very rash of Mr. Newman to leave his friends', said Mrs. Scarvell. 'It is not as if he were a great traveller. He had never been abroad before, I understand. I hope he has not been wrecked.'

'I really must call on the Newmans', said Lucy, plainly avid for more news. 'I have neglected them lately, but then I have been so unwell.'

She poured out her woes to Clem later, when they were alone. The chief of them was having to endure her mother-in-law's perpetual presence, so that she could not feel her home was her own.

'Mamma would be less hard on me if I had a son', she grumbled. 'Clara should have been a boy; she has such high spirits. I wish I had spirits like hers.'

Clara, flaxen-haired and blue-eyed, was as imperious as her grandmother, the only person who could quell her. She was three or four years old, and since then Lucy had had a miscarriage; she felt that her only chance of Mrs. Scarvell's approval would be to produce boys to carry on the Earl's noble line.

Lucy did not after all call on the Newmans; Clem found she was apt to propose things and then put them off, for no apparent reason. Instead, she invited her brother George Pierce to stay, and as she did this immediately after asking Clem whether she had ever been in love, Clem thought it probably a piece of matchmaking on her part. George Pierce was a curate in a poor London parish, but Clem was ready to admire any brother of Lucy's, until he arrived and turned out to be fat and solemn, with a bad stutter. It was a disappointment, but George's arrival meant that she saw something of Oxford, for he had a great admiration for the place and was always suggesting a walk to look at the colleges. He also had a great admiration for Bertram, who was not unwilling to gratify such an appreciative audience with his opinions, so that the conversation was as interesting to Clem as the views of the city.

One morning at the beginning of July they were all four strolling down the High Street when suddenly Bertram cried, 'Newman!' He dropped Lucy's arm to dash across the road.

They all stopped to look and there was John Henry Newman indeed, tall and thin in his black coat, striding along in a purposeful way, with his head thrust a little forward, as if he could not keep up with himself.

Bertram seized his arm and shook his hand and in a moment was hauling him back across the road, Newman smiling and blinking behind his spectacles.

'But where have you been all this time?' Bertram was saying. 'Pickpocketed in Naples? Turned brigand yourself?'

Newman laughed. 'No! I've been ill. In Sicily I had a fever, bad enough. But it's gone now.'

'Indeed, you look very thin, Mr. Newman', said Lucy.

'And my hair's falling out!' he said, pushing his hand through it with a smile. 'But I hear that's common after a fever.'

'But were you alone?' Bertram asked.

'Except for my Italian servant, who was wonderfully good to me', said Newman. 'And we had got right away into the country, too. They all thought I would die, but somehow I felt I should not, because there was something I had to do first, work to do here in England.'

'Aha, do I scent battle?' Bertram said. 'What now? A blow at the government for suppressing our bishoprics in Ireland? But what can be done?'

Newman smiled and quoted a line of Greek, almost with flamboyance.

'How unfair!' cried Lucy. 'What does it mean, Bertram? Have pity on us poor dunces!'

'It is Achilles', said Bertram with a chuckle. '"You shall know the difference now that I am back again." Is that who you are, Newman?'

Newman laughed. 'Count Froude as our Achilles', he said. 'We remembered that tag in Rome.'

'I hope the voyage has done Froude some good', said Bertram.

'I hope so too', said Newman. 'It seemed to be I who kept getting ill all the time! But with him it is a deep-seated thing, I fear, and he may have to winter abroad again. There's some talk of Barbados.'

'Mr. Froude always looks such an active man', observed Lucy, as if she did not quite believe in the delicacy of Newman's friend.

'He is', said Newman. 'That makes it all the harder for him, I'm afraid.'

Just then another man in clerical black came hurrying towards them, young too, but with rather a solemn face.

'Here's your curate, the poetic Welshman', said Bertram.

Newman turned round. 'Williams!'

Williams wrung his hand. 'Χᾶιρε, πόλυ χᾶιρε, my dear Vicar!' he said with emotion. 'How delightful to have you back amongst us again!'

This Oxford greeting amused Clem; she wondered if they all *thought* in Greek. 'My dear Vicar' seemed inappropriate to Newman, she could not quite think why. She was surprised by him, somehow. He was still the same person she had met in Brighton, and yet he was different. Perhaps it was only the difference between an earnest young man in his twenties overworking to keep up with heavy family commitments, and a man of thirty-two who had found his place in the world; yet she felt the change was deeper than this. The signs of illness were still on him, yet she had an overwhelming impression of energy and power. And she felt what she had not felt before, a strong charm in this singular man, whom she could not think of as 'John' in spite of knowing his family, but only as 'Newman'.

At St. Mary's Newman and Williams left them, going into the church.

'Who is to preach on Sunday?' Lucy asked as they went on.

'Keble', said Bertram. 'It's the Assize Sermon.'

They went to hear the sermon; although term was over, the church was full of dignitaries, university, clerical and legal. Clem, for the first time, got the feeling of Oxford from the inside, a close enclave, living in a strong tradition of its own, of classical learning and Church of England religion. The University might be small, but through its members its influence extended over all the country, so that she had the feeling that Keble's words would reach far beyond the walls of the ancient church where they sat, that warm summer day. For though he was a quiet and unpretentious man, about forty years old, there was controlled passion behind all he said; England, it seemed to him, was deserting the principles of the Christian Faith to follow a nebulous liberalism, which, in allowing all opinions, would favour, finally, the lack of any.

Clem, who did not much like listening to sermons, lost the thread sometimes. She fell back on mere staring; what a kind, good face Keble had; just the man one would choose for one's parson, understanding, but comfortably conventional. You would know where you were.

Then her eyes wandered and she found herself looking at another face: Newman in his place, quiet and intent, with his drooping eagle head. The dim light glanced off the small lenses of his spectacles as he suddenly looked up, his attention caught by some phrase that chimed with his own thoughts. She again felt the power alive in him, like a river building up against a dam. What was it? With him, she thought, far from knowing where you were, you did not know what would happen next.

After the sermon they went out into the sunny street, dusty and hot, and Bertram was full of enthusiasm.

'Keble is too meek, though, he will never *do* anything', he said. 'But I believe Newman is going to act. There is something strange in his manner since his return; it almost makes him look different—like someone come back from the dead.'

'He certainly does look terribly thin', said prosaic Lucy.

Bertram made a laughing face at Clem.

The next day they all called at Rose Bank, even Mrs. Scarvell, who still disapproved of the Newmans for what she considered their lowly origins, but visited them, she said, to please Bertram. In private she called Harriett a minx and Jemima sullen, expressing the opinion that they had come to Oxford to get husbands, but were unlikely to achieve their object. To Clem the sisters seemed much the same; five years had perhaps sharpened Harriett's tongue and weighed down Jemima's heavy lids a little more, but just now they were overflowing with happiness, for not only had John come home, after months of silence and anxiety, but Frank too, on the very same day, all the way from Persia. But Clem again missed handsome and clever Frank; he was not there during their visit. Jemima whispered that he was dreadfully in love, but she was not at all sure Maria would have him, beautiful and enthusiastic Maria Rosina Giberne, she explained, who had been staying in their house when poor Mary died, and who was a great admirer of John's, of his work and ideas, she hastened to add. Clem breathed a small sigh as her vague dream of falling in love with Frank Newman receded, and turned to listen to the conversation of the others.

Bertram was pressing Newman to disclose his plans.

'I haven't any plans', he said, smiling. 'There's some notion of publishing poems and articles setting out the idea of the church as an autonomous divine society; that has so fallen out of people's minds that it will come as quite a novelty.'

'Writing?' said Bertram, dissatisfied. 'What about some sort of Association?'

'There is talk of that', admitted Newman. 'But talk is all those sort of things amount to, in my opinion. The main thing is to get into touch with the clergy directly, an appeal of one person to another.'

'So you are going to raise the country!' Bertram said, with a laugh, but he seemed excited. 'You and Froude are going to start a new reformation, are you?'

'A better one', said Newman confidently. 'Because it will go back to the seventeenth rather than the sixteenth century.'

'Mr. Froude will not be content with that', remarked Harriett. 'He will want to go back to his beloved Middle Ages, and as for you, John, I cannot see you stopping short of your holy Fathers in the fifth century!'

'The English divines of the seventeenth century had the Fathers behind them', said Newman emphatically. 'Our church was aware then of its Catholic heritage—'

His mother interrupted him. 'John,' she said, changing the subject abruptly, 'have you told Mr. Scarvell your plans for a new church at Littlemore?'

John, after a momentary pause to collect his thoughts, obediently began to outline his parish plans, and Mrs. Newman, well aware of Mrs. Scarvell's unconcealed distaste for her brilliant son's opinions, glanced anxiously in her direction.

When Newman made some reference to having a cross put on the wall behind the altar in his new church, Mrs. Scarvell could contain her indignation no longer.

'It seems, Mr. Newman, they have made a papist of you in Rome.'

'Indeed, ma'am, that is not so', he said gravely. 'I am well aware of the corruptions in the Creed of Rome, but we must remember it is still part of the Catholic Church, and a great part too.'

'What!' cried Mrs. Scarvell. 'Do you mean to deny that the Pope is Antichrist and Rome the woman we read of in Revelation, drunken with the blood of the saints?'

'I am sure John means no such thing', interposed Mrs. Newman hastily, and she postponed Armageddon by sending for wine and sponge cake, so that religious subjects had to be dropped forthwith.

Presently Newman came over to Clem, to fill her glass. He put the wine down and leant on the window sill near her. 'I met you before, did I not? At Brighton that Christmas, just before dear Mary died.'

'Yes, that was it', said Clem, surprised that he remembered.

'You were Mary's friend', he said slowly.

'I wish I had known her better', said Clem. 'I saw her so little and liked her so much.'

His eyes lighted as he looked at her. 'Did you? Yes, she was always loved, dear Mary! The wonder was not that she went so soon but that we kept her so long. I thought of her so much when I set out last year. You know, to start on a voyage must bring before one the thought of death, of leaving all we know to face the unknown.'

'I think I should have been looking forward to what I was to see', said Clem.

'Perhaps I'm inclined by nature to look back', he said thoughtfully. 'Memory means much to me.'

Clem smiled. 'I'm surprised you remember me', she said. 'You must meet so many people in Oxford.'

'Anything to do with Mary cannot be forgotten', he said. 'Not only for her own sake, but because her death, coming after that illness of mine, made a great break, a deep change in my life.'

'What sort of change?' she asked, wondering, watching his brooding face.

'I think, before that, I had begun to care too much for intellectual excellence', he said. 'But when it comes home to you that reason may as easily be lost as bodily health, and when someone goes from your world whose mind you trained and could enclose in your own, and yet whose soul has its own being and destiny, perhaps much higher—well, that opens your eyes to the value of the heart and will.'

'But you don't despise intellect, surely?' Clem said.

Newman smiled. 'Oh no! I am a real don!' he said, and then added, 'But I am a priest first.'

Somehow Clem had not thought of him as a priest. The idea was anyway unfamiliar to her. Officially her father was a priest too, yet she always thought of him, and he thought of himself, as a clergyman. It was merely a point of language, and yet it carried overtones.

Newman was still brooding. 'It is strange how new events in one's life can illuminate what is past', he said. 'My illness in Sicily has somehow done that for me. You know, to come so near to death is almost to die. And yet the experience is such that however minutely one can describe it, one cannot wholly understand it. I think it is like the view of some great sight; it seems to have a meaning that cannot be altogether grasped with the mind. The image remains, like that temple at Segesta. . . .'

A look came into his eye as if he saw something a long way off, a sacred vision.

'Where was that?' Clem asked, interested, but not at all sure why she should find it interesting.

'In Sicily', he said. 'It was the first time, when I was with Froude and his father. We went up from Palermo through wild country, the valley rich, even in winter, but the hills most desolate. We came to a place and stood among ruined stones; opposite us a precipitate rock started out of the ravine below. There was only one building on it, one temple standing high up, alone, gigantic doric pillars, no roof. The whole place is one ruin except this in the waste of solitude.'

Clem saw it in her mind, the air singing through the broken stone, far away there on the ancient island, in those distant seas. She almost felt the coldness of the place, and shivered.

'Did you like that?' she said uncertainly, looking at him.

'It gave me a most strange pleasure', he said slowly. 'Once those hills were full of life, men thought their greatness would stand for ever. And now there is only this, a great ruin in the wilderness.'

Clem said, 'I think I should be sad. It would make me feel time was taking away all things, as if it were my town lying there abandoned.'

Newman stood looking down at her, but perhaps he still saw the lonely temple on the mountain.

'It is', he said. 'It is man's tomb.'

After he had said that, in spite of the talk in the room, Clem felt herself suddenly alone in silence. She felt strange, as if she were standing on a hill looking into a new country, but it lay in mist. Newman looked out of the window suddenly and so Clem looked too, and the sunny Thames country came as a shock to her, with this picture of grand classic desolation before her inward eye. The fields, heavy with summer, looked unreal as a dream. Suddenly the whole world, near and far, appeared a dream, vivid, miraculous, ready to vanish.

'Did you go back to Sicily just to see that place again?' she asked him on impulse.

He looked at her, startled, thoughtful.

'I don't know. Perhaps I did. What a strange place it was: I cannot put into words all I feel about it. I thought of it again and again till I went back and fell ill. Was I wrong to go back? It was self-willed; all my friends were against it. It was almost an obsession. Yes, I felt God's hand too was against me, and he stopped me.' He paused, and then added, 'And yet I felt that in my inmost heart I had not sinned against the light. I had obscured it; I was in a cloud, and yet it was not deliberate. You see, they all thought I would die, but I knew it was not death. I was thrown down, but I was raised up again.'

Clem, fascinated, out of her depth, asked tentatively, 'And after your illness, did you still want to go back to Segesta?'

Newman came out of his thoughts with a laugh. 'No! I was cured of that! I just wanted to get home as quickly as I could. I felt there was a work waiting for me in England, the work of my life, what I was meant to do, made to do.'

Fired by his enthusiasm Clem said, 'You mean this new reformation in the church?'

'I mean we must wake people up', Newman said. 'We are all going away from the city of God. The further we go, the less we can see of his light. We are already a long way off in the dark, a long way from home.'

'I don't see why', Clem said, bewildered. 'Why are we going the wrong way?'

'Because we are all children of Adam', said Newman. 'We want to be like gods, we want to be saved from suffering instead of from evil, and what is so dangerous, men are beginning to believe, because of their increasing power over nature, that they can do it by their own efforts.'

'Is that so dangerous?' Clem said.

'Of course it is! The devil is always ready to promise kingdoms, and perhaps he can give them, since he is the prince of this world, but his palaces are all of dust and the shadow of them is everlasting loss at the end.'

In a momentary lull of conversation the name of the devil sounded in the neat drawing-room and Mrs. Newman turned anxiously towards them.

'John, whatever are you saying to Miss Burnet? We cannot allow her to be made a victim to your views on so fine a summer morning!'

'Don't be taken in by John's views, Clem!' cried Harriett. 'He is always so sure he is right!'

'I am sure the church is right', Newman answered, with a smile.

Church still meant to Clem grey stones, preachers, Mr. Beer the clerk saying Amen and the poor curtseying to her father when he came in.

So she could listen no more to strange talk of man's tomb and God's city and the promises of the prince of this world. But she long remembered it, all the more because the next day came a querulous letter from her father, summoning her home to Cornwall.

## II

## "LIFE IS AT ONCE NOTHING AT ALL, AND ALL IN ALL."

# I

Mr. Burnet had written that he was ill, in very shaky writing, but it turned out to be little more than irritation because a few mishaps had upset his regular life. His headache and cough soon vanished when Clem returned, so that she felt she had been recalled on false pretences.

If she had found it dull in Cornwall before, she found it far more so now that she had seen something of life in other places. Oxford was always in her mind, and in retrospect it seemed an immortal city set in unfading fields of summer light. She kept up a correspondence with Lucy, eagerly demanding news of all her new acquaintances, even George Pierce.

One day in September Clem came down to breakfast to find her father surveying with distaste a printed pamphlet headed in black type: 'A Tract for the Times'.

'What is this nonsense Bertram has sent me?' he said and read out, '"I am but one of yourselves, a presbyter." Presbyter! God preserve us!' He hummed and clucked his way through the pages, none the less. 'What's all this about Apostolic Succession?' He jabbed a thick forefinger at the page. 'Does the fellow want to make bishops into little kings? Bishops are made a great deal too much of already, in my opinion.' He gave a short laugh. 'If this presbyter wants to be one he had better keep quiet! Bishops have to get on with the government, whatever it does.'

'May I read it, please?' Clem asked, wondering if Bertram had written it.

'You read it? What, is little Clem to turn blue-stocking?'

But he threw it over and Clem studied it, and the others
that Bertram sent during the next few months. The writer
of the Tracts made the church seem an exciting thing, a
castle embattled against the world with flags flying in a golden
heaven. The writer, she soon discovered, was John Henry
Newman.

'There are several men meeting and discussing things',
wrote Lucy. 'But Bertram says Newman has written most
of the Tracts so far. There's no stopping him.'

Clem could not help smiling at the idea of Newman writing tracts, like any evangelical with his pockets stuffed full
of *Are You Saved?* to hand round in the street or push under
the front door. Apparently he and his friends were doing
just this, sending or taking round bundles of tracts to all the
clergy they could think of, High or Low. Yet this was not
an appeal to emotion, but to the mind. They were very
Oxford tracts.

They soon became notorious, and so, to a certain extent,
their authors too. The newspapers were full of them; they
caught public attention just at the moment when people
had stopped taking authority for granted, either in government or in religion. Clem enjoyed the fun of knowing some
of the principal men involved in the controversy, and longed
to go back to Oxford to hear more about it. Lucy often
asked her to stay, but every time Clem suggested it her father
fretted and grumbled himself into a minor illness, so for
the sake of peace she gave up trying. Lucy's gossip was better than nothing, though she was always jealous of Bertram's friends in 'the Movement' so that her picture of them
was not very sympathetic. When Newman's dearest friend,
Hurrell Froude, died of his consumption at the beginning
of the year 1836, Lucy wrote, 'None of us can imagine

Newman without Froude, they were inseparable, and of course Froude was by far the cleverer man, though too conceited and rude to be generally likeable.'

Yet Harriett Newman, who had often argued with Froude, wrote of him as 'that bright and beautiful Froude', lamenting his loss. He had died in his Devonshire home, still young, unknown to any but his friends. His father, Harriett said, had sent all his papers and notebooks to John; reading them was not only a solace but a strange voyage of inward discovery: the grave had opened a deeper communication between the two friends than they had ever known in life.

Lucy's next news was more cheerful: Jemima Newman was marrying one of her brother's ex-pupils, John Mozley. But only a few weeks later came Mrs. Newman's death; Clem could imagine the shock it must have been to Newman to lose this loving mother, who had been his first care now for so many years. Yet Lucy could write, 'I hear that at the last she was much upset by his opinions, but it was partly her own fault he was so headstrong; "dear John" was allowed to be perfect too long at home not to lord it even over her.'

Lucy's triumph over the Newmans was complete when soon after the mother's death, much too soon in Lucy's opinion, Harriett decided to marry her brother-in-law, Tom Mozley.

'He's three years her junior and she'll be buried in the depths of Wiltshire', she wrote. 'But I suppose it's her last chance—she must be thirty if she's a day; more, I daresay.'

Clem, twenty-six this year, was irritated. She felt she could easily forgive Harriett, even if her marriage was as calculated as Lucy suggested. Clem saw herself stuck in her father's vicarage till she might well have no chance of marriage, and as he was not well off, an uncertain future, probably as a governess, when he died. She sighed impatiently, put down Lucy's letter, and went out to walk on the cliffs. It was a clear day at the end of summer, the seas were peacock green, bursting in showers of snow on the long rock teeth of the lonely Atlantic shore.

'Why do I complain?' she said to herself. 'The sea is wonderful.'

But the wild sea was no substitute for human love.

Would it be better to marry fat George Pierce than not to marry at all? He was good-natured, and it would mean a new home and children perhaps; she wanted children so much that once she woke in tears because she had dreamt she held her baby in her arms. But even stolid George was out of reach.

She turned away from the brilliant, the cold, salt, shining sea, with a heart as restless as those everlasting waves, breaking their sighs through all her days and dreams.

A little over two years later, in the beginning of the year 1839, the Reverend Samuel Burnet suddenly died, sitting at his desk with his specimens arranged in rows before him.

It was, to Clem, as if the house had suddenly fallen down.

Aunt Scarvell came to the funeral and told Clem she was to come home with her until her future was decided. Clem at once determined to decide her own future, but for the present she obeyed, packing her things, finding it hard to believe she was leaving the familiar house for ever.

It was now over five years since she had seen Lucy; querulous letters had somehow not prepared her for the change she saw. Lucy was only thirty, but she had grown thin and yellow and listless and spent most of the day on a sofa by the fire. It was evidently an accepted thing for her to be an invalid and have nothing to do with the running of the house; Mrs. Scarvell was now completely in command there. Clara, eight years old now, was still the only child and likely to remain so. Lucy begged Clem to stay on and take charge of Clara's education, and Clem felt so sorry for her that she had not the heart to refuse. After all, her only alternative was to accept a similar post in a stranger's household. Bertram insisted on paying her a salary; she accepted, and settled down to a new life.

But now everything was different from her earlier happy visit. Bertram, though he was as strong and handsome as ever, was much less at home, perhaps because it had become a place of trials to him. His mother would leave nothing alone; she made barbed comments about Lucy and persistently attacked his friends in the Movement. Lucy wept and complained, and there were perpetual small rows among the servants. Sometimes Clem longed for tempers to break out, but Lucy was too timid, Mrs. Scarvell too insensitive and Bertram too self-controlled for more than quiet chilly arguments which reached no conclusion and left a sour taste in the mouth. Life in the vicarage, on the surface so gracious and high-principled, was embittered by these poisoned undercurrents. Clem often had to escape to her own room to calm down; here she could look across the garden and the churchyard to the quiet green meadows, and achieve a measure of freedom.

Spring came at last, and that was some relief, releasing them from the close quarters of the house. Leaves came rushing out of the trees, flowers were starting up everywhere; Clem felt herself coming to life again. One fine afternoon Bertram took her and Lucy out for a drive. They passed Rose Bank, and Clem thought how suddenly that busy feminine household had been emptied, by death and marriage, leaving John Newman a lonely bachelor living in college. But then perhaps that was the life he liked best.

They went through a dull little village and Clem asked what it was.

'Littlemore', Bertram said.

Lucy insisted on his stopping, so that Clem could see Newman's chapel, built a few years ago to serve these outlying parts of his parish.

It was plain and bare inside, almost like a barn with its wooden hammer-beam roof. Light wavered on the walls, slanting sideways through the long lancet windows. There was an austere stone arcade behind the altar and in the central arch a plain cross was carved on the wall. There was nothing on the altar at all, and in spite of rumours of Roman practices, no candles or statues in the church.

It was very quiet in there, as if the stone were thinking.

They went out into the spring sunlight and Bertram cocked his head. 'Well?' he said.

'It's very simple', Clem said at last.

'Yes, it is truly primitive', said Bertram with satisfaction. 'We want none of the corruptions and additions of Rome, but the real ancient thing, the Church of the Fathers.'

'But isn't the church in the medieval style?' Clem said, puzzled.

'I mean in principles of faith, not in architecture', said Bertram, irritated.

Clem felt a fool and was glad to see Newman himself approaching, riding along the muddy road. He dismounted to greet them and much to Clem's surprise remembered her without any prompting.

'Mary's friend', he said, shaking her hand warmly.

Bertram began to tell him about an article he had read on Froude's 'Remains', which Newman had been editing and bringing out, volume by volume. The notice was unfavourable, accusing Froude of levity, scruples, superstitious practices and treachery to the land of his birth and the church of his baptism.

'Keble and I never expected this outcry', said Newman. 'Dear Hurrell, why should they sneer at his fasting and discipline of conscience?' He sighed. 'I can tell you, Scarvell, going through his papers has been a revelation to me, and reading the Breviary he used.'

'I don't know that I approve of that', Bertram said. 'It's full of saint worship and idolatry of the Virgin.'

Newman shook his head but did not answer.

Bertram invited him to dinner, but he refused, saying he had a guest in college. 'In any case,' he added with a smile, 'it is better not to come while your mother is at home. I know she does not approve of me.'

He was right; Mrs. Scarvell strongly disapproved of Mr. Newman, who had added to his initial disadvantage of low breeding the intolerable crime of upsetting the Establishment.

When they got home she was sitting in the drawing-room, upright in her black silk dress, doing a petit-point design for a footstool.

'I have had a letter from poor Eleanor', she announced.

'Who is Eleanor?' Clem whispered to Lucy.

Unfortunately Mrs. Scarvell heard her.

'Lady Gornal is my sister-in-law', she said sternly, as if Clem ought to be ashamed not to know this. 'She is dear Sidney's sister, grand-daughter to the Earl.'

Clem dared not ask what Earl.

'She married a dreadful manufacturer called Frederick Firle', went on Mrs. Scarvell, with acute distaste. 'Of course he has a great deal of money, from his father's ironworks, or whatever it is. The late King made him a Baron, I cannot imagine why. I suppose he had done a good turn to some scheming politician. Lord Gornal, indeed! Poor Eleanor!'

'I expect Aunt Eleanor would rather be Lady Gornal than Mrs. Firle', Bertram remarked, with a smile.

'That is unfeeling in you, Bertram', said his mother. 'Eleanor has a great deal to bear, though I admit she is not the wisest of women.'

'She's the silliest woman I know', said Bertram cheerfully. 'And how are the Dear Boys?' He added, aside to Clem, 'The Dear Boys must both be over thirty by now.'

Clem smiled; Bertram in high spirits was very engaging.

'Eleanor writes mostly about her new doctor', said Mrs. Scarvell. 'Oh yes, she says Augustine has been spending the winter in Italy, for his health, and is not home yet.'

'For his health!' jeered Bertram. 'For his amusement! He does it every year. That little cousin of mine is nothing but a waster. I saw what would happen years ago, when they sent him here for me to keep an eye on his studies.'

'It is a pity he did not stay', said Mrs. Scarvell. 'You might have put some principle into him, Bertram.'

'A pity!' said Bertram. 'I was glad to get rid of him. He stayed in bed half the morning, read all the books I told him not to read, and none of the ones I recommended, and invited undergraduates to wine parties in his digs whenever he knew I was safely in college.'

'Wealth is a great temptation to a weak nature', said Mrs. Scarvell. 'How differently he has used his opportunities from you, dear boy!'

'He had better be careful', said Bertram. 'He's a younger son and his father could cut off supplies if he chose.'

'Frederick is not a very moral man himself', observed Mrs. Scarvell.

'He is disappointed in his sons, all the same', said Bertram. 'He told me once he considered Alexander feebleminded, and Augustine nothing but a dandy.'

'It's disgraceful for a man to waste money on his appearance', said Mrs. Scarvell.

'Augustine is a conceited ass', said Bertram. 'Though I don't know what he has got to be conceited about, for he looks like a monkey.'

Clem and Lucy both laughed, but Mrs. Scarvell looked doubtful. Scarvell blood, she evidently felt, should not be mocked. But Bertram, a Scarvell himself and a great-grandson of the revered Earl, could afford to laugh at his cousins if he pleased.

A few days later Clem was in the High Street with Clara when they met Bertram, alone.

'Ah, now I shall get a lift home!' he said, joining them.

Clara, who was swinging happily on his hand, cried, 'Oh, Papa, look! There's Mr. Newman coming out of Oriel Lane. Oh look, he's going to be knocked down by the baker's cart!'

Newman indeed narrowly missed being run down; he paused in mid-road to collect himself and apologize to the baker, and then came rapidly on, books under arm.

Bertram hailed him joyfully.

'Newman! Do you want to make murderers out of your parishioners? Why do you wear those spectacles? I don't believe you ever look through them!'

'I forget to take them off', said Newman, removing them.

Clem noticed the fine lines of his face; it had never occurred to her to think of him as good-looking, but now she suddenly saw that he was, with those strong bones and clear meditative eyes. It was a surprise.

He seemed in a very good humour and began to talk at once about various men she did not know. Someone called Johnson was made University Observer; Newman was delighted. Someone called Ward of Balliol was said to have changed from bad to good principles.

'By which I mean from Arnold's to ours', he said, chuckling.

'Ward is an unknown quantity', said Bertram. 'It's hard to believe someone so fat can be such a clever metaphysical thinker, as they say he is.'

'I cannot help liking him', Newman said. 'Though he was a great trial at my lectures, so staring me in the face that I had to have the seats turned the other way.'

'He's another trophy to your influence, then', said Bertram.

Newman laughed. 'Dear Froude used to say, "What is the use of influence if not to influence?"' he said. 'Do you know, the Tracts, the bound volumes, are selling beyond every expectation? Yes, we have made a beginning!'

Bertram was looking over his shoulder. 'Who are these young men hovering in the background?' he said.

Newman looked round, squinting against the sun. 'Oh, they are some undergraduates who come to my Monday evening tea parties. Will you excuse me? I had better see what they want.'

As they went on, leaving him surrounded by eager young men, Clem laughed and remarked, 'So those are some of the incense-breathing acolytes we hear so much about!'

Bertram was not too pleased. 'Newman won't stand silliness, you know', he said. 'They talk politics and poetry as much as religion.'

'People will be silly all the same', said Clem. 'I'm told that young men even copy his walk and his way of reading the service.'

'More fools they', said Bertram. 'He would hate it if he knew.'

'But he is the leader of this new Movement, isn't he?' said Clem. 'So he must put up with notoriety.'

'It is one of the good things about the Movement that there is no one leader', Bertram added, with satisfaction. 'Though I suppose it could be said that Keble, Pusey and Newman are the three men chiefly behind it.'

'The Oxford Trinity', Clem murmured.

But Bertram, she noticed with confusion, was shocked at her frivolity and affected not to hear. Clem did not like to displease someone she admired as much as Bertram, and was silent, embarrassed.

Bertram passed over her solecism kindly.

'Newman is certainly the driving force', he allowed. 'He defers to Keble and asks Pusey's advice, but neither of them has the power to move people as he has. It may be a dangerous gift, but he can make people listen. He is almost like one of the prophets of old, his ideas are like a wind blowing through people's minds.'

Words from the Bible sprang to Clem's lips, the Bible authorized by King James, which had sounded all her life in her ears, beating a double fugue with the thunder of the Cornish seas. 'His fan is in his hand, and he shall throughly purge his garner.'

When she hesitantly began the quotation Bertram took it up with enthusiasm and spoke it aloud in ringing tones, and as if he had touched a hidden spring all the clocks of the city began to chime.

A shiver ran through Clem's flesh, so curious was the effect. She almost saw God like a great giant standing in the blue sky, with his iron flail in his hand, and people flying in the beating whirl of it, falsehoods and hypocrisies, vanities and greeds blown off them like chaff, and they left naked and small and still on the ground, cold as dead things, and yet that was the real seed, the bread to come.

'How big your eyes are!' Bertram teased, looking down into her face and smiling. 'Mind they don't pop out!'

He spoke as if she were Clara, but her heart jumped, like a bird startled in its bone cage.

May ended, term drew to a close and people went away. When the weather was fine Clem took Clara's lessons in the garden, and sometimes Bertram would see them there and come and lay himself down on the grass and listen. He liked poetry, and could recite long passages of Southey and Wordsworth.

'Poetry garden time', Clara called it.

September began; evenings and early mornings grew sharp and misty, but the days were still warm and the sky seemed a deeper clearer blue. Clem felt very happy, she did not know why.

One evening when the equinoctial light was falling side-ways and golden through the row of elms between the garden and the churchyard, she stood in her cool dim room in her white petticoats, brushing her brown hair, getting ready for dinner. Half singing to herself, she was gazing out of the open window down into the bright and shadowy evening garden, where yellow and purple autumn daisies stood high in the fading green, when she saw Bertram crossing the lawn to the churchyard gate.

He walked over with his usual purposeful stride and bent to lift the catch.

Suddenly in Clem's heart a warm fountain rose and a heat like the sun flowed through her. She gazed at Bertram; he went through the gate and it clicked shut behind him. He went between the yew trees.

'I love him', she whispered. 'I love Bertram.'

It was such a surprise. She felt as if a great weight, whose pressure she had long suffered but never before noticed, was lifted off her. Her spirit bounded; happiness flooded through her, tears of joy came into her eyes. Bertram! She loved him.

It was not for minutes that she remembered Bertram was married and she ought not to love him like this. Even when she did remember, it did not deeply disturb her. His marriage was simply a fact, shutting off the possibility of love being returned, but not preventing her own.

'I'll never let anyone know it!' she told herself, floating still in a golden heaven of delight which she did not need to share. She had no intention of suppressing her love, only of hiding it. She thought she would be perfectly happy just loving him, and her love already seemed to be growing, from the moment of her realization.

She dressed herself carefully, joyfully, and went downstairs to dinner. Nobody noticed any difference in her. Yet she felt herself totally changed: a new being.

And now October was beginning and a great moon rose and filled the night, and so slow was its huge transit that in the morning it was still there, no longer a shining orb of power but a pale puff of down, the ghost of a face looking out of the blue air. In the night Clem often knelt by her window, her arms on the sill, staring out at that high moon riding above the waving grey trees, gleaming down on the leaded roof of the squat church, on the leaning dark tombstones of the dead.

She thought of her love.

Her love became an aching in her heart and throat, because she must be silent. Her silence was like a silk cord strangling her, but she must learn to live with her neck in the noose. So she stared and stared at the moon, and at the world under the moon, a different place, and at her hands, somehow not hers in that strange light but just human hands that one day would be bones. There was no happiness or unhappiness for her, but an intensity of awareness that made every day as long as the first day of creation.

And by day, luckily, there was plenty to do; Clara took most of her time. One afternoon she took the child into Oxford and they walked through Christ Church Meadow in the bright slanting light; all the leaves were shivering in the gusts of wind, a thousand thousand little windmills of yellow and fading green.

Clem saw Newman coming down the Broad Walk with a magazine in his hand, folded back, but he was not reading it.

Clara ran up to him, her fair curls bobbing in and out of the sunlight, for he was a great favourite with his friends' children; Clem had seen some of the littlest Puseys pulling his spectacles off and putting them on with great delight. He stopped now and gravely shook hands with Clara when she held hers out to him.

'Was it lovely in the New Forest, Mr. Newman?' she asked. 'Did you see the ponies?'

'Ponies?' he said vaguely.

'The wild ones', said Clara. 'I'd like to have a wild pony and tame it.'

'Would you?' said Newman, smiling. 'You are rather a wild little pony yourself, aren't you, Clara?'

He turned and walked along with them, but he seemed abstracted.

'Miss Burnet', he said suddenly. 'Do you know what it is to find yourself at a crossroads, a turning point in your life? When you come suddenly upon a new view, that may change all?'

Clem stared at him, startled. Could he have guessed her secret? But he was looking ahead, absorbed in thought.

'I do know', she said aloud, and sighed. 'Yes, I do know.'

Newman gazed at her pensively. 'Yes, I expect everyone must feel something of the sort at one time or another.'

There was a long pause while he still looked at her and then, as if he must speak, he went on quickly, 'I do not expect you to enter into my views, Miss Burnet, but I fancy, perhaps because of our link in dear Mary, that you sometimes enter into my feelings, as a friend.' He paused again, only a moment, and then said slowly, 'I have had a great shock.'

'I am sorry', said Clem, wondering what could have happened.

'Yes, I have had a hit', he said. 'The first real hit I have had from Rome.'

'Oh, Rome!' said Clem, quite relieved.

'Yes.' Newman tapped the magazine in his hand. 'There's an article here by Dr. Wiseman, a learned Roman divine, that touches on the very thing I have been studying, the heresies of the fourth and fifth centuries, and the way in which they were settled. Do you know, he uses words of St. Augustine's which I have read, of course, many times, and yet till now they never struck me in this way. And now I can't get them out of my mind. *Securus iudicat orbis terrarum.*'

He pronounced the marble Latin words so gravely and slowly that Clara, who had been skipping ahead, chasing leaves, looked round in surprise.

'What does that mean, Mr. Newman?' Clem asked him.

'In effect, it means there is safety in the judgement of the whole world; in this case, the world of the Catholic Church', he said. 'In those early times I see the divisions of our own reflected, and I find that it was not the middle way that proved right, but extreme views, Roman views. I have appealed to Antiquity and now Antiquity seems to be speaking against me.'

Clem tried to grasp it. The question seemed to her academic, historical; yet it was so urgent to Newman that he was in a state of high nervous tension, excited, uncertain of everything. Dr. Wiseman's was almost the part of one who first gives a man the suspicion that his wife is untrue.

'It makes a great difference to you?' she said, hesitantly, but with sympathy, because she was sorry to see him so worried.

Newman gazed ahead, down the avenue of trees.

'A vista has opened to me,' he said at last, almost in a whisper, 'to the end of which I do not see.'

In the pause after he spoke the Merton bells struck out the chime of the hour, the notes, with their haunting irregular intervals, sounding in the cool autumn air.

Then all the bells came in with their resonant tongues, reminding the ancient city of the passing of time, the hundreds of hundreds of hours gone by, time like a wind blowing over the stones, leaving walls and towers standing but carrying away men like leaves, turning even their delicate bones to dust. But inside those walls their ideas remained in the long shelves of books, so that words of men who died over a thousand years ago could spring again in this man's mind now, could strike him a blow to make him turn pale and wonder where he would be led, following the clue of truth.

Clem said, haltingly, 'I hope you will see your way clear, Mr. Newman.'

'Thank you', he said, pulling himself together. 'No doubt I am too startled to see things straightly. I must have made a mistake somewhere.'

They came to the end of the walk and Newman stopped.

'I must go back to college', he said. 'Will you be so kind as not to mention what I have said to anyone? But I must thank you for your attention and sympathy. I miss Jemima's presence so much; Derby is so far away. You are a kind listener!'

He said goodbye and went off with his long rapid stride towards the gate in the wall, back into the citadel of Oxford.

Clem gazed at the pale and smoky honeycomb of stone rising against the clear blue sky and thought how strange people were, what different worlds they lived in. Oxford was Newman's world, he was in his right place there, at home in the city of ideas and ideals. Then suddenly she remembered his telling her of the ruined temple in Sicily, the image of the desolation of mankind's ideas. There were the bare mountains and the broken temple; here was Oxford city alive, a golden head pulsing with thoughts: but time went on passing and the stone decaying.

The bells struck out again, the short tones of the quarter, and a coldness pierced her.

'I shall grow old', she thought. 'I shall not be loved. I shall have no children.' Because she had set her heart where there could be no answer to her longing.

She felt that she too had looked down a long avenue where she might have to go, but did not want to go, because it ended in mist and loneliness.

'Come on, come on!' Clara cried impatiently, tugging at her hand.

She was glad to go, running away from that ghostly inward place where the crossroads lay. No need to look ahead! She ran with Clara along the bank of the river, laughing, trying to catch the falling leaves for luck, and one fell right in her face. She felt young and strong again as she ran and did not care when elderly persons turned round to stare at her in shocked amazement.

# 2

Clem was a tenacious person. Loving Bertram might be a hopeless business, but she did not give it up. She went on all through the winter. It was only too easy to hold to her decision to let no one guess her feelings; nobody appeared to think she had any. Certainly Bertram never noticed; he treated her as he always had, in an easy, friendly way, relying on her for things Lucy could not do and which he did not wish to confide to his mother. From Bertram, too, she learned more of the Oxford controversies, but not much, for hers was the sort of mind that found ideas difficult and was opened only by the personal touch. She was interested in anything that concerned Newman, because she knew and liked him, but on the whole she felt more sorry for him when he caught a bad cold in March than when, about the same time, he confided to them some of his increasing anxiety of spirit.

'I am afraid that no religious body may be strong enough to withstand the league of evil but the Roman Church', he said once, gloomily. 'At the end of the first millenary it withstood the fury of Satan, and now the end of the second is drawing on.'

'Why, that's a hundred and fifty years ahead!' Clem cried.

'Not a long time in the history of the Church', he observed. 'What we see now is only the beginning. I expect a great attack on the Bible. Indeed, I have long expected it.'

Bertram laughed. 'You don't imagine Rome will be a defender of the Bible?' he said. 'Why, their people are not even allowed to read it!'

'The Bible has come from the Church, not the Church from the Bible', Newman said. 'I do not see how it can stand alone.'

After he had gone Lucy remarked, 'Mr. Newman talks quite as if he were a Roman Catholic. Don't you think he'll go over?'

'Nonsense!' said Bertram. 'You don't suppose they make their converts out of learned and mature minds? Romantic boys, women and artists, those are the only converts of our class. As for Newman, he always has had an exaggerated sense of the evils of the time. Besides, he's overtired. I wish he would rest at Littlemore, as he's going to be there till Easter, but now he's taken to catechizing the children on Sundays.'

'Yes', said Lucy. 'And I hear half of Oxford goes out to hear him.'

Clem was one of those who went, out of curiosity.

There was no sign of despondency in Newman while he was with the children. His cold was gone, he seemed full of life and taught with great spirit; he interested the children and they answered eagerly. One Thursday, too, Clem went into the Littlemore schoolroom and found them all singing, Newman leading them with his fiddle, his hair flopping energetically in time to the music. He was pleased to see Clem and made the children sing a psalm to show her how clever they were at it now.

As they all flocked away he said, 'I think they *do* look tidier, don't they? I had to lecture them about keeping their work clean, not to mention their hands and faces! That's the sort of task that makes me miss my dear mother and the girls. They did so much for me at Littlemore.'

'You like it here, don't you?' Clem said, glancing round the bare schoolroom. Littlemore's poor and dirty cottages, the new plain chapel, seemed to mean more to Newman than beautiful St. Mary's and the crowds of well-fed, well-educated people who hung on his words when he preached there.

'It is a haven, a retreat, dear Littlemore', he answered. 'Perhaps I'll come and live here altogether, some day. It gets more and more difficult for me in a public position, now that people in authority are beginning to turn against me.'

'But are they really doing so? I think you fancy there is more opposition than there is', said Clem, repeating what Bertram always said.

Newman smiled. 'Oh, I know I always croak! I hope you are right, but whatever happens I would like to come here, with perhaps one or two friends, and live a more regular life.'

'What, in a kind of monastery?' Clem asked.

'Sometimes I call it that, but it would be more like a miniature college of a religious kind.'

Talking to Bertram about it later, Clem said, 'I think it's a good idea. He needs somewhere to retire and rest.'

'Rest!' said Bertram. 'Do you know he has been living on bread and tea and very little else this Lent? Newman takes everything too far, that is his trouble.'

But after Easter Newman did buy some land and begin to plan his 'monastery'.

It was a beautiful spring, the first really good one for four years; May was so brilliant, so green and flowery, that Clem could not feel sad. She had got used to her love, got used to her silence; it was only sometimes that she was sensible of the wound of it.

One fine evening when they were all in the drawing-room after dinner, the maid announced the arrival of the

Honourable Augustine Firle, and in walked a small young man, wrapped up, in spite of the warm weather, in a great many clothes.

'Augustine! What a surprise!' said Bertram, rising.

'Is it? Oh dear!' said Augustine Firle sadly. 'You didn't get my letter then? That's the worst of posting things in France, they probably end up tucked inside a lady's garter. Well! Shall I go to the Mitre to stay?'

'Certainly not', said Bertram. 'Of course you will stay here, won't he, Mamma?'

'Dear Aunt', said Augustine, going up to her. 'How tremendously regal you look, much more so than our little Queen. What a pity you aren't a Queen!'

Mrs. Scarvell rose to greet her nephew, towering above him, so that Clem wanted to laugh at the ludicrous sight. When Augustine was introduced to Clem he said, 'How do you manage to have such charming cousins, Bertram? When I have only horrible ones—excluding yourself, of course.'

He unwound a very long muffler from his neck. 'Perhaps I had better unveil', he remarked. 'It was the boat, you know. Water is such cold stuff; I do hate it.'

Mrs. Scarvell asked Clem to go and see about a room for him, so she went and supervised some hurried activity on the part of the maids, and watched the Honourable Augustine's boxes brought up. He had an Italian manservant, a small nimble fellow whom she at once christened Figaro. This little man fussed about, getting his master's things arranged to his liking.

'The signore likes this so, so', he kept saying, while the maids glanced at each other and giggled at his foreign ways.

When Clem went down to the drawing-room again Augustine Firle was sitting in a large armchair, looking smaller than ever, since he had divested himself of his big overcoat.

Bertram had once said he looked like a monkey; Clem felt she would have called him a goblin, because his head, covered with thick black curly hair, looked large for his small thin body. His forehead, his whole face creased up when he smiled, which he often did; he had a wide mouth and eyebrows that bent up in the middle, so that it would have been difficult for him to look solemn if he had tried. It seemed strange that Bertram, who was so tall and fair and strong, should have such an odd little cousin, with small white hands like a delicate boy's.

The family were asking him about affairs abroad.

'I daren't join in politics', he said. 'What would happen if I was challenged to a duel? If I fought I'd be bound to get spitted and if I didn't my favourite hostesses would refuse to receive me. So I cultivate the arts and look silly when the Austrians and the French are mentioned.'

'It's the duty of every responsible person to take an interest in public affairs', said Bertram.

'But then I'm not a responsible person, am I?' said Augustine cheerfully. 'I go to Rome because the winter is short and there are so many pleasant people to talk to there.'

'I hope you are in good health, Augustine?' said Mrs. Scarvell, solicitously.

'Alive is all I care about', he answered. 'But that boat made me wonder whether death was not preferable after all.'

Presently he said that if his room was ready he would like to go to bed, and so left them.

Mrs. Scarvell remarked, 'He looks better than he did last time I saw him.'

'Pooh!' snorted Bertram. 'His illnesses are largely imaginary, an excuse to do as he pleases.'

The Honourable Augustine did not come down to breakfast. Later in the morning Clem was bringing Clara back from a walk when she came upon him in the churchyard, peering at a tombstone.

'Pretty little cherub there', he observed, taking off his hat to her. 'Only head and wings, of course: the English imagination is so chaste, especially where religion is concerned.'

Clem did not know what to say, so she laughed.

'What a relief!' said Augustine. 'I thought you were going to be shocked when I'd said it. I always forget to think before I speak—it leads to bizarre situations sometimes.' Clara was staring at him, and he suddenly put down his head and stared back, and then laughed. 'I can't have you growing like this, Clara', he said. 'You're nearly as tall as me and it's impossible to retain any dignity if one is not taller than mere children.' He turned to Clem. 'It's one of the advantages of living in Italy, Miss Clem, that I don't feel a dwarf more than half the day there.'

'I'm not as tall as you', Clem observed with a smile.

'I noticed that', said Augustine. 'That is one reason why I am flinging myself at your feet without delay. The other is because you laughed at my remark on the cherubs. It shows you have a kind heart.'

'We had some funny ones on the tombstones at home, in Cornwall', said Clem.

'Cornwall? Is that where you come from?' said Augustine. 'I thought everyone in Cornwall was gaunt and beetle-browed, romantic to the last drop of blood.'

Clem laughed.

'You do laugh in a nice way', said Augustine. 'Do it again.'

Of course Clem could not help doing so. 'Do stop talking such nonsense', she said.

'I can't help it', said Augustine. 'I don't know any sense to talk and I must *talk*. Do you like Oxford? Do all the young dons, if there is such a thing as a young don, fling themselves at your feet?'

'Of course not', said Clem.

'I hear they're all too busy flinging themselves at the feet of one John Henry Newman', said Augustine. 'Is he going to turn Catholic, by the way?'

'Good gracious no', said Clem. 'That is, he is Catholic already, but not Roman. Bertram is always having to deny rumours like that.'

Augustine nodded towards the church. 'I've been in there. I see old Bertram's got ideas too. A cloth on the altar and no box pews to go to sleep in. I hope his sermons are worth it!'

A little annoyed at his tone, Clem said, 'It's a serious matter to Bertram.'

'Everything is always a serious matter in England', said Augustine, sadly. 'That's why I don't live in it much. I doubt if I'd come back at all if it weren't for my brother. Have you any brothers, Miss Clem?'

'No', said Clem.

'How splendid!' said Augustine. 'They won't come wanting to knock me down for dallying with you in the churchyard.'

Clem could not help laughing.

'Dalliance with me is plainly a comic notion to you', said Augustine. 'Perhaps our conversation has been too impersonal? Is your name Clementina, by the way?'

'No, Clemency, unfortunately.'

'Why not pretend it is Clementina?' he suggested.

'I never thought of it.'

'Ah, you have an innocent mind', said Augustine. 'I've often thought of pretending my name was different, but too many people know it. It's a relic of my mother's Catholic phase. In fact, I am a relic of it myself, and so is my brother. We are Catholics because she went through a conversion; she has gone right through and out the other side, but here we are, like pickled onions, or pickled relics perhaps I should say, perpetuating the time when she was never happy without a Monsignor in the house.'

'Are you serious?' said Clem doubtfully.

'No, not at all', said Augustine. 'I never am if I can help it.'

'You're not a Roman Catholic then?'

'Oh yes, I am, but that's not serious.'

Clem did not know what to say. She was used to households where it was so extremely serious to be a Roman Catholic that people were turned out for becoming so.

'Oh, dear Clementina, do laugh!' begged Augustine, clasping his hands and sending Clara off into helpless giggles. 'It doesn't suit you at all to try to look like Cousin Bertram.'

Clem blushed and smiled. 'I suppose he can't mind about you', she said. 'As you are his cousin.'

'They don't mind when we've always been Catholics', said Augustine. 'It's like being born black, something you can't help. It's deciding to be one that upsets them so, like saying you *will* be a negro and no one is going to stop you.'

Clem now laughed aloud. They had wandered to the gate into the garden and saw Bertram and George, who was staying, pacing the drive, two black figures, one lean and one fat, deep in earnest discussion.

'Two holy Fathers', observed Augustine. 'Cyril of Oxford and Cyril of London.'

Clem was giggling cheerfully when Bertram turned round and saw them. He looked at her in surprise.

'Good morning, Augustine', he said in a chilly voice. 'What do you find so amusing?'

'I was comparing you to the reverend and learned Fathers of the Church', said Augustine solemnly.

Clara's squeak of laughter annoyed Bertram and he sent her indoors to get ready for luncheon.

George Pierce said, 'Are you familiar with the F-Fathers, Mr. F-Firle?'

'I wouldn't dare to be', said Augustine. 'They turn up in the missal from time to time, but I quickly flip over the page and find a nice little virgin martyr. Much more in my line.'

Bertram and George both looked so shocked that Clem wanted to laugh more than ever. She caught Augustine's bright eye fixed on her and he gave a discreet wink. It was too much, and she burst into a wild chuckle.

George looked astonished and Bertram extremely displeased. After lunch he took Clem aside and said, 'Clem, I was sorry to see you laughing at Augustine's vulgar nonsense.'

Clem turned hot all over, hating to be disapproved by Bertram.

'I'm sure you didn't mean to encourage him', Bertram went on. 'But he has no idea what is proper conversation for an English lady's ears. No doubt it comes from living so much abroad.'

Clem rebelled. 'But he didn't mean any harm, Bertram. It was just fun.'

'I don't like the way he has immediately tried to ingratiate himself with you', said Bertram. 'I have heard nothing but bad reports of his behaviour and I consider him an utterly untrustworthy person.'

Clem, looking up covertly into his angry face, suddenly wondered if he were jealous. Of course not, she told herself quickly. But he was certainly more annoyed than the occasion warranted.

'I'm sorry, Bertram', she said meekly. 'I just met him by chance in the churchyard. I didn't know you thought him untrustworthy.'

Bertram was mollified. 'So long as you realize he should not be encouraged, that is all right', he said. 'It's a great pity Aunt Eleanor was perverted to Rome and had the boys put to school with the Jesuits. It has obviously destroyed Augustine's judgement completely. It is a very sad thing.'

It might be a sad thing, but Augustine was not a sad person. Although Clem had now been so long, as she felt it, in love with Bertram, she thought him a little heavy-handed where his cousin was concerned. Of course men ought not to waste their time in Italy amusing themselves (and she wondered what his amusement was, whether he kept a mistress abroad, as people in books sometimes did), but still it seemed unnecessary to go so far in deference to Bertram as to refuse to laugh if Augustine said something funny. She laughed.

Augustine was only staying a few days, and he did not divulge what had brought him to Oxford; whatever it was did not take up much of his time. The second afternoon of his visit he came out into the garden, where she was sitting alone, for the Scarvells had all gone into the country on an invitation accepted long before, and suggested a drive into the town. Since there was no one to forbid it, she agreed. After all, nothing very wicked could happen in Oxford.

It was a warm June day and they walked slowly up the High Street and went into St. Mary's, because Augustine said he had forgotten what it looked like inside. It was large and dim and cool, so cool that after a little Clem, in her thin muslin, began to shiver. Augustine at once apologized and took her out again into the Radcliffe Square and the hot sun. He squinted up at the spire.

'Really, it's nicer outside', he pronounced. 'So that's where the famous Mr. Newman spins his theological webs. What a pity he should waste his time constructing that paper religion of his—neither Catholic fish nor Protestant flesh!'

'I think that's a very insulting thing to say!' cried Clem indignantly.

'Have I made you angry, Clementina? And merely about religious opinions? Oh do forgive me!' he said. 'I didn't say he was a paper person. I know he's a very good man, much better than wretched me. I told you I couldn't talk sense. You must forgive me or I shall burst into tears.'

Clem smiled. 'Don't do that', she said. 'But Mr. Newman is so tried with people attacking him and misrepresenting what he says, that I don't like to hear him mocked.'

'I won't mock him, I promise', said Augustine. 'What shall we do now?'

'Whatever you like', said Clem, with another little shiver, for the chill of the empty stone church was still on her.

'Still cold?' said Augustine solicitously. 'Let's find a seat in the sun.'

This turned out more difficult than he supposed, but they did find one at last, in Christ Church Meadow, and though Clem was quite warm then from walking, they sat down. The sun beat steadily down from the middle of the blue still sky.

'Clem,' said Augustine suddenly, 'don't you ever get tired of this high-minded vicarage life? Don't you ever feel the need of a little fun?'

Clem had not thought about it before, but now she had to admit to herself that sometimes she longed to escape the physical ease and mental unrest of Bertram's home. But she said, 'I am lucky to be able to live with my cousins. I've no money and no one else to go to, and anyway I like them very much.'

'I know you do', said Augustine. 'But you must wish sometimes that your life was your own.'

'Only sometimes', said Clem firmly.

Augustine leant his cane carefully against the end of the seat.

'Well, this may not be fun for you, but it is for me', he said, and put his hands on her shoulders and kissed her.

Clem was very surprised. No one had ever kissed her like that, on the mouth.

Augustine laughed at her expression and kissed her again.

'No! Stop it!' cried Clem, breathlessly.

'Not fun?' he said, smiling and mischievous.

'No', she said firmly.

'Liar!' said Augustine cheerfully.

'Aren't you conceited?' she said, recovering herself a little.

'It wasn't me I thought you would like, so much as kissing', he said. 'You do.'

'No I don't', she retorted quickly. 'It was very—it was quite wrong of you, and right out here in the Meadow, too.'

'More fun in private, you think?' he said hopefully. He did not seem to be taking any notice of what she said, and was holding her hand, she suddenly discovered.

'Augustine, let go of my hand.'

'Clementina, it just doesn't suit you, being prim. That nice little snub face was made for kissing. I wish you would let me do it again.'

'I won't.'

'As nicely as possible', he pleaded.

'Certainly not.'

Augustine laughed and kissed her hand instead.

Clem suddenly remembered Bertram's warning. He had said Augustine was utterly untrustworthy. Now he was behaving just like that. And what about her own behaviour? She had just called him by his Christian name, which was not at all proper.

'I think we ought to go home', she said.

'And *I* think that's a horrid idea', said Augustine. 'I can't possibly kiss you there with Bertram waiting to battleaxe me.'

'You're not going to kiss me here either', said Clem. 'Suppose somebody saw us?'

'If that's your only objection, we could find a more secluded corner', said Augustine.

'Of course it isn't my only objection!' cried Clem hotly. 'Why should you think I like being kissed by you, when I know perfectly well you're only doing it because you're bored and there isn't any prettier girl to kiss?'

'How do you know why I'm kissing you?' he teased her. 'I haven't told you.'

'You don't need to', she said. 'I know the kind of person you are.'

'How can you?' he demanded. 'I met you only the day before yesterday.'

'A really good person wouldn't start kissing a girl he has known only that long.'

Augustine smiled. 'But you get to know girls only after you start kissing them', he said. 'Especially English girls. They don't even know themselves till they start.'

'Thank you', said Clem coldly.

'Oh, Clem, do laugh!' he pleaded, as he had in the churchyard. 'Don't be so high and mighty about two little kisses, really hardly kisses at all, were they? Just two little appetizers. Do laugh, Clem.'

She tried hard not to, but she could not really take it so seriously. She laughed.

'Bless you! Now we'll go home if you like', said Augustine. 'Unless you will give me the lucky third after all? Do!'

'I can't think why I should.'

'Because it's fun.'

Clem suddenly abandoned propriety. 'All right, I will', she said, boldly.

'You blessed little cherub, you!' said Augustine, delighted.

He did not take his kiss in a hurry, but put his arms round her and prolonged it.

Clem felt so many different things all at once she was quite bewildered. She realized she was being embraced by a man she hardly knew and that she was liking it. She was deeply shocked at herself, so much so that when Augustine stopped kissing her and looked in her face, he said in a changed voice, 'My dear girl, what's the matter?'

'It's me', Clem said, incoherently, struggling against a rising tide of tears. 'How dreadful of me! How could I?'

The tears overflowed.

'My dear sweet Clem, don't cry', said Augustine anxiously. 'I didn't mean to make you unhappy.'

'No, I know you were only amusing yourself', she sobbed. 'But I—I shouldn't be kissing someone I don't love—it ought to be—'

She stopped, just in time. It ought to be Bertram he was kissing, not the cousin he said was untrustworthy and looked like a monkey.

Augustine still sat with his arm round her, nor did she mind it.

'I'm sorry, Clem', he said gently. 'I didn't know you were in love with someone else.'

'I'm not!' she cried wildly. How could he have guessed that, her deepest secret?

He did not press the subject, but said presently, 'Don't worry about it, will you? It was not at all your fault, but only mine. You can forget it, if you like.'

'That's easy for you!' she sobbed indignantly. 'You're doing it all the time!'

'Am I?' said Augustine. 'Who said so? Well, never mind that now. No one, not even a jealous lover, could call your behaviour abandoned. Clem! Do laugh!'

'I can't!' she cried, gasping. 'I'm miserable.'

'Clem, I won't let you be miserable for such a little thing', he said. 'You're a dear sweet girl, and he's lucky, whoever he is—not dear old George, I hope? He's good, but dull as a dumpling. Clem, come, you needn't tell that lucky fellow— what a slow one he must be! You needn't tell him you've been kissed before.'

'Oh don't!' she cried in despair. 'It's not like that, nothing like that.'

Augustine looked at her so keenly she felt he must be reading her mind, but again he dropped the subject.

'Do you know what?' he said. 'We are going to walk about and look at the flowers.'

'There aren't any flowers', Clem said dismally.

'At the trees then.'

She submitted to being walked slowly along by the river, Augustine holding her arm and solemnly pointing out with his cane the daisies and buttercups, loading them with long Latin names.

'Here's a very rare one', he announced, poking at a small faded buttercup on a bent stalk. 'Ranunculus ridiculosus toomanynightcapsknocksusover.'

Clem realized then he was inventing the nonsense to make her laugh. And in the end she laughed. After all, what did it matter? She never could be in Bertram's arms, so why be miserable for this?

'That's better', Augustine said.

By the time they were driving home she had quite recovered, and even apologized for making such a fuss.

'I shall be thankful if you don't hate me for ever', said Augustine. 'You don't, do you?'

'No, of course not', she said, smiling.

'All's well that ends well', he said.

Unfortunately the episode did not end there. Someone who knew Clem by sight had seen them in the Meadow and made it her business to let Mrs. Scarvell know at once, and she, of course, told her son.

Clem was ready early for dinner, and found only Augustine in the drawing-room. She discovered she was not at all embarrassed by his presence, which surprised her. They were soon amusing themselves picking out the tunes of their favourite songs on the piano, and as neither was an able performer the results led to some hilarity. Suddenly there was Bertram in the doorway, looking very tall and stiff, his blue eyes blazing.

'Augustine!' he said. 'I am ashamed to have you in the house!'

Clem jumped and felt herself turn scarlet, but Augustine said easily, 'Bertram, calm down. There's no harm done.'

'No harm!' Bertram glared at him and then turned on Clem. 'I don't know how you could go out with him, Clem, after my warning.'

'Now don't lecture Clem', said Augustine. 'It's not her fault if her admirers start kissing her. She put up a good fight and she has won her case. I won't do it again.'

'It's a disgrace', Bertram said. 'And I am responsible for not looking after Clem more carefully. I should have known better than to leave her exposed to your attentions. I wish you to leave this house immediately.'

'Now?' said Augustine, raising an eyebrow. 'Before dinner?'

'To-morrow', emended Bertram, deflated and annoyed.

'I am going to-morrow in any case', Augustine pointed out. 'Clem has forgiven me; why can't you?'

'I'm certain Clem has done nothing of the sort', said Bertram crossly. 'Why you had to go into Oxford and behave like that in public I cannot imagine.'

'It wasn't a premeditated crime', said Augustine. 'It was a *crime passionel*, the inspiration of the moment.'

'How can you speak of it in that flippant manner?' said Bertram fiercely. 'It disgusts me! An English gentleman to behave in such a vulgar way in public! I don't know that I can bring myself to sit at the same table with you.'

'Then I shall retire gracefully to my room', said Augustine calmly. 'We mustn't have digestions upset by a few pleasant kisses. If you wish to repeat your strictures on my conduct in more detail I shall be happy to listen to you while lying down in comfort.'

'It's as much as I can do not to knock you down', Bertram growled.

'I know', said Augustine. 'That's why I am going to put myself in a recumbent position at once. Goodnight, Clem. I'm sorry to have stirred up the wasps' nest for you.'

He went out, and they heard him going upstairs, whistling.

'He's not even ashamed of himself!' Bertram said furiously. Then he turned to Clem and took both her hands. 'My dear little cousin, I cannot tell you how sorry I am that this should have happened.'

'Oh, please don't worry, Bertram', she said, overcome with embarrassment, but liking to have him hold her hands and speak so tenderly to her. 'I made him understand he must not do it again. Perhaps they go on like that in Italy. He did not mean anything by it.'

'That's exactly what is so despicable', said Bertram.

The dinner bell rang, and the moment of contact was over. As soon as she could, Clem fled to her room. She opened the window and gazed into the cool dim evening. One star was out, very high up. The scent of flowers hung in the still air. All sorts of feelings chased through Clem's heart, but most of all surprise. She was surprised at herself still for not minding Augustine's kisses.

He left the next day and she saw him for only a moment, as he was coming downstairs in his ridiculous big coat, ready to go. She hesitated as to whether to go on and meet him, or retire and avoid him. He smiled at her in a friendly way, so she went on.

'Goodbye, Clem', he said. 'Don't be too high-minded!'

That was all, except that he gave her arm a squeeze in passing.

Clem tried to feel relieved that he was gone, but in fact the vicarage seemed suddenly dull, and the conversations interminable, as she sat over her sewing and remembered that Augustine had nicknamed Bertram and George Cyril of Oxford and Cyril of London. She tried not to smile at the memory. But she smiled.

# 3

The next winter Lucy was seriously ill and Clem had to run the house, since Mrs. Scarvell, to everyone's relief, was abroad with an ailing sister. Clem was now looking after Bertram's home, his child, and even his clothes, and yet she was no nearer to him than before. She could not help knowing that Lucy's death might mean future happiness for her, and she hated herself even for thinking of it. It made her feel guilty, and the burden of this guilt so oppressed her that sometimes she hardly knew what to do with herself. Her room was no longer an escape; it was too much hers. She went out looking for peace, sometimes going into the old churches of the city, but she could never find what she wanted, or even be sure what it was. Once she tried kneeling down to pray, but a verger came in and stared suspiciously at her, so that she felt a fool and went disconsolate away.

Going to the Sunday services in Bertram's little church was no help; her feelings and thoughts were so concentrated on the man that the words of God did not come through to her. Worse still, she discovered that the Christian religion, which she had lived in so casually all these years, and which she did not now doubt, or even examine in an intellectual way, somehow had no real meaning for her; at any rate it was not as real as her love and her guilt and her unhappy loneliness.

Once or twice she went to the afternoon services at St. Mary's to hear Newman's sermons. When he preached he stood very still, he made no gestures, he read what he had prepared with a curious delivery: a rapid and clear sentence would come out, followed by a noticeable pause, and then another sentence. In this way what he said was like a flight of arrows to the heart, each one found its target. When he started he was cool, but often as he went on, what he was saying began to affect him too, so that his words seemed to grow and quiver with intensity; yet there was never any hint of dramatic effect, or of what is generally called self-consciousness. Clem always felt that Newman was acutely conscious of himself, but that his consciousness of his Creator was so much greater that when he spoke of him he was able to be absolutely simple and direct. He never mentioned the questions of the day, as they were discussed in newspapers and common rooms; always he spoke of Christ and his redeeming power, and how this could change and govern the lives of all. Clem was sometimes surprised at the way in which he could penetrate the thoughts and feelings of other people, particularly in revealing self-deceptions that commonly went unnoticed. He would never allow his hearers to imagine themselves virtuous; at the same time he put Christ before them as the source of life and courage.

But what was so real to Newman was not truly real to Clem; when she went out of reach of his voice she slipped back into her own meaningless misery. Sometimes she wished she could tell it to him, and yet it was not a thing she could tell anyone, really. She must go through it alone, seeing no end.

Lucy began to recover as spring returned to the earth and the air. Clem's load of guilt lightened a little, though her heart did not. Bertram looked less strained and began to take an interest again in outside affairs, especially in religious controversy, suddenly raised again by the outcry which greeted the publication of Newman's latest Tract, No. 90, in which he had tried to interpret the Thirty-Nine Articles in a Catholic sense. In March Clem met Newman in the street and asked him how the sales were going.

'Too well!' he said, with a smile. 'Do you know I am getting into a scrape over that Tract?' The wind blew his hair about and Clem thought he looked almost boyish, certainly not forty years old; his birthday, about which he had groaned heavily, had occurred last month. 'Yes! I fear I am clean dished!'

The slang made her laugh. 'Why are you dished, Mr. Newman? Your head in a dish, like John the Baptist?'

He laughed, but then said seriously enough, 'I'd no idea it would attract so much attention. I daresay I've got Golightly to blame for a good deal.'

Golightly had been Newman's pupil years ago, before Clem had met him; he was an ebullient character, full of opinions and fond of pulling strings.

'Oh dear', Clem said. 'Has he got a bee in his bonnet about you?'

Newman laughed. 'He certainly has! He's sending the Tract to everyone, bishops and all, with red-pencil warnings, of course. Well! Golly wouldn't be Golly if he didn't *goliare*! But Lord Morpeth's attack on us in Parliament, just before the Tract came out, has made everyone so frightened that anything may happen.'

'But what could happen, except a lot of talk?'

'People are so angry they will attempt anything', he said. 'The Heads of Houses are on the move. I believe they are at this moment concocting a manifesto against me.'

'But what would that *mean*?'

'My Tract might be condemned in Convocation', he said. 'If my bishop condemns me, that *would* be a blow. I should have to withdraw it then.'

'I hope it won't put you in a bad position', said Clem, wondering if the frightened authorities could possibly expel him from the University.

But typically he took her to mean his mental rather than his physical position.

'Oh no, now I am in my right place', he said. 'I've long wished to get there and did not know how to; I hate being in a false position. Now it has happened, without my intention, providentially, I believe.' He looked positively happy to be in danger of losing his job, his reputation and his home all at one blow. 'Of course,' he added suddenly, 'I know the trouble of it is also a punishment, for my secret pride and sloth.'

'Mr. Newman! How can it be both?' Clem cried, touched, but on the verge of laughter.

'But it can, you know', he said earnestly. 'That is just how God deals with us. The hardest trials are often his greatest providences.'

'Well, I hope they will not censure you', said Clem, smiling. 'You may be ready to be martyred, but how your friends would miss you!'

'I don't mind if they censure *me*', Newman said. 'So long as no doctrine is censured.'

Clem looked up. 'Because that would mean the Church of England did not believe itself to be what you believe it to be?'

She saw a look of uncertainty and unhappiness in his eyes, but it passed quickly.

'That cannot be', he said. 'There are *people* in our church who do not see it as we see it; that is why I believe my writings have been necessary, even though full of my own imperfections, to put forward the Catholic view. And I include this Tract, for I do not repent it in the least, whatever happens.'

Clem laughed. 'I believe you enjoy these battles, Mr. Newman!' she teased him. 'You are always more cheerful while they are on!'

She said goodbye and left him standing there, gently protesting, the March wind ruffling his thick straight hair into untidy plumes.

She mentioned her encounter to Bertram and was surprised to find he was upset by the publicity of the Tract row and indignant with Newman for causing it.

'Why can't he leave things alone?' he complained. 'We should do much better if he did not go on so fast. These extreme views will put all sensible people against us and the mob will begin to howl "No Popery", not without cause. What is it about Newman? Why must he go on so far?'

This was how all the Tractarian friends talked, as if the church were a road along which they were progressing. Steps forward were in getting people to understand the meaning of sacraments and the reason for the authority of bishops; to some, even crosses and candles in church were steps forward of a symbolic kind. But angry remarks by bishops who did not realize they were the apostles' successors, or by clergymen who baptized but did not believe baptism effected anything, were steps back, a sad reverse. And men like Newman, if there was anyone quite like him, who had been marching with the banners in the vanguard, were now rushing on rashly alone, leaving the main body far behind. And yet to Dr. Arnold's liberal followers, as Clem knew, all this progress was regress, and the Tractarians were all hurrying headlong down the slope of reaction, like the maddened herd of Gadara, and would undoubtedly end up by falling into the black and bottomless sea of the Roman Catholic Church, drowned in superstition and dogma, beyond reach of the clean wind of enlightenment and freedom that was blowing through the world with the promise of spring, the vision of the earthly paradise.

Here was a conflict of ideas, but most of the people Clem knew were less concerned with the ideas than with their effects. Mrs. Scarvell, who had now returned home, was very pleased to find Bertram dissociating himself at last from Mr. Newman.

'Now perhaps he will get some preferment', she said. 'Of course no one could advance a man who held such opinions as Mr. Newman's. I consider him an extremely dangerous man, and it is shocking to think of the influence he has on unformed young men.'

Several ladies, who were taking tea at the vicarage, began to join in with the latest gossip.

'Someone told me she actually heard Mr. Newman say a prayer to St. Mary', hissed one of them. 'In the *service.*'

'And he's been seen in St. Mary's Church with a large cross down the back of his surplice.'

Clem could not help laughing at this nonsense. 'Don't tell me poor Dr. Pusey sacrifices a lamb every Friday', she said. 'I've heard that one before.'

Mrs. Scarvell reproved her for such levity. 'Of course that is not true', she said, and Clem tried not to giggle at the inward vision of kind, serious Dr. Pusey performing this pagan rite in his respectable household. 'But it is true that their opinions, if followed to their conclusion, would lead to all the superstitions of Rome.'

Clem worked away at her mending and wondered idly what these Roman superstitions were of which everyone

was so frightened. But the only Roman Catholic she knew
was Augustine Firle, who seemed to be more interested in
kisses than idols.

The Tract battle, after the first flare-up, sputtered on without definite conclusion, like so many Anglican battles. Nothing drastic happened to Newman, but his position became
slowly more and more difficult, beset with problems within
and without. And after this he was marked down as dangerous; suspicions surrounded him. He, the most unsuspecting of persons, was suspected of every kind of hypocrisy
and subtlety; sometimes the insinuations were base, sometimes merely ridiculous. Clem often wondered why people
minded so much what he said and did; somehow this rather
shy, courteous man, only keen and fearless, as after all a
clerical don should be, in pursuit of truth, had become
a figure of importance to the educated public of England, a
figure who unexpectedly focused on himself all kinds of
violent, contradictory and often irrational feelings, which
he was beginning to be aware of, with bewilderment and
anxiety, almost fear, for although he wanted his cause to
win he never thought of himself as a leader, the head of a
party. And indeed, he shared the unpleasant surprise of notoriety with his friend Pusey, who deserved it even less, since
his opinions had been more fixed than Newman's when he
had cautiously added the weight of his learned volumes to
the lighter stream of the first Tracts; Pusey was more of a
scholar and less of a preacher than Newman; perfectly at
home in the past, he could not understand when the present
jumped up and hit him. Newman told Clem that his only
anxiety over the Tract row was that it would bring more
trouble on Pusey, who had enough to suffer in his loneliness after his loved wife's death, with his young daughter so
delicate. But however strange it was that England should be

troubled by these Oxford divines, troubled it was. They struck at something in the public mind that was deeper than perhaps they knew themselves. It was certainly a mystery to Clem at that time.

As the weather got better Lucy Scarvell began to make an astonishing recovery. Everyone was surprised; Bertram overjoyed. His fond love for his sick wife was admirable, Clem knew; it made her feel worse than ever. She was afraid of her own heart, afraid she was not as glad as she ought to be when Lucy got up. And Lucy, now that she was about again, began to be jealous of Clem's place in the household, the way everyone, even Bertram, referred things to her. Clem would sometimes look up and find Lucy's resentful blue eyes fixed on her; she would go hot all over and wonder if her secret were discovered. She hardly knew how to speak to Bertram in Lucy's presence, and everything he said to her seemed to suggest some meaning Lucy might misinterpret.

She knew she ought to leave, but she could not make up her mind to it. Oxford contained all that she loved, and this year she would be thirty; after that, people said, there was no chance of marriage. She thought of herself as an ageing governess in a stranger's house and put off the decision, though she knew that the longer she stayed the worse things would be in the end.

One hot day in August she was walking alone through the town when a voice called from behind her, a man's voice, pleasant and somehow familiar to her.

'Miss Clem! Don't run away from me so fast!'

She turned round and saw it was Augustine Firle. He came up to her with his hat in his hand, smiling, and she felt pleased to see his cheerful face again.

'I'm so glad to have caught you alone', he said. 'I was wondering how I should see you, since Bertram forbade me ever to darken his doors again—not that I should block them up very effectively, should I? How are you, Clem?'

'I'm very well', she said, aware that he was holding her hand and looking closely at her, and surprised to find how keen his grey eyes were.

'You don't look it', he said. 'You look strained and unhappy, and tired too. It's very hot. Now will you come into the Mitre and drink some tea?' Clem hesitated, and he went on at once, 'Of course I know it isn't done for young ladies to take tea alone with gentlemen in the Mitre, but why not start a precedent?'

'Very well', said Clem. 'After all, I'm not such a very young lady now. I'll be thirty next month.'

'Will you really?' said Augustine, interested. 'You don't look it. Well, I'm thirty-three, I may tell you, so you're not to make me feel old by saying you're no longer young! Come along.'

It was very nice, Clem thought, to sit and drink tea with Augustine, and no one, not even Mrs. Scarvell, could have called his behaviour or his conversation improper. In fact, he was so friendly that Clem found herself telling him she was thinking of going away to teach in a school.

'I told you that you ought to live a life of your own', he said. 'But I can't see you as a schoolmarm.'

'It's the only alternative', said Clem wearily, not weighing her words.

'To marriage?' said Augustine. 'And is that altogether unthinkable?'

'Yes, it is', said Clem and then, to her horror, she found herself adding weakly, 'And yet I should so much have liked to have some children.'

She was so overcome at the impropriety of saying such a thing that she turned crimson and stared at the floor, murmuring, 'I'm sorry.'

'Why be sorry?' said Augustine. 'It's natural, isn't it? Have some more tea?'

He began to talk of other things, much to her relief. Later he escorted her most of the way home.

'What are you doing in Oxford out of term?' she asked.

'I came to see you', said Augustine at once. 'I wondered how you were getting on.'

'Oh', said Clem. She wondered if that were the truth, or just an idle compliment. 'How long will you be here?'

'I must leave directly', said Augustine. 'But I shall come back before I go abroad.'

'When will that be?'

'About October, I expect.'

In the weeks that followed Clem found herself vaguely looking forward to October and when it passed without a sign of Augustine she felt aggrieved. 'He just says things without meaning them', she told herself. But though she would not admit it, she was disappointed.

It was November, and a cold spell of frost and fog had set in, when one afternoon a card was brought in to Mrs. Scarvell which caused an exclamation of annoyance.

'Augustine! What can he want? How unfortunate that Bertram is out! I suppose I must see him, for poor Eleanor's sake. Clem, I think you had better go up to your room.'

'But I don't mind meeting Augustine again', said Clem, irritated, because her heart told her that Augustine had come to see her, rather than her aunt, and it pleased her.

'But I do not wish you to do so', said her aunt firmly. 'I shall refuse to see him unless you go upstairs.'

So Clem had to go, for she did not want to make an issue of it. She stood in her small cold room, half expecting to be called downstairs, but no message came, and presently she heard the front door shut and a carriage drive away. Disappointment closed in on her like the damp fog outside. She moved slowly to the window, as if the sight of the dark trees in the dun clouded air could dispel the coldness within. Everything was black or white in that winter world; the churchyard grass covered in a faint rime, the tombstones like black cards stuck this way and that.

Suddenly she saw a small dark figure coming out of the mist, in and out of the tombstones, coats and scarves flapping. It was unmistakeably Augustine. Surprised but pleased, Clem pushed up the window.

Augustine looked up and waved.

'Clem!' he called softly. 'Come down. I want to talk to you.'

Clem knew it was not the proper thing to do, but she caught up her cloak, ran down the back stairs and out of the garden door. She ran across the whitened grass in her light shoes, leaving shadow steps behind her, to the little iron gate, which Augustine was holding open for her. When she arrived, face to face with him, she was shy suddenly and angry with herself because she felt her cheeks burning.

'How nice of you to come', said Augustine. 'Now let's just get out of sight of the house, because if Aunt Scarvell caught us my life would not be worth living.'

He took her arm and guided her through the tombstones to the other side of the church. Its ancient mouldering bulk stood between them and the vicarage, and on the other side mist swirled softly between the great thick yews. It was very still.

'Clem', said Augustine. 'I've been thinking about you.'

'Have you?' she said, still shy.

'Yes. Have you made up your mind to leave here?'

'I don't know', said Clem feebly. 'I suppose I must.'

'Of course you must', he said. 'You can't stay on, feeling as you do about Bertram.'

Clem felt faint. 'You guessed', she whispered.

'Yes, of course', said Augustine. 'But he hasn't—yet.'

'I think Lucy has', she murmured, hardly audible.

'It will be bad for you all if this goes on', he said. 'Have you made any plans yet?'

Clem sighed. 'I must go to some school, I suppose.'

'Listen', said Augustine. 'I've got a much better plan. You marry me and come abroad. Make a complete break. Say yes, Clem.'

She stared at him in astonishment.

'What are you talking about?'

'Marriage!' he answered, with a grin.

'Augustine, do be sensible', said Clem crossly. 'You have just guessed my secret, the one I—I love.' It seemed odd to say that, after her long silence.

'Oh bother love!' he said impatiently. 'I'm not asking you to fall in love with me on the spot, that would be too tall an order altogether. There are other reasons for marrying; you told me one yourself once. But look at it this way. You don't want to teach in a school, and Bertram would never let you. There would be a terrible row and it would all come out and then where would you be? Whereas if you married me you would be free at one stroke. I've got one advantage, you see: money. Father's, of course, but mine to all intents and purposes. Oh, isn't it cold here?' He stamped his feet impatiently in the creaking snow. 'Do say yes, Clem.'

Clem stared at him. 'What are you asking me to do, Augustine?' she said at last. 'I don't believe you've thought about it for five minutes.'

'Yes, I have, for months', he said. 'Listen, Clem. I think we could be happy married to each other, but all I'm asking now is that you should let me make you legally my wife. That will give you a breathing space, and a chance to find out whether you can stand the sight of me for more than a few hours at a time. Later, you might feel able to make a new start, with me, I hope. But if not, a merely legal knot could be untied; it would be easy to get a decree of nullity and then you would be free of me too. Do you understand?'

Clem still stared at him, unable to believe what he was saying.

'I understand that you've thought out this mad idea to the last detail.'

'Mad idea? It's eminently reasonable', complained Augustine. 'And why lecture me for being methodical about it? It shows I mean what I say, doesn't it?'

Unreasonably, Clem turned haughty. 'It's kind of you to take so much trouble about me', she said. 'But it's much too generous an offer.'

Augustine refused to answer her tone of voice; there was no sign of emotion in his cheerful reply.

'Oh, come on, Clem, why make a fuss? It would be a nice holiday in Italy, because that's where we're going.'

Clem said feebly, 'It would be mean to say yes.'

'If you say no I shall scream the place down', he said. 'The elopement is all arranged, tickets waiting, horses pawing the ground. I propose to leave the marriage ceremony till we get abroad, because I know the law better there. Now, Clem, I'm freezing to death. Say yes, there's a dear girl.'

Clem stood among the tombstones, irresolute. And then she knew she was going to do it. She was going to run away from Bertram and her unlucky love, away from Lucy's watchful eyes, from Aunt Scarvell's domineering voice and Clara's teasing, from the vicarage and the parish and all the rest of it.

'Yes, then!' she said.

'*Bene!*' cried Augustine, and kissed her. 'Oh, I'm sorry, I forgot. I'm going to be extremely proper, really. You'll never know it's me. Run along, Clem dear, and fetch your jewels and pocket handkerchiefs.'

'Now?' she said, aghast.

He nodded. 'Yes, now, quickly, before you change your mind, or anyone finds out I'm here making improper suggestions.'

Clem laughed.

Yes, she thought, running back to the house, here I am, laughing. But as she went up to her room a feeling of anguish took hold of her. She was leaving her love, however illicit, leaving Bertram, giving him up for ever.

'Oh, Bertram!' she whispered and pressed her lips to the wood of his door as she passed.

But once in her own room she did not delay. She pulled out from the cupboard her father's old leather bag, and hastily packed all the things she thought she would need for the journey. Then she put on her walking shoes and her bonnet and went downstairs, lugging the bag, her heart in her mouth.

In the hall she met Lucy.

'Where are you going?' Lucy demanded suspiciously.

'Some things for the Higginses', Clem muttered. 'I shan't be long.'

'It's getting dark', Lucy said, peering at her through the evening gloom.

'Not outside yet', said Clem.

She hurried out of the door, shutting it behind her. She could not believe in what she was doing; her actions were unreal to her. She went up the drive, her heart hammering uncomfortably, and out of the gate, and there was Augustine waiting round the corner. He took her bag.

'Augustine', she said breathlessly. 'I lied to Lucy!'

'Splendid!' he said cheerfully.

'How shall I let them know I am all right?'

'We'll send a message from Dover', said Augustine. 'That's what they brought in the penny post for, didn't you know?'

He addressed his note to Bertram. Clem read it over his shoulder.

'Have eloped with Clem. Marrying abroad. Hope you don't mind.

Augustine Firle.'

# 4

On the boat crossing the Channel Clem had misgivings. When Augustine was not actually beside her she took fright at the thought of him, at having gone off like this with a stranger, trusting someone whom Bertram had several times told her was untrustworthy. But when he turned up again, looking very green because he had been seasick all the way over, it was difficult to be frightened of him. It surprised her when he drank some brandy out of a flask, and more still when he offered her 'a swig', but somehow he did not look very wicked, nor did the brandy make him drunk, as she had always imagined brandy did.

They travelled in Augustine's own carriage, and they went rapidly down through France, changing horses and stopping only for meals.

'Are we going on all night?' Clem asked at last.

'Yes, if you can bear it', he answered. 'I want to get home as soon as possible, so that we can be married before they catch up with us.'

Clem had not thought of interference. 'But who will come after me?'

'Bertram', said Augustine.

Clem felt herself blushing and was glad the coach lamp was so dim.

'I don't see why he should', she murmured.

'Of course he will', said Augustine. 'He's your cousin and feels responsible for you, and he has a very low opinion of me. He's bound to try to stop us.'

'Oh', said Clem, wondering if she would like Bertram to stop them.

'We can't let him do it', said Augustine, as if he had guessed what she was thinking. 'He doesn't realize how miserable he would make both you and his wife if he took you back.'

It was true, she could not gainsay it.

'Where's your home?' she asked, presently.

'Have I omitted to tell you?' said Augustine, smiling. 'In Rome.'

It was a long way to Rome. Clem thought she would never be able to sleep, bumping along foreign roads in the dark, with a stranger beside her, but sleep she did, heavily, and was surprised to wake up in broad daylight with her head on Augustine's shoulder. He was wide awake, which made it worse.

But he only said, 'Look, the sun! No more fog!'

Down they went through Italy; everything seemed strange as a dream to Clem. The brown hills crowned with little towns were all like so many pictures, and yet real people, dirty and laughing boys, girls with great solemn eyes, old women in black shawls, went walking about the streets. At last, tired with so much looking, she leaned back and shut her eyes.

The wheels, rattling and shaking on stones, woke her from her doze. It was late, the light was going. Blinking and yawning, she looked out of the window again. Out of the darkening air a vast decayed circle reared up before her. She gasped.

'It's the Colosseum!'

Augustine chuckled. 'Yes, there it is. You really are in Rome, Clem.'

She could not believe it. They went through streets crowded with people, hundreds of dark foreign people, all talking their unknown language, and turned in through a narrow gateway. The carriage stopped in a cobbled court-yard with a fountain in the middle. Tall walls rose up on all sides, with rows of long sashed windows. Clem stared round.

'What a huge place!'

'I don't live in all of it', Augustine assured her. 'The first floor along one side is ours.'

Smiling servants came running from every direction.

'They seem to know all about it', Clem said, bewildered.

'They do', he said. 'I told you I had been arranging this for months. They think it is very romantic and are having the time of their lives.'

'But suppose I had said no, Augustine?'

'I knew you were too sensible to refuse a real chance to get away from that impossible situation', he answered.

She could not quarrel with that.

They went up wide marble stairs and through a big dou-ble door. The rooms were large, the furniture old, stiff and gilded; the drawing-room ceiling was painted with pink gods and goddesses disporting themselves with garlands of flow-ers and cups of wine in a careless kind of way. Clem gazed all round. Everything was as different as possible from an English vicarage, and she was glad of that.

'Clem,' said Augustine, 'I hope you don't mind having the room next to mine, but it's the only one suitable for you.'

Clem said she did not mind, but all the same it startled her, and when she saw there were connecting doors between her room and his she was not exactly reassured. She said nothing, but Augustine walked up and examined them.

'I'll have the key put in for you', he said casually.

Clem blushed and turned away to hide it. It was annoy-ing to be so easily embarrassed, when he was not; it was silly and schoolgirlish.

'It's a lovely room', she said quickly. 'Thank you, Augustine.'

'Don't thank me', he said, coming up and putting his arm round her waist. 'It's wonderful to have you in it. Oh dear, here I am breaking the rules again!' All the same he kissed her cheek. 'Don't be nervous, Clem. You're to do just as you like. I won't bully you, I promise.'

He left her alone and Clem began to look at the room. She soon saw that it had been newly painted, and all the curtains and bed fittings were new too. It was all got ready for her. She was touched at the care Augustine had taken, but she could not help feeling he was very confident of himself.

Above the fireplace was a little picture of the Virgin and Child, painted on wood in a carved and gilded frame. It was an early Renaissance picture, stiff and springlike, by someone whose name had disappeared altogether in the long landslide of time, as she learned later. Now she just looked at it, pleased that it was there, waiting for her.

Presently in came an old woman in black, smaller even than Clem, smiling all over her wrinkled yellow face and holding up a big key, which she shook at Clem.

'Signorina! Till you be Signora', she said, grinning a toothless grin. She stuck it noisily in the lock and turned it with a flourish. Then she came close up to Clem and patted her cheek.

'*Bella Inglesa!*' she said '*Poverina!*' And off she waddled.

Clem was amused and stopped wondering what was going to happen to her. In fact, she almost felt as if she had really eloped with Augustine.

Later, when he tried to explain the legal and religious regulations about marriage, she got very confused.

'Are we to be married in a Roman Catholic church, then?' she asked.

Augustine smiled. 'They mostly are, in Rome', he said. 'Do you mind? But the English chaplain might make difficulties, and besides, if I get married by a heretic I excommunicate myself.'

Clem was horrified; it sounded terrible to her. But Augustine only laughed and tried to reassure her. She need not turn Catholic herself unless she wanted to, need not wear a white dress, which somehow worried her just as much; he fetched in a dressmaker who made her a dove-grey one trimmed with crimson, the prettiest dress she had ever had.

Somehow he arranged things so that they were married only a few days after their arrival. They went into a dark church, and then into a side-chapel, where an old bald-headed priest rattled through some Latin and faltered out in almost incomprehensible English a vow which sounded very much like the one in the Prayer Book. Clem found it difficult to believe in what she was doing, even when, in a small voice, she made her assent, and Augustine put the gold ring on her finger.

The church was so near the house they walked back, and there in the courtyard was a strange carriage, all splashed with mud.

Figaro, whose real name was Benedetto, came running out to them.

'The Signori Inglesi!' he said dramatically, in a voice hoarse with excitement. 'They have come!'

'Just in time!' said Augustine, coolly. 'How many of them?'

'Two, signore.' Benedetto held up two fingers. 'One fat, one long, two Protestant *pastori*.'

'George Pierce has come too, evidently', remarked Augustine.

Clem clutched his arm. 'Oh, please, I don't want to see them.'

'My dear, I'm afraid you must', he said. 'Or they'll think I've walled you up alive or thrown you in the Tiber.'

'All right', she said, reluctantly. 'If you say so.'

'How very wifely that sounds!' said Augustine, amused, tucking her arm more firmly in his. He was looking particularly trim this morning, with a flower in his buttonhole, and he did not seem to mind meeting Bertram and George at all.

There they were, looking extremely English, and quite out of place in Augustine's very Roman apartment.

'Good morning, Bertram', said Augustine. 'I'm sorry I was not here to receive you, but I was out getting married.'

'Too l-late!' cried George, unexpectedly dramatic.

'Nonsense', said Bertram crisply. 'I don't suppose for a moment it is valid. Clem, I have come to fetch you home.'

Clem looked despairingly at Augustine.

'Don't be silly, Bertram', he said calmly. 'It's a perfectly legal marriage.'

Bertram ignored him, fixing his eyes on Clem, so that she felt as if she had done something cheap and shameful.

'I'm very disappointed in you, Clem', he said in his deepest voice. 'How could you have listened to him after what I told you? To run away with a worthless idle fellow because he flatters you, it's not like you; it is not, indeed.'

Clem, though still burning with shame, faltered out what she felt to be fair. 'If he's so worthless, why should he run away with me? I'm plain, and nearly as old as he is, and I haven't a penny.'

'Plain? Nonsense!' said Augustine. 'That's the nicest little face I know.' And he gently pinched her cheek.

That enraged Bertram. 'Augustine, you ought to be ashamed of yourself!' he shouted. 'Fooling the poor girl with sham weddings and silly compliments! Clem, how can you be taken in so? When he's tired of this whim, what will happen to you? Then you'll find this "wedding" is not as real as you thought, you will find yourself alone in the world, your good name lost for ever. Don't you understand your danger?'

'Bertram, you ought to write melodrama', said Augustine. 'Have a glass of Marsala and remember you are a rational animal.'

Bertram turned away from the proffered glass with an exclamation of impatience. Augustine shrugged and offered it to George, who refused with a heavy sigh.

'Well, Clem, love, you have it', he said, putting the glass in her hand. 'Don't look so worried and frightened. I've no intention of playing Maria Marten with you—do I really look the part, now?'

He made her sit down and stood by her, with his hand on the back of her chair.

Bertram was pacing angrily up and down.

'Now, Bertram', said Augustine. 'You are quite at liberty to examine the lawfulness of the marriage. You had better engage a lawyer to look into it, and mine will answer any inquiries he wishes to make. Ask the Church of England chaplain to recommend a lawyer, if you do not choose to accept a recommendation from me.'

Bertram glared at him, momentarily at a loss. George said, 'That's a f-fair offer. If the m-marriage is valid there is n-n-nothing we can do.'

'I don't believe he hasn't left himself a loophole', Bertram said. 'Probably English and Italian law don't coincide.'

'At least in Italy I shan't be able to get an Act of Parliament to divorce my wife', said Augustine. 'That is a privilege reserved for English Protestants, if they are rich enough.'

'Are you insulting our country's laws?' Bertram cried.

'My dear Bertram, you are certainly insulting me', said Augustine. 'Even a worm will turn. Why should you suppose I am the sort of fellow to sham marriages with defenceless girls? I've never done it before. Why should I begin with Clem, bless her?'

Bertram stopped opposite him and looked down from his full height, with angry scorn.

'Because Clem is not like the women you are familiar with here, and you know it', he said. 'She would never have left England with you if you had not promised marriage. Thank God we have come soon enough to stop your game.'

'Thank God you have come too late', said Augustine, with spirit. 'Since I have not only promised marriage but effected it.'

Bertram turned to Clem. 'My dear', he said, speaking quite gently. 'If you will come with us now we will put you in the care of the English chaplain's wife till this business can be cleared up. Even if this marriage proves valid according to law, you can refuse to live with him.'

Clem gazed up at him in bewilderment. His whole behaviour was so vehement that she half believed he must love her after all, yet his eyes seemed innocent of any such knowledge. Because he so evidently despised Augustine her own confidence was shaken. Why had the marriage service been such a hole-and-corner affair? What about the doors between their rooms and the servants' laughing complicity? What was she letting herself in for? Was she a fool to trust a man she hardly knew because he kissed her and made her laugh?

She hesitated and Bertram saw her hesitation. A look of relief, almost of triumph, came into his set face.

Clem tried to look round at Augustine, but as he was standing behind her chair, it was too difficult.

'What shall I do, Augustine?' she whispered.

'Don't ask him', said Bertram, irritated.

Augustine said quietly, 'You must do what you want to do, Clem.' But he moved his hand from the chair to her shoulder and she felt the gentle pressure of his fingers. 'If you stay, I shall do my best to make you happy.'

She did not know what to say or what to do. Bertram had destroyed her faith in Augustine.

'Come with me, Clem', Bertram pleaded, and he held out his hand.

It was too much to have him ask her that. She took his hand and stood up, trembling.

'Are you going with him, Clem?' said Augustine sadly. She looked round at him then and could not believe it was his cheerful goblin face looking so sad. She saw it was a serious thing to him that she was going, and it disturbed her.

But Bertram said firmly, 'Don't answer him, Clem', and led her away at once, out to the carriage, with George, silent and gloomy, lumbering after.

Clem felt dreadfully sad as they drove away. Why had she given up her adventure? Or why had she ever started on it? Tears rolled down her cheeks. If Bertram noticed, he said nothing. But she did not think he noticed. Augustine would have tried to make her laugh, and probably kissed her. Bertram sat upright, victorious but aloof.

The English chaplain and his wife were kind, but behind their kindness Clem sensed keen disapproval. At dinner there was a good deal of talk about Roman morals in general and Augustine's in particular, though not, of course, in detail. Somehow the polite hints and meaningful reticences built up a nasty little picture of a spoilt idler flirting with rich old princesses and pursuing low-class dancers whose southern beauty was not matched by virtue. Clem had no means of knowing how true it all was, but the more they disapproved, the more she remembered what she liked about Augustine; at least he was never pompous or priggish, as these good people seemed to be. To fit with their conversation the rooms were furnished in English style; the old familiar vicarage atmosphere was round her again.

She cried in bed.

The next day Bertram plunged into long sessions with lawyers. Clem had to stay indoors and she felt she was back in England already. The day seemed never to be coming to an end as she sat yawning by the window, and at last, in despair, she asked George to take her for a walk. George was always obliging to her, and as they set off she wondered idly why he had come with Bertram, if he himself felt any interest in her, as Lucy desired he should.

'What are you thinking of?' she said at last, after a long silence.

'I was w-wondering how my vicar would manage on S-Sunday if we are not back', said George. 'He's not young, and has very d-delicate health.'

Clem wanted to laugh; at the same time she felt a little ashamed of herself. It was ridiculous to imagine people cared for her like that.

It was afternoon; a pale winter sunlight slanted through the bare plane trees as they walked along by the Tiber. The stream swirled slowly, thick with yellow mud, under the bridges.

Suddenly across the road Clem saw Augustine. He was ahead of them, going the same way, so he had not seen her. His small figure, weighed down by the usual enormous caped coat, was unmistakeable. Almost without conscious decision Clem dropped George's solid arm and raced across the street, nearly getting run down by a cab. She slipped and stumbled in the gutter; the cab driver shouted and Augustine turned round. He ran back and caught hold of her, pulling her onto the pavement.

'My dear Clem! Killing yourself? For fun, or intentionally?'

Breathlessly she cried, 'Augustine, please, may I come back?'

What would she have done if he had greeted this request coldly or solemnly? But she saw his eyes brighten.

'Tired of the vicarage already?' he said.

'Yes, yes! Dreadfully!'

'Oh, how very gratifying!' he said, holding her arm tight.

George Pierce came lumbering across the road with an expression of puzzled anxiety on his broad pale face.

'Miss C-Clemency', he said doubtfully. 'Is this w-wise?'

'Perhaps I'm not a person who ought to be wise', she said. 'I've decided to go home with Augustine. Will you tell Bertram?'

'He'll be very angry', said George.

'Are you angry, George?' she asked him, suddenly curious.

George blinked. 'It is a wife's d-duty to s-s-stay with her husband', he pronounced finally. 'I t-trust all will be well. Good-day.'

He solemnly raised his hat and walked ponderously away.

'Good old George', said Augustine. 'But then he hasn't lived in a chaste harem with you, like Bertram.'

'Augustine, really!' cried Clem.

'Don't pretend to be shocked when you aren't', he said, smiling, and he tucked her arm in his.

Clem said, 'You know, Augustine, I'm getting so used to your kind of talk I am quite bored with the other.'

He began to laugh. 'That's a step in the right direction! Were you bored at the chaplain's?'

'Dreadfully!' she said. 'And Bertram never took any notice of me once he had got me away from you.'

'Ah, that's one advantage in an immoral man, isn't it?' said Augustine. 'He does like talking to women.'

Clem laughed. 'But you're not as immoral as Bertram thinks, are you?' she said. 'I couldn't tell him how kind you have been, because he would see some dreadful motive behind it.'

'Are you sure you don't, Clem?' Augustine asked her, quietly.

'Well, he made me wonder', Clem said, honestly. 'But I've decided I don't mind.'

'You're a wonderful girl', he said.

They had reached the house now; night was coming on fast. Augustine stopped at the gateway.

'Clem', he said seriously. 'If you come in now, you won't let Bertram take you away again, will you?'

'Did you mind it, Augustine?'

'Of course I did, and you know it', he said.

'But in England,' Clem objected, 'you said it was marriage you were talking about, not love.'

'Ah, that was just one of my immoral wiles', said Augustine.

Clem looked at him uncertainly. It was getting too dark to see clearly. 'Are you joking?' she said.

'If you like', said Augustine.

They stood looking through the gloom at each other and then he asked, rather hurriedly, 'Do you still think you're in love with Bertram?'

Clem blushed hotly. 'I don't know', she murmured. 'I wish I could forget about it. It's so wrong.'

'You do still think you are', said Augustine, with a quick sigh. 'Of course you can't get over it all at once. But are you sure, quite sure, that you want to come in?'

Clem thought of the vicarage.

'Yes', she said firmly.

'Good', said Augustine, cheerful again. 'I can't carry you across the threshold, I'm afraid, but consider yourself carried.'

They went into the house laughing.

Not very much later Bertram called. Augustine told Clem to stay in her room, which she thankfully did. She wandered restlessly about, listening to Bertram's strong determined voice, raised in the drawing-room. She did not hear Augustine's soft replies. His voice had no carrying power.

It was over an hour before she heard the servant show Bertram out. She waited, expecting Augustine to come, but as he did not she went into the passage. The drawing-room door was ajar and she gently pushed it. She saw Augustine lying on the sofa with his eyes shut, unaware of her, and she thought how tired he looked, almost ill.

'Are you all right, Augustine?' she asked, in a nervous little voice.

He jumped and sat up, beginning to apologize. Clem went and sat down on a little stool beside the sofa.

'Lie down again', she said. 'You look ill, Augustine.'

He did lie down, but propped up his head to look at her.

'I'm only a bit tired', he said, smiling, so that his face came alive again, much to her relief. 'I like talking, not listening.'

'What is Bertram going to do?' she asked.

'There's nothing much he can do', Augustine said. 'He's given me a powerful sermon on the duties of a husband and a eulogy on the worth of little Clem, which I know quite as well as he does, if not better. But short of beating me black and blue, which he was longing to do, there was no real possibility of action. We are married and that's that. I wasn't going to tell him it was optional on your part.'

'On yours too', she said. 'You might want to marry someone else, someone more suitable.'

'There couldn't be anyone more suitable', said Augustine. 'Don't you realize I'm wooing you, my dear Clem? I admit it's unconventional to get married first and woo afterwards, but I never have been a stickler for convention. In some ways it's convenient to have you permanently at hand to woo, though it makes a romantic approach rather difficult to sustain.'

Clem decided he was not serious, and laughed.

'Don't you believe me?' he said. 'You are the most difficult girl to woo I've ever met! Never mind, it will make a great interest in my life. And in case you can't forget Bertram's tragic picture of the betrayed girl abandoned in the snow, I want you to know that I've made a will in which I am leaving you some money which is strictly my own, not Father's, Scarvell money. It's yours if I die, or if we separate. That makes you a free agent, doesn't it?'

Clem gazed at him thoughtfully.

'Why do you put all the weapons in my hands?' she said at last.

'Because I'm so cunning', said Augustine, trying not to smile, but soon failing. 'We're going to have some fun, Clem, whatever happens.'

And as far as Clem was concerned they began to have fun at once, for Augustine insisted on having a lot of new clothes made for her, and took her to a concert and to the opera and to a big ceremony in St. Peter's, where she saw the Pope and any number of Cardinals, and was only for one moment embarrassed, when she was left standing while everybody else fell on their knees. Hurriedly kneeling, she whispered to Augustine, 'Why didn't you warn me?'

'I forgot you didn't know the routine', he said.

The next day Bertram and George called to say goodbye, and they remarked on her having been at St. Peter's: evidently the word had gone round.

'You must not let them m-make a p-papist of you', said George earnestly.

'Augustine says I don't have to be', said Clem. 'But I like the churches, they are so full of pretty things.'

This remark did not seem to reassure George, who shook his head sadly.

Bertram said little on this occasion, but gazed gloomily at Clem, who felt remarkably cheerful, considering that she would soon see him no more. She could not explain this to herself; perhaps she was just relieved to know the thing was settled.

Bertram held her hand for a moment when they parted, but he did not say anything. He went away and somehow Clem hardly thought about him any more. There was such a lot to do.

Christmas was coming, and there were endless parties and entertainments. Clem was shy at first of going into society, but she soon discovered that Augustine was a very popular guest and that she was accepted and welcomed because she was his wife. One old princess patted her hand and said, 'Augustine always said he would never marry, but we are so glad he has.'

Clem was flattered, but puzzled. Perhaps he had a mistress, a lady who was married already. Or perhaps he liked only the sort of vulgar girls gentlemen were not supposed to marry. She was so curious that as they drove home that night she asked him point-blank, 'Why did you say you would never marry?'

'Couldn't find anyone small enough', he said, putting his arm round her waist and giving her an affectionate squeeze.

So that did not get her much further.

On Christmas Eve she remarked gloomily, 'I suppose I ought to go to church to-morrow.'

Augustine laughed. 'Don't you want to?'

'I don't much want to meet the chaplain again', said Clem.

'Come with me to Midnight Mass, then', he suggested.

'If you tell me when to kneel down and stand up.'

But when they reached the church it was so full they could hardly move at all.

'This won't do', said Augustine. 'We're the wrong size for crowds.'

Clem thought she saw some coins changing hands; at any rate they were soon up in a gallery, and from here she could see everything, as if she were in a theatre. She thought it was like that, too. The sanctuary was bright with candles and the three priests in stiff gold vestments moved and turned and bowed, and attendant boys in white cottas scurried to and fro, just as if they were acting a play. Clem supposed she ought to be shocked, but in fact she enjoyed watching. The music sounded loud and glorious in that great shining place, turning into a wild fantasy at the Gloria when bells were rung without stopping and the organ pealed at full blast so that she could hardly hear the choir, though they were singing at the tops of their voices with all their mouths wide open. And then there was a sudden silence, which took her by surprise, when the white Host was lifted up and all the dark heads went down.

Augustine went down to Communion, telling her to wait for him, and she sat with her elbows on the edge of the gallery, and her chin on her hands, and fell into a dream, remembering all those Oxford men who were so fascinated by the early Christian centuries.

'It must have been very like this', she thought, and wondered why they were always so angry about Rome; even Newman had said some very angry things about Rome. They seemed to expect it to be as it was in St. Peter's day;

but after all, St. Mary's in Oxford probably wasn't like that either. In fact, why should it be? Unless a thing died, it must change.

At last Augustine came back and soon they were surging out of the church into a midnight full of bells and people. Augustine gave her a kiss, for Christmas, he said.

'You must be happy for Christmas', he said. 'Are you happy?'

'Well, yes, I think I am', said Clem, surprised to find that it was so.

She now discovered that Augustine went to Mass every Sunday. This also surprised her; he had never seemed to her a religious person. Now, when she expressed her surprise, he only said, 'It's a sin not to, you know.' She thought this was the reason he went, but it was still a puzzle why this sort of sin should worry him, more, it appeared, than the things she was accustomed to consider as sins. She did not go with him, but neither did she go to the English church; she knew the English atmosphere would make her feel guilty and embarrassed. She was really quite pleased not to have to bother with church at all.

The Christmas season was very gay and she began to enjoy herself. It was like a belated youth to dress up in new clothes and go to theatres and parties.

Augustine used to go with her to the dressmaker, and Madame, a dark little Frenchwoman with gold teeth, always paid attention to his comments.

'How do you know more than I do about ladies' dresses?' Clem teased him once, as they walked away, arm in arm in the bright January sunlight.

'Ah, it's my misspent youth', Augustine said. 'I fancy they let you know all about that at the English chaplaincy.'

Clem did not quite know what to say.

'They didn't say anything very definite', she said at last, but the hints about sordid affairs with dancers came vividly back to her.

'On the whole I think that would give a more sinister impression than any details', said Augustine calmly. 'I'm not very sinister really, Clem. I used to pursue some silly, pretty girls, not with much success, because there were usually better-looking candidates with just as much money as I had. I dropped it when I realized I wasn't getting much out of it but indigestion and insomnia. Are you horrified? I'm sure you're not.'

'No, I don't think I am', said Clem. 'Of course, I might be if I were really your wife.'

'I suppose you wouldn't like to try it, if only for the sake of having a scene about my past?' asked Augustine hopefully.

'Augustine, you are ridiculous!' said Clem, and she laughed.

She could never quite make up her mind whether he meant what he said, but then she did not want to. Her sudden freedom and riches went to her head like wine; she wanted only to enjoy herself and not worry about anything. She did not worry over Augustine; he was always cheerful and seemed to have nothing to do but take her about Rome. If they were out late he stayed in bed till midday and only laughed when she teased him for being lazy, calling her his Puritan Girl. She did not realize that she found it dull when he was not with her.

Suddenly, at Easter, her careless world was shattered. A black-bordered letter arrived from Aunt Scarvell. Lucy had died.

Clem wept. She felt guilty about Lucy, longed now to see her, tell everything and beg her pardon. But it was too late, and beautiful aimless Lucy was gone. And even while

she wept for Lucy, the thought of Bertram came disturb-
ingly into her mind. She forgot the difficult scenes with
him here in Rome; it was the Oxford Bertram who appeared
in all his splendour, fair and ideal, and now she kept remembering his protective tenderness to her, his disproportionate
anger with Augustine, and began to wonder if, after all, he
had not a special feeling for her. And if she had not been
such a coward and run away, she would have been there,
ready to comfort and console him! She felt she had betrayed
the best in herself and lost her chance of real happiness.
The old love stirred; Rome was an alien place and Augustine's marriage of convenience had turned into a trap. She
grew silent and melancholy, unlike herself.

Augustine, of course, knew of Lucy's death; in fact the
letter had been addressed to him. One day when Clem was
standing and staring, unseeing, out of the window, he came
up beside her and said abruptly, 'Are you thinking about
him? Bertram?'

'Yes', she said, with a despairing sigh.

Augustine was silent.

Clem turned to him. 'I'm sorry. I can't help it', she said.
'I do want to see him so much.'

Augustine still said nothing.

'If only I could go', Clem said, sighing.

'You can go, Clem', he said at last. 'Of course you can go.'

'Do you mean that?' Hope sprung within, making her
feel as queasy as if she had eaten dangerous food.

'I did not think of poor Lucy's dying', he said, not looking at her.

Clem persisted in what was most urgent to her.

'You would let me go and see him?' she said.

'You are free', he answered. 'I promised you that, at the
beginning. But it's not worth starting a nullity suit till you

have seen him. He may not—he may not feel the same as you do.'

'No, he may not', said Clem. 'But I must know. I must go to him.'

'Yes, well, go then', said Augustine abruptly, turning away. 'Go when you like, to-morrow if you want to. You can write about the decree.'

Clem was suddenly panic-stricken.

'Augustine! Go back to England alone? Must I do that?'

'My God, Clem, what do you expect of me?' he cried, turning round in a passion. 'Do you want me to take you to Bertram and give you to him?'

Clem jumped backwards, startled by his look and his voice. She had never imagined Augustine was capable of that kind of anger.

'I—I didn't know you would care', she faltered.

'Care? Of course I care!' said Augustine. 'You know I love you. Why else do you think I have done all this? I thought I could win you in the end, I thought I could get through all those prejudices and opinions they have put in your head, a lot of nonsense, not true to life or to your own nature. I might have won too, if poor Lucy had not died. But am I to take you back to Bertram, who's more in love with himself than he'll ever be with any woman, and say, "Here's your bride, I've kept her for you"? Be damned if I will!'

He pushed back his hair with a shaking hand and walked away from her, back into the room. Clem stood by the window, trembling with surprise.

Augustine recovered first. 'I'm sorry, Clem', he said, after a moment. 'I beg your pardon for shouting at you like that.'

'I didn't know', she said. 'I didn't understand.'

'Never mind', he said shortly. 'Forget it.'

'I'll stay if you like', she said anxiously. 'I'll be your wife, Augustine.'

'No! Don't!' he said. 'The thing's impossible now; you must see that. Don't try to please me with any stupid sacrifices, I don't want any of that. Of course you must see Bertram. I ought to go to England in any case. I'll take you as far as London and send Benedetto with you to Oxford. Will that do?'

'Oh yes', she whispered miserably. 'I'm sorry, Augustine.'

'You can't help it', he said. 'It was a mad idea of mine to think I could compete with Bertram.'

He went out of the room and Clem had never felt so uncomfortable in her whole life.

# 5

The days were miserable to Clem till they left, and although Augustine recovered his temper, she felt it was an effort to him to maintain his usual good humour. She could not forget his outburst, or anything he had said; she lay awake at night, remembering it.

It was May now and their journey north was not difficult, nor was the Channel crossing too bad, though Augustine was sick, as usual. They went directly on to London and he put her on the coach for Oxford. He said goodbye to her, suddenly kind and gentle again.

'Clem, if anything goes wrong, come and see me here, in London', he said. 'I'll try to help.'

He looked so ill, shrivelled up by the cold English wind, that Clem felt an unexpected pang of anxiety.

'Where will you be?' she asked.

'At Father's house, a horrid big place near Eaton Square.'

'Augustine, do look after yourself.'

He smiled and held her hand for a moment, but made no attempt to kiss her, and somehow she missed it. She looked back as the coach drove away and saw him standing there, a small figure weighed down with clothes, his hat on the back of his head. She felt as if she had left behind something vital to herself. 'He has been so kind', she told herself, as a sort of excuse for this surprising feeling.

It was late when she arrived in Oxford, but light enough to see the familiar streets as she went through, the decorated skyline; and she heard the bells too, like souls haunting the damp evening of the town. Yet it was strange to be back; everything seemed unreal, as if it would vanish at a touch. Or was it she who was the ghost, invisible to the place she revisited?

At the Mitre she scribbled a note to Bertram and sent it by Benedetto; he was glum and silent, and she felt sure he had guessed what she intended and did not approve. To Bertram she simply wrote that she was in Oxford alone and would like to see him.

Bertram himself arrived in answer, just after breakfast next morning. He walked into her private sitting-room with an anxious frown on his face. When she saw him she felt strange, as if he were not the same person as the man in her mind. He was somehow more solid than she remembered, more rigid, middle-aged; nothing of the lover about him.

'What are you doing here alone?' he demanded at once. 'Has that man abandoned you after all?'

'Oh no', said Clem. It had never occurred to her that he would imagine that. 'He's in London.'

'Thank God for that!' said Bertram, with a relief that did not augur very well for her hopes. 'But he should not have let you travel alone.'

'He sent his servant with me', Clem answered, quite annoyed at his critical tone. 'Augustine did what I asked him.'

Bertram relaxed a little and sat down. They began to talk about Lucy—now she had been dead nearly three months—and about Clara's future. Clem asked him then whether he would not marry again, if only for the child's sake. 'Lucy would surely have wished it.'

As soon as she said that, she felt a hypocrite. Lucy was exactly the sort of woman who would have liked to imagine her husband going to his grave a widower for her sake.

Bertram shook his head. 'Don't mistake me', he said. 'Although I could never love anyone as I did dear Lucy, I see that a second marriage might be almost a duty, for my little motherless Clara's sake, as you suggest. But I have long felt that for a clergyman singleness is the higher state. Fortunately my mother is well able to bring up my daughter, and so I have determined to dedicate my life entirely to the service of God and my people.'

Somehow the measured easy way in which he made this announcement convinced Clem that he had made it before, to others. It was uncompromising, and she knew she ought to say no more. But all her long suppressed feelings, revived more by his voice than the sight of him, rose up and demanded utterance. If she did not speak now she would suffocate under the unspoken weight of emotion. And without realizing it, living with Augustine, she had become accustomed to saying what she felt straight out.

'Bertram,' she said, 'you may feel like that now, but if you ever feel differently, if you ever do want someone to share your life and work, I am ready to be that one.'

Bertram stared at her.

'Clem, have you gone mad? You are married!'

It was ridiculous, but she had quite forgotten he did not know what her marriage had been. The blood rushed to her face, but she could not stop now. She would have to explain herself.

'My marriage is not, never has been a real marriage', she said, as coolly as she could.

'What! You mean Augustine has cheated you after all?' Bertram cried, jumping to his feet. 'I never did have faith in those foreign lawyers.'

'No, I don't mean that', she said. 'I mean that we have not lived together as man and wife, and that makes a marriage null, Augustine told me. I can be free whenever I wish it.'

Bertram gazed at her, and then rubbed his lips with the tip of his fingers.

'You can't expect me to believe that, Clem', he said at last.

'It's true, all the same', said Clem. 'He offered to take me away from your house because he guessed I was in love with you.'

'Clem!' Shock almost took Bertram's voice away. 'Don't say such things!'

'Lucy knew', Clem said desperately. 'It was because I couldn't bear the strain that I agreed to go away with Augustine. I should not have gone if he had not promised to leave it to me whether our marriage should be a real one or not.'

'I don't believe it!' Bertram said, wildly. 'I certainly can't believe it of Augustine. Anyone could see what he wanted—he couldn't keep his hands off you, even in the drawing-room.'

Clem suddenly felt very queer, stifled and nauseated, as if she were going to faint. She had meant to bring her emotions into the open, but now she hardly knew what they were. The way he spoke made her realize that his controlled manner hid some violent feelings, all the cruder, perhaps, because he so sternly suppressed them. At the same time what he said affected her attitude to Augustine, but she was too excited and confused to understand what was happening in her. She thought Bertram, roused as he was, might be even now realizing that after all he loved her. Almost without knowing what she was doing she went close to him, put her hands on his arms and looked up at him. It was a long way to look.

'Why don't you believe I could love you, Bertram?' she said, breathlessly.

But with horror stiffening his hands he pushed her roughly away.

'I won't listen to such a story', he said hoarsely. 'You, my little sister, as I have thought of you so long, to imagine such things! Poor Lucy's friend—no! It's disgusting, it's horrible to me.'

They stared at each other across the room. Clem could not say anything; she thought she would die of shame.

'This is not you, Clem', Bertram said at last, more calmly, though he was still breathing heavily. 'Augustine, I see, is tired of you already, and has put these monstrous ideas into your head.'

Clem was suddenly furiously angry.

'Is love so monstrous?' she cried. 'Why are you so horrified because I've said I love you?'

'Love!' said Bertram, disgusted. 'What do you know about love? You cannot have learned much from Augustine but these twisting Roman ways, married and not married—oh, it is altogether unspeakable! Poor little Clem, how he has corrupted you.'

'I won't have you blame him like that', she said, still angry. 'Why do you always think the worst of him? It was my idea to come, not his.'

'Don't!' Bertram said, holding up his hand. 'Don't say any more. I don't wish to discuss this any further. I hope this is the last time we shall speak of it, Clem.'

'It is the last time', she said, and sat down. She felt very tired.

Bertram stared at her uncertainly. At last he said, 'You must not come to see me, Clem, do you understand?'

'I will not come to see you, Bertram.'

'You must leave Oxford at once.'

'I won't compromise you; don't worry', she said coldly.

Bertram hesitated, and then picked up his hat. 'I wish I could forget what you have said to-day.'

'I expect you will', said Clem wearily.

'Goodbye', said Bertram, and he went out without looking back.

Clem sat still, in a cold rage. Love Bertram! Of course she did not love him! Once, long ago, she had fallen in love, more with her own ideal than with him, her loneliness an easy victim to his forceful charm, but the Bertram she had loved had been the last image of youth, his as well as hers. She saw him now as he was, not transfigured by her own immature adoration, and she felt no point of contact with him at all. Nothing in his mind or heart corresponded with hers, and now she knew too that nothing was left of the vague desires the splendid look of him had once raised in her. She knew she had been a fool, enchanted by an idol all this time. She was angry with Bertram for his hardness, but more bitterly angry with herself for entertaining so long this stupid and deceptive dream. And because of it she had made Augustine very unhappy.

And now what was she to do? Go back to Augustine and say, 'Bertram won't have me, will you?' It would be so humiliating for them both that she doubted if she could make herself do it. But if not, what was left? She was over thirty, and had no money, for of course nothing would induce her to take Augustine's. The thought of starting to teach in a girls' school now made her feel weary and depressed.

There was a discreet tap on the door and Benedetto entered.

'The Signora called?'

She had not called and he knew it; but he wanted to speak to her, having guessed, she felt sure, most of what had happened.

'The Signora will go to London now?' he asked hopefully.

'I don't know, Benedetto. I don't know what to do.'

'It is better to go to London', said the little man gently. 'Signor Agostino, he is a good man, and he is *molto simpatico* to the Signora, *evvero*? And so much he loves you, Signora!' He clasped his hands and rolled up his eyes.

Clem could not help smiling. 'I don't deserve it', she said.

'That will not worry him, Signora', said Benedetto eagerly. 'He is not a proud man, like this one who is gone. He will be glad because you come back, believe me, I know him. And you too, Signora, when you have your *bambino*, you also will be happy. Pardon me, if I have offended.'

'No, Benedetto, I am glad to hear what you think', said Clem.

'We go to London, then, Signora?'

'Yes, we go to London.'

They went to London, but Clem was much less sure than Benedetto that she would be well received. And she felt shy of meeting Augustine now, because she realized how blind she had been, what a silly way she had behaved; it seemed to her that no other woman in the world would have behaved quite so stupidly.

They arrived in Eaton Square late in the afternoon. An intimidating butler informed Clem that 'the Honourable Augustine Firle was at the office'. She was too tired to laugh, but it seemed an extraordinary place for him to be. She said she would wait and was shown into a small room, obviously unused, formal and cheerless. Although it was May the weather was cold and there was no fire. She sat and shivered for a long half-hour, and then the door opened. She looked up, but it was not Augustine.

A tall thin man stood on the threshold and gazed uncertainly at her. He had large vague blue eyes, tired and pouched, and a long drooping nose. He almost backed out of the doorway at the sight of her, but then stopped and murmured diffidently, 'Can I do anything for you?'

'I'm waiting for Augustine', said Clem.

He seemed relieved. 'Oh well, he'll soon be back, I expect.' He looked doubtfully at her and then hazarded, 'You're not—that is, are you by any chance Clementina?'

Clem smiled to think Augustine had called her that. 'Yes, I'm Clem.'

'Oh', he said. It was evidently a favourite noise, avoiding the definition of speech. But then he added, 'I'm Augustine's brother, Alexander.'

'How do you do?' said Clem politely, but she was astonished that Augustine should have a brother so unlike himself. 'What is this office where he's gone?'

'Oh, the firm's', said Alexander, surprised. 'I'm afraid it means nothing to me, iron and so on.'

'I don't imagine it means much to him either', said Clem, amused at the idea of Augustine, a dilettante if ever there was one, faced with a Midland ironworks.

'Oh, but he takes an interest, when he is in England', said Alexander. 'Of course, his health won't stand the winters here.'

Clem, who suspected that Augustine's Roman winters were kept up mainly to escape from his family, said nothing.

Alexander Firle took fright at her silence and withdrew, shyly murmuring something about fetching his daughter from a music lesson.

The next person to come in really was Augustine, swallowed up in a huge overcoat, with his nose sticking out above a muffler, which he unwound as he opened the door. Here he was, and Clem was speechless; she was half afraid of him suddenly, dreading another emotional scene.

'My dear Clem, how nice to see you again so soon', he said. 'Have they been freezing you to death in here? How bitter England is in May! I always forget that. Come and have a cup of tea in my room.'

She was relieved not to have to do more than accept this invitation and go upstairs with him.

Augustine's sitting-room was light and comfortable, and a bright fire was burning. Clem sat down beside it, and Augustine took off his armour of outdoor clothes. He gave her a cup of tea and sat down on the other side of the fireplace.

'You look very peaky, little Clem', he said. 'What's happened?'

Clem murmured, 'I'm ashamed of myself, Augustine.' She dared not look at him.

But he said without emotion, 'Was Bertram unhelpful?'

His matter-of-fact tone cheered Clem. 'He was shocked', she said, in her normal voice. 'Horrified.'

'I thought he might be', said Augustine. 'Imagination has never been Bertram's strong point. He didn't soften at all?'

'No', said Clem. 'He ordered me off from Oxford.'

'I hope he didn't turn biblical and call you a harlot', said Augustine.

'He treated me like one', said Clem, still angry at the memory.

'Too bad', said Augustine, very cheerfully. 'Well, Clem, I can't pretend I am sorry Bertram has refused his chance. I don't think you would be happy with him, you know.'

'No', she said. 'I realize that now.'

'Do you?' said Augustine at once. 'How would I do instead? Or what do you want to do now?'

Clem meant to make a sensible answer, but tears rose up against her, could not be held back, overflowed helplessly. Augustine jumped up and came over to her. He sat on the chair arm and began to comfort her.

'Poor little Clem! Of course you don't feel like discussing it now. It was stupid of me to bring it up like that.'

'Oh! I'm ashamed to come back like this', she sobbed. 'You must hate the sight of me by now. I just don't know what to do, that's all.'

'Stay here, that's what you'll do', said Augustine firmly. 'There's no need for any decisions to be taken yet.' He kissed the top of her head. 'That's how much I hate you, *carissima*.'

Clem, feeling better, blew her nose.

'Now you stop worrying', said Augustine. 'You can have a nice peaceful time, because my parents are away and I'm having all meals sent up here, as the dining-room is so vast and draughty. Alexander may drop in, my brother, you know, but he's quite harmless.'

'I've met him already', said Clem, and described Alexander's visit.

Augustine laughed. 'I hope you won't mind his moony habits', he said. 'I'm rather fond of him; we've always been allies.'

Already Clem began to feel at home; it was hard, now, to imagine living anywhere without Augustine.

As the days went on, however, she began to wish she had made some sort of decision at once, because now she could not accept their odd situation, as she had when she had fancied herself in love with Bertram. Augustine baffled her; he seemed as cheerful as ever, but somehow more distant; for instance he never kissed her now, as he used to before Lucy had died. Nor did she know what she felt about him, with any certainty.

Now the weather, with English inconsequence, turned suddenly hot, so hot that even Augustine left off his winter overcoat when he went to the office. Clem was becoming very curious about this office which he visited every day; she suspected that Augustine did not spend long in it, but went on to some club or other. One afternoon when she was doing some shopping she suddenly decided to go and look for it. She took a cab to the corner of the street and walked down it till, much to her surprise, she came to a large brass plate: Firle and Sons, Engineers, Dudley and Birmingham.

Having found the place, she was much too shy to go in, and would have gone away if the door had not suddenly opened. Augustine came out, cramming his top hat on the back of his head as usual and talking hard to another, much larger man, also in a top hat. It was strange to see him here in the city and hear all those engineering terms coming out of his mouth, and he looked very funny in his top hat, Clem thought.

Just for a moment he did not see her, and in that moment Clem suddenly knew she loved him, and always had, without realizing it, ever since he had kissed her in Christ Church Meadow, saying it would be fun for him. It had not been so much fun for him so far, she reflected.

Then he saw her.

'Why, there's my little Clem', he said in great surprise. 'How did you get here, Clem? Is anything the matter?'

'Oh no', she said quickly. 'I just—I just happened to be coming this way.' It was, she knew, very unlikely that she should come into the city by chance, perhaps it was even improper. She felt a fool.

Augustine gave her a keen glance and excused himself to his top-hatted companion. He took Clem's arm.

'It's a very hot day for the streets', he said. 'Let's get a cab and find a park to cool down in.'

In the cab she had nothing to say. Augustine asked again why she had come and she could only answer, 'Curiosity. I didn't really believe in your office.'

'Come, I'm not a liar, am I?' he said, mildly hurt, rather to her surprise. 'If I hadn't been so busy I would have been taking you out, which would have been much more fun.'

They reached the park gates and Augustine paid off the cab. They began to walk along the paths under the plane trees; the crinkling shades of the leaves slipped and quivered like a reflection of water under their feet.

Augustine had tucked her arm in his. 'It really is so nice that we are the same size', he said contentedly.

Clem giggled suddenly. 'Augustine! Why didn't you ever laugh at me for imagining I was in love with a great tall creature like Bertram?' she said. 'I never thought of it till this time in Oxford when I went close to him and his face was quite out of reach! I could have laughed myself if I hadn't been in such a temper. I wonder you never did.'

'My dear girl,' said Augustine, 'I find a lot of things amusing, but not your love for Bertram, whatever the oddities of your respective sizes.'

'Well, laugh now!' she said. 'I don't love him a bit, and I believe if he had ever shown any sign of returning it I should have been horrified. I don't know why I couldn't see that till I'd shocked him and humiliated myself and caused you, I'm afraid, such unnecessary pain. I can't forget what you said in Rome, how hurt you looked. I would give anything to make up to you for that.'

'Would you?' he said, so huskily that he had to clear his throat. 'Anything, Clem?' He stopped still.

'Not that I have anything', she said, knowing it was a stupid thing to say, but confused by the tumult of her feelings.

'Yourself', he said. 'That's all I want.'

In the middle of the path they stood close together, their arms still linked. Clem put her other hand on his shoulder and looked in his face.

'Well, here I am', she said, in a whisper.

'Do you mean that?' he said, with a hesitation that hurt her. 'You don't have to take me on just because I'm always here, like a dog begging for his bone.'

Clem did not feel she could convince him with words. She kissed him instead. 'You see I do like kissing', she said. 'I like kissing you, anyway.'

'Oh my dear little Clem!' Augustine said, nearly squeezing the breath out of her body. 'Nice, fat little bone!'

Laughing, they walked on, talking it all out.

'You knew all the time', Clem accused him. 'You knew I was falling in love with you when I thought I was in love with Bertram.'

Augustine only laughed, but he said presently, 'I thought I'd lost the game when you wanted to go back to him.'

'But, Augustine, why weren't you serious with me before?' she demanded. 'You never were serious!'

'I don't know how to be', he teased her. 'I think love is a comedy, not a tragedy; sometimes it's a farce, especially when I am involved.'

And he laughed helplessly when she bewailed their wedding day. 'I've wasted it!' she lamented. 'Now I don't feel really married to you at all!'

'We can't have that', he said. 'Let's have a private rite, make our vows again.'

He took her to a large unfinished church, dark on that bright day, and empty except for an old woman in button boots saying her Rosary in a corner. He hunted among some dog-eared pamphlets till he found one with the marriage service in it, and then led her to a side-chapel. Above the altar was a life-size statue of the Mother of God, holding up the Divine Child, and both were crowned.

'It's fearfully dark', Augustine remarked. He stuffed some coins into a box, picked up some candles and started lighting them and sticking them all round the rings of the votive candlestand.

'Let me do some', Clem whispered.

Absorbed in the beauty of the flames softly flowering out of the waxen stems, she did not look at Augustine till their hands met at the last candle, and then he took hers away and held it, and she was happy because there was so much happiness in his eyes.

They knelt down and Augustine held the tattered little book and they repeated the words to each other. Clem, who had started by feeling embarrassed, ended in great contentment. This, after all, was what she meant; she had made her vow with all her heart and it was addressed to him, in the presence of God.

Augustine had taken her ring when she was lighting candles and now he put it on again and held her hand in both his.

Presently he whispered in her ear, 'Thank God for my good wife, Amen.'

She was trying not to laugh as he helped her up. The old woman smiled as they passed her; Clem was so glad she smiled. Augustine put the rest of his change in the boxes at the back of the church as they went out.

The sun seemed dazzling outside.

That summer it seemed to Clem that till then she had been asleep and dreaming. She woke up in a world in which she was at home, and wondered how she had managed to live so long without Augustine. And yet it was some time before she could believe he was as happy as she, because he was used to the society of clever cosmopolitan people.

'But I'm not clever, you know', he told her, much amused. 'I just talk a lot.'

Clem still did not believe he had a real interest in the family firm, since he said now he could not be bothered to go to the office, and instead took her down to stay at Sandgate, in lodgings kept by an old Mrs. Salt, who had been his nurse. Mrs. Salt approved of Clem and regaled her with stories of Augustine's childish mischief; she could easily believe he had been a naughty little boy.

'But we never did think he'd have lived to grow up', said Mrs. Salt. 'That sickly he was, a regular misery every winter with his coughs and colds and bronchitis.'

Clem wondered if it was the memory of these bedridden winters which drove Augustine south every year.

But now it was fine and warm, and they used to wander along by the sea and sit on the brown shingle banks, watching the narrow waves of the Channel glint in the sun. Clem felt as if she had known him always, and yet in another way that she hardly knew him at all. He was always surprising her. When the weather suddenly changed again and sea and sky turned grey, he grew restless.

'I ought to go up to the Dudley works', he said.

'But, Augustine, what on earth can you do there?'

'Well, I shan't roll the iron, of course', he said, smiling. 'But would you mind if I went?'

'Not if I can come too.'

So they went up into the Midlands, by railway, to Dudley, and Clem had her first sight of the industrial landscape on a gloomy, steamy, summer day. The town itself was old, crowned by its castle, high up, but it stood in a great torn and blackened tract of country, forested with smoking chimneys and lit by the glare of furnaces, and over these waste places flickered the 'gob' fires, turning even the earth into a ground of hell. The very air was bitter in Clem's mouth.

Although this strange sight frightened her, she said nothing, and insisted on seeing the ironworks. But she did not know enough to sort out her impressions; the dun smoky air, the glare of the furnaces where dirty brawny men were shovelling coal into the roaring red mouths, the rolling mills, the noise of engines thumping, the clangour and shouting, it was all a nightmare to her. She held tight to Augustine's arm, but he too seemed different here. He was no stranger to the place, evidently; everybody seemed to know him, and he not only knew their names but what they were doing. Men came up and started conversations with him, unintelligible to her, full of technical terms and carried on in a variety of accents, the squeezed Midland talk, high singing Scots, and thick Irish from some of the labourers. She watched their faces, brown, worn, keen, patient, bold, shrewd; so many, so different. They went into sheds and looked at plans, and Augustine talked away, pointing at this and that with his thin white finger alongside the brown and stubby ones, and he asked questions and argued answers in such a way that Clem knew without a doubt that he was just as much at home here as in the palaces of Rome.

When at last they were back in their hotel Clem let out a long, astonished sigh.

'Well, Clem?' Augustine said, cocking an eyebrow, interested in her reaction.

'It's like hell!' she burst out.

'Oh come, not as bad as that, surely?' he said, evidently quite disappointed. 'We've put in a number of improvements lately.'

'I'm sure it's a splendid works', said Clem weakly. 'It's just the idea of people living in all this smoke and din that appals me.'

Augustine agreed, but even so his attitude was different. He was full of plans to improve things.

'But you can't improve desolation', Clem said, gazing at him.

'Why not?' said Augustine. 'It's the only thing you can do with it.'

'Except not to make it in the first place', said Clem.

'I didn't make it, my love', he pointed out.

'But your family did.'

'And if they did?' he retorted, pugnaciously. 'Don't you know my people have been ironworkers for centuries? In Sussex once, now here. We've built this up from the ground. It's our trade.'

'Laying waste the country!' Clem cried. 'And to produce weapons!'

'And who used them?' he demanded. 'All those precious Scarvells no doubt, and your gentlemanly ancestors too, I daresay. But in fact we don't make weapons here. We roll iron for boilers, engines, that kind of thing. And who uses them? You do! Everyone does. Why blame us?'

Clem gazed at him in utter astonishment, speechless.

'What's the matter, Clem?' he asked at last, anxiously.

'It's you!' she said. 'An ironmaster! I can't get used to the idea, that's all.'

'I don't look the part, do I?' said Augustine, with a half smile. But then he came over and took her hand. 'Does it worry you, Clem, that I am involved in all this?'

'Doesn't it worry *you*?' she said. 'That all your money comes from this?'

'No', said Augustine bluntly. 'Why should it? Money is just a thing to use. It's how it is used that matters.'

But Clem said, 'To me it's riches from slavery.' She was thinking of the dirty toiling men at the furnaces.

Augustine dropped her hand and walked to the window and stared out, silent, with his hands in his pockets.

Clem felt tears coming into her eyes.

'Oh dear', she said, in a small voice. 'Now I've made you cross.'

He turned round at once. 'Dear Clem, no you haven't', he said. 'You think I am very hard-hearted, but what do you want me to do? It wouldn't help anyone to disown the works, would it? It seems to me that in this world we are put into such situations to do what we can with them, not to refuse both guilt and responsibility. Maybe I have been too lazy and selfish about it; you can help me, you know, unless you think I am corrupted beyond hope of guidance.'

Clem jumped up to embrace him.

'I'm just stupid', she said. 'I'd never thought about it at all before. I'm sure you're right, Augustine.'

'The perfect wife!' he teased her.

But she was happy again. 'What a funny person you are', she said tenderly. 'I shall never get to know you.'

When they went back to London Augustine's parents were there; secure in her love, she did not mind meeting them now. Frederick Firle, Lord Gornal, was still a handsome man, though getting somewhat pop-eyed and red in the face; he had black curly hair like Augustine's, only a little grizzled, but he was so large and strong that it was ludicrous to see his son beside him. Clem was rather taken with his bluff cheerful manner, but she found it hard to forgive him when she realized he was ashamed of Augustine's insignificant physical appearance, and he showed it by making continual half-joking references to his size, his odd face, and his supposedly delicate health. Augustine took no notice of it; he teased his father in a good-humoured way, and championed the vague melancholy Alexander, who suffered even more from Lord Gornal's irritable dissatisfaction with his heirs.

Lady Gornal, Bertram's aunt Eleanor, was a great invalid, spending most of her time on an elegant sofa, dressed in cloudy pinks and blues. She had the long, beautiful Scarvell face: Alexander's was a pathetic travesty of it. She had their blue eyes too, though hers were pale. Clem saw a likeness to Bertram in both of them, but she now realized that Bertram had inherited his strength and determination from his mother, and that the Scarvells were a weakly stock; Augustine seemed to have got nothing but his childhood's illnesses from them, for his looks, she felt sure, came from the iron-working Firles. Lady Gornal evidently thought so too, for she plaintively lamented Augustine's interest in the works.

'You are some kind of throwback', she said. 'Holy Flower says that earthbound souls cannot keep away from their old haunts, and even their bodies take on the look of former incarnations.'

Clem was astonished, never having met with a spiritualist before, but Augustine only laughed at his mother. 'Is Holy Flower very expensive?' he teased her. 'Give her a guinea from me and you'll find my character and spiritual prospects will improve immediately.'

Lady Gornal was not too spiritual, Clem soon discovered, to consider a poor clergyman's daughter an unfortunate match for her second son, however eccentric he had turned out. Clem once heard her complaining, 'But my dear boy, if you insist on remaining in that antiquated and materialistic religion, you might at least have married an Italian princess. It isn't as if the girl is pretty.'

'I'm not pretty either', said Augustine. Then he saw Clem coming, and afterwards apologized for his mother. 'Don't take any notice of her', he said. 'It doesn't matter what she thinks.'

Clem did not much mind Lady Gornal's snobbish disapproval.

'Why didn't you marry a princess?' she asked him.

'Because I'm so earthbound', he said, grinning. 'But Clem, give the princesses a chance! They're not so kind-hearted as you.'

He suggested that they go back to Rome, and she agreed gladly. But she refused a visit to Oxford first, even though Bertram was out of it now, gone to a fashionable London parish. Oxford had become unreal to her.

'I hear Newman's living like a hermit at Littlemore', said Augustine. 'He won't see anyone, Catholic or Protestant.'

But Newman too seemed far away to Clem. He belonged in the dream of Oxford.

# 6

Clem's second winter in Rome ended, to her great happiness, with the discovery that she was going to have a child. As it was not due till December they spent the summer in England, as usual, and while they were there Augustine bought a house. Clem had expected it to be in London, but it was in a new suburb of Birmingham. It turned out that the Firles owned a presswork factory there, and an old uncle was retiring from its management, a Midlander who had thought it ridiculous of his brother to send Frederick to school with the upper classes, and was not impressed by the title he had afterwards gained. Augustine wanted to try out his favourite improvements, mechanical and social, and he knew he would have a freer hand there than in the ironworks. From Birmingham he could go to Dudley whenever he wished, and in Edgbaston they would be out of the smoke and noise of industry. When Clem wondered if this was fair Augustine said, 'I don't propose to shorten our lives in the cause of justice. Who's going to benefit if we do?'

The house was large and white, with a pillared porch and a little hamlet of outhouses and stables, situated in a big comfortable garden. The richer people of Birmingham were putting up houses like this all round.

They went back to Rome in the autumn, taking a stout English nurse, a niece of Mrs. Salt's. The baby, born a fortnight before Christmas, turned out to be a boy, fine and strong, with tufts of black hair and a hearty yell. Augustine was delighted that he was so lusty and, when he was

christened Felix Frederick, nicknamed him Fortissimo; Clem
discovered that he had been worrying for fear the child
should inherit his own weak constitution. She always wondered why he worried about his health; it was unlike him
to be so cautious of himself, when he was, as far as she
could see, never ill at all. Perhaps he had never got over the
fears inspired by adults in his sickly childhood.

The baby was strong, and Clem was happy. There was
nothing to warn her of what was coming. He was six months
old and they were preparing to go back to England, in May,
when he fell ill. She did not worry at first, but Augustine
called in a doctor at once, and the Italians were all whispering about the fever.

The baby's illness grew rapidly worse; it was pathetic to
watch his struggle against it, but Clem could hardly bear to
leave him, even for a moment. They did all they could but
the fever ran high. On the fourth night he died.

Clem lay down on her bed; she felt like stone. It was too
sudden, too terrible a shock to feel; she could do nothing
but stare at the ceiling. Augustine came and tried to talk to
her, but she could not answer. She lay all that long day,
hardly moving, not eating, only trying to drink what Augustine brought her, to please him. In the night she slept fitfully.

The next day, which seemed centuries later, Augustine
came and told her that she must get up and come with him
to the church, where Felix's requiem was to be sung.

'I can't', she said. 'I can't bear it.'

'For your own sake, Clem', he said gently.

'Don't make me', she whispered.

But he would not listen to her and she was too weak to
fight. He helped her to get up and put on her things; it
was like a dream. He took her downstairs and along the
street, brilliant with irrelevant sunlight, and into the dark

church where they had been married. Clem, staring ahead, became aware of light; there were candles everywhere, it seemed to her, and little boys in white cottas singing, and in the middle before the altar the tiny coffin covered with a white satin pall. The surprise that shook her then was her first real feeling since her child died.

'It's all white', she whispered to Augustine, bewildered, clinging to him.

'Dear Baby had no sins to suffer for', he said, with his arm round her, holding her close. 'He's gone straight to our Lord like the little child in the Gospel.'

Clem stayed quiet, on her knees beside him. Eternal rest and perpetual light for Felix, but she had to come back to life on earth, where the shadows were cold, and there was always change, and no peace.

When they went home and she saw Felix's little coats and dresses folded up in the drawers, she began to cry, and now she realized how badly, too, Augustine missed his baby son, and they were able to suffer it together and comfort each other.

In a few days they left Rome and went to England, to Birmingham and the new house, and tried to forget how last year they had planned everything thinking of the child who was to be there with them. But Clem knew that nothing would be the same again for her; until now she had never really felt the cruelty of life, how terrible it is to lose what you love. It was the end of being young, of trusting the future.

Autumn came, and the leaves began to turn yellow, but she did not want to go back to Rome, to the place where they had been so happy and where everything would remind her of Felix, who was gone. Augustine yielded, saying there was plenty for him to do in England. He had certainly been working hard all the summer; there was much less for her to do. She longed for another baby, but the months went by without a sign and sometimes she used to cry, when she was alone, afraid they would never have another.

It was some occupation, even if a tiresome one, making the acquaintance of their neighbours, the wives of Birmingham magnates. They were all very curious about these new arrivals and Clem was amused at the fascinated suspicion with which Augustine was regarded. Indeed, he could hardly be more unlike the Midland men of business who were now his rivals and colleagues. They did not know what to make of him, his flippant talk, his smart clothes, foreign tastes and aristocratic cosmopolitan background; last, but not least, he was a Roman Catholic, an unheard-of thing among these solid ranks of Dissenters and Low Church people. Clem's nearest neighbour and greatest trial, Mrs. Bodley, took advantage of the fact that she was a good deal the older, to pry into Clem's affairs and give her good advice and unwanted sympathy. She belonged to the Church of England, but many of her friends and relations went to chapels; Mrs. Bodley took more interest in religion than anything else outside her home, and was shocked because Clem hardly ever went to church.

'Doesn't your husband let you go, dear?' she asked, solicitously.

'I go with him, sometimes', said Clem, evasively. In fact, she had been once to Pugin's new cathedral down in the black middle of the town, and once, rather bewildered, to Mass celebrated in a schoolroom crowded with coughing people; that was all.

'Oh my dear Mrs. Firle, is not that very wrong?' cried Mrs. Bodley. 'Surely you, a clergyman's daughter, ought not to countenance such things? Why, I could not bring myself to enter one of those dreadful places.'

'Nothing very wicked goes on in them, you know', said Clem, smiling.

Mrs. Bodley cried out at that. 'My dear, how can you defend them when you know they are full of images and people worshipping the Virgin Mary?'

'She's not a bad person to worship', said Clem, mischievously.

Mrs. Bodley was greatly shocked. She was enjoying herself. She leaned forward and said, almost in a whisper, 'My dear, I'm afraid your husband is perverting you.'

Clem began to laugh; she looked forward to telling Augustine this.

Mrs. Bodley shook her head. 'Excuse my mentioning it, but as we passed Mr. Firle's study I could not help seeing that he has one of those images set up on a shelf in there, and I cannot bear to think he should persuade you to worship it too.'

Clem was amused at the notion of Augustine's bowing down to his little French porcelain Madonna, but she was annoyed, too.

'Mrs. Bodley,' she said firmly, 'I'm sure your intentions are kind, but your ideas are quite ridiculous. My husband is a Christian, just as you are, and he does not interfere with my opinions in the least.'

Mrs. Bodley was not to be put off. 'I daresay he hides the worst from you, my dear', she said. 'Why, Amos, my husband, has actually seen, with his own eyes, Mr. Firle going down on his knees to one of those priests, in the street, too.'

This sounded so unlike Augustine, who was extremely careful of his trousers, that Clem could only stare at her in astonishment. Later that evening, when they were sitting by the fire after dinner, she told him this incredible story as a joke.

But Augustine said, 'Of course I knelt down because he had the Blessed Sacrament with him.'

Clem was surprised; she had imagined only Italian peasants did that kind of thing. She sat looking at him and then said, 'I think I like that, I like you for doing that.'

Augustine smiled. 'You silly Clem! It's only what any Catholic would do. You don't think we could meet our Lord in the street and not kneel down?'

'Do you know, I believe I thought it wasn't a thing *gentlemen* did?' said Clem, laughing. 'I should think that's as silly as Mrs. Bodley's conviction that you are an idolater.'

'Mrs. Bodley was probably brought up to think the Pope was anti-Christ', said Augustine, good-humouredly.

'So was Newman', Clem pointed out. 'But he didn't go on believing it.'

'Mrs. Bodley hasn't the advantage of an Oxford education', said Augustine.

Clem laughed. 'She hates the very name of Oxford! I think she would like to have Newman and Dr. Pusey hanged, drawn and quartered, as traitors to the Queen and Jesuits in disguise! It's ludicrous to hear her talk, but it's a little frightening too. Why do people hate them so?'

'Because they are afraid of them.'

'Afraid!' she repeated. 'But you know Newman, don't you? Who could be less frightening?'

'Not him, his ideas', said Augustine. 'England had almost forgotten what Catholic ideas were till he and his friends dug them up out of the fifth-century Fathers.'

'What's the harm in that?' Clem said. 'Ideas don't hurt anyone.'

Augustine smiled. 'Oh yes they do! Those same ideas once turned the Roman Empire upside down.'

Clem brushed history aside. 'But if you could hear her, Augustine! It was like—like a witch hunt must have been.'

'Of course', he said. 'To people like her the Church is simply a witch, something both malicious and powerful. It's not what we believe that they hate, but what they think we believe, and not what we do but what they think our ancestors did. To them Newman is the Judas inside the castle, selling the postern to the enemy.'

Clem gazed at him. 'You're very calm about it', she said at last. 'But it's a dark thing, a nasty, horrible thing to come up in the minds of ordinary decent people.'

'I don't suppose anything unpleasant will happen in this enlightened age', said Augustine. 'Though of course old people can just remember the Gordon Riots, not that they were anything like the Popish Plot business.'

Clem was surprised; she had not been thinking of anything so definite. She realized suddenly what a long history of secrecy and anxiety lay behind the remnant of Catholics in England; a continual expectation of violence and injustice, a deep suspicion of Protestant talk of tolerance and a habit of hiding all religious feeling. Augustine escaped some of this by his wealth and his residence in Rome, but it was still there, even for him.

November came and the leaves began to fall. It turned cold and wet, and Augustine caught a cold and began to talk about returning to Rome. But Clem could not bear the thought of going back now, just before Christmas, when everything would remind them of last year's happiness.

'Can't we wait till the new year?' she pleaded.

Augustine gave in at once. 'Winter doesn't really begin till after Christmas', he said hopefully. 'My cold does seem to be going.'

'What a fuss you do make', Clem said, half teasing, half irritated.

They went to Oxford in November, as Augustine wanted to see someone there, and they drove out to Littlemore to call on Newman, who had now been living there some years. It was a damp, chill, gloomy afternoon and Littlemore village looked particularly dreary, and the cottages of Newman's 'monastery' when they came to it, dull and comfortless.

They were received by a serious fair young man, in his early twenties Clem guessed, and there was a moment's embarrassment when he went to find Newman, for they could hear him saying, rather fretfully, 'No, no, I don't want to see them. I don't know them. Why should strangers keep coming like this to pry upon me? Tell them please to go away, St. John.'

Clem would have withdrawn, but Augustine immediately called out, 'Mr. Newman, you are mistaken. You do know my wife: she was Miss Burnet.'

Newman came hurrying from his room to greet them, full of anxious apologies. 'My dear Miss Burnet, Mrs. Firle, I do beg your pardon. I did not know you had married, please forgive me. Come in, indeed, you must come in after my rudeness.'

So they went into a small room, rather cold, and sat down on some upright uncomfortable chairs. The place was certainly more austere than a college, though even in Oriel Newman's rooms had been furnished for work, not for comfort. In the rainy November light Clem watched his face, gone thin and pale and lined by the mouth. There was a look of such deep weariness in him, even in his eyes, usually so clear and alive, that she remembered all her old sympathy for him and said anxiously, 'Mr. Newman, you don't look at all well.'

'I don't think I am ill', he assured her. 'My doctor says I shall be if I don't eat what he tells me and take more rest. You would think that easy enough, wouldn't you, now that I have resigned St. Mary's and have so few commitments of a public kind? But you would not believe how I am pursued by people, how they come poking and prying, and even looking in at the windows, expecting to see monks in habits and I don't know what nonsense.'

'It is you who have taught people to expect that kind of thing from you', said Augustine, smiling. 'You have defended monastic ideals and they expect you to practise them!'

'I know, I know', Newman answered. 'I have taught people to look for the Catholic Church *somewhere*, and the bishops are busy teaching them not to look for it at home. They have all made charges against my Tract 90: that is a condemnation, isn't it? Even though I have remained silent, they are not silent. And not only the bishops, but everyone thinks he has the right to accuse me of treachery and duplicity, and every other base motive. But what have I done to be treated like this? Can't a man retire to his own house, to study and pray in peace?'

'Perhaps it would be better to leave Oxford altogether', Clem said, realizing that he must have suffered a great deal of petty impertinence and intrusion of his privacy to talk like this.

'I suppose it may come to that', he said wearily. 'I had hoped to live and die here, but I fancy I am getting changed. When I go into Oxford I find myself out of place. Everything seems to say to me, "This is not your home." ' He sighed.

Augustine asked, 'Why do you stay here, then?'

Newman put his hand over his eyes. 'I am so afraid', he murmured. 'I am so afraid I may be under the power of a delusion.'

Clem, with a chill of apprehension, wondered if he feared a nervous breakdown like the one he had suffered in his youth; surely the strain now was even more intense?

But Newman went on in his puzzled, gentle voice, 'Yes, I was certain once and found I was wrong, when I believed the Church of England was a branch of the Catholic Church. May I not be wrong now? I must stay here till I am sure I am not under a delusion.' Then, suddenly and desperately, he said, 'But what have I done to be given up to a delusion, if it be one?'

Augustine said, gravely, 'Perhaps you give too much weight to what your friends suggest, in their anxiety not to lose you. I am sure your reason is as clear as your conscience.'

Newman looked at him uncertainly. 'It is kind of you to say so', he said at last. 'But I believe you are a Roman Catholic.'

'I am not speaking for religion but for common sense', said Augustine, smiling. 'Too much indecision will make you ill.'

'I am going to write a book', Newman said, suddenly. 'And when it is done, if I have satisfied myself it is the truth as far as I can know it, I will make a decision.'

'What will the book be about?' Clem asked.

'It will be on the nature of development in Christian doctrine', he answered. But then he sighed. 'God help me when I make that decision, for I know only too well how I am watched, how what I do is taken up and made a cause of unsettlement and pain in others. I can hardly bear to hurt people so, my sister—she writes me such sad painful letters, I cannot tell you ... and what if I am wrong? Yet it seems to me that all along I have only looked for the truth, and not to follow it is surely that sin against the Holy Spirit of God, which is unforgiveable. It is hard, it is hard indeed.'

But when they began to sympathize he said hastily, 'What a lot about myself! Now let me hear about you. Why don't you write to me? I have often thought about you. I fear your cousin Bertram Scarvell will have nothing to do with me now. And he has married a bishop's daughter.' His eyes brightened with the old ironic gleam and a mischievous smile twitched the corner of his mouth.

'Married? Bertram?' cried Clem. 'Why he said—' she stopped in confusion, remembering the occasion on which Bertram had declared his intention of leading a celibate life.

Newman said, 'Yes, I should have felt it as a desertion once but Scarvell gave me up over Tract 90, and I did not expect him to continue in all our principles. And somehow, that is always the first one to go!' He smiled.

Clem glanced at Augustine and saw he was looking at her to see how she took this news, but when he caught her eye his own merely twinkled.

'I'm sure a bishop's daughter is just the thing for Bertram', he said.

As they drove back into Oxford Clem looked out at the tower of Magdalen College, rearing in the cloudy sky, and remarked, 'Fancy Bertram marrying again after all!'

Augustine chuckled. 'I thought he would', he said. 'I'm glad I got you first.'

'Oh', cried Clem passionately. 'I couldn't have borne to be married to anyone but you!'

Augustine laughed, but she knew he was pleased she had said it like that.

They could not escape Newman's problems while they were in Oxford. A Catholic acquaintance annoyed Clem by saying he could not make out what all the fuss was about.

'If Newman no longer has faith in his heresy, why doesn't he submit and have done with it? Why sit there doing nothing?'

'It's not easy to give up your whole way of life when you are over forty', Augustine pointed out. 'Especially if, like Newman, you are not convinced you are always and infallibly right.'

His friend merely snorted and said it was intellectual pride; Newman did not want to give in and admit he was wrong. 'What's he giving up, anyway? That dreary hermitage at Littlemore? Nobody is going to martyr him for coming over. I can't stand dither.'

Quite as irritating was another acquaintance, not a Catholic, who remarked, 'I can't understand why he doesn't go over to you openly. Everyone knows he's a secret Catholic. I've heard he has even been ordained and told to keep as he is, subverting people.'

Clem mentioned this accusation when she saw Newman again, alone, for Augustine dropped her at Littlemore while he made a business call.

'That's not new to me', said Newman wearily. 'People even believe I have taken money to advance the cause of Rome while still a member of the Church of England.'

'Surely no one could believe that of you?' Clem cried, incredulous.

'I should say, no one who knows me', he said, with a flash of pride. 'But people in general have no means of checking such tales, and so the dirt sticks. And perhaps they would rather think me dishonest and a hypocrite than allow that I may be right. If you call a man a liar and a cheat it saves you the trouble of considering what he says, especially if you take care not to say it to his face, so that he has no chance to defend himself. Cowards, they are, the lot of them!'

Clem wished the anonymous slanderers could meet him now; she thought few would have the courage to repeat their insinuations.

'It is so unfair', she said, full of indignation. 'Can't anything be done?'

'You can't fight rumour', he said, more quietly. Then, after a moment of silence, he spoke in quite a different voice. 'No. I am not unwilling to be in trouble now, and the more of it, the sooner over. It is like drinking a cup out.'

The image remained in Clem's mind, even when they went on to talk of other things. Because he had used it, she knew that this gathering of people against him, their suspicion and crude scorn, even hatred, was a source of pain second only to the anguish of finding himself separated from his dearest friends in the very things nearest to his heart. People had sometimes said to her that he was cold, an academic at home only among abstractions; perhaps because he so resolutely kept to his ideal of a single life, and lived it with an unobtrusive but unmistakeable austerity. But Clem never felt he was cold-hearted; rather, she sometimes wished for his own sake that he could feel less. She had known no one so tenacious of friendship, and with so many different kinds of people, of both sexes and all ages; no one who suffered more at the troubles of his friends, or when he lost them, by the changing of minds, or by death. Mary had gone, and Hurrell Froude, and now this year Pusey's daughter Lucy, whom he had baptized and played with in her childhood, and in September his oldest Oxford friend, Bowden, with whom he had shared his undergraduate days and thoughts.

At last Clem told him how she had lost her baby.

'To lose a child must be the greatest sorrow', he said, full of sympathy, and after a moment added, 'That was St. Mary's part, to suffer the death of her only son.'

Somehow this had never come home to Clem as it did now.

'It is a crucifixion of the heart', Newman said.

She was silent, and he too said nothing more. It was very quiet in the house.

She suddenly had an overpowering sensation, indescribable, even to herself, of her heart opening; she felt she was seeing things from another angle, herself in a new light, the whole world larger and more mysterious. The pain of the loss of her child did not lessen, but became intense with meaning, a meaning she felt but could not quite grasp with her reason. The place of the skull was here, but it was a tomb opening; Christ was on the everlasting tree and it was flowering.

She could not speak.

Presently Newman, unaware that his words had touched a spring in her, said slowly, 'Sometimes it is very dark, but we must trust God to bring us through. He knows the way.'

The bell rang; Augustine came in to fetch her.

Newman came to the door with them. 'I hope it will not be so long before you come to Oxford again', he said.

'Do you know, when I first came back I felt most strange', said Clem. 'As if I were not myself, or the city were unreal. I think I know what a ghost feels like!'

Newman was interested. 'Curious', he said. 'It reminds me of a time, some years ago, when I happened to ride down to Alton, where I lived as a boy, before I came up to Oxford. It seemed to me then so very strange that everything was in its place after so long a time. As I came near and saw Monk's Wood, the church and the hollow on the other side of the town, it was as fearful as if I were standing on the grave of someone I knew and saw him gradually recover life and rise again.'

The skin of Clem's neck tingled; she remembered suddenly how he had spoken of the ruined temple in the Greek wilderness, years ago. He seemed to have the power of seeing visions in the mere seeing of places; the images remained, indestructible, mysterious.

'When was that?' she asked him.

'I think it must have been the year after I came back from my illness in Sicily', he said.

They said goodbye and drove away. Clem looked back and saw Newman still standing there in the gloom, thinking, remembering. His face showed pale, and his hands too, but the rest of him vanished, a shadow in the shadows.

'He's a strange man', she said, turning away.

Night was coming down in a soft drizzle.

'He's a kind of poet of living', said Augustine. 'A seer, but he doesn't always know what it is he sees: perhaps they never do. What was he telling us about just now?'

'The dead town coming to life again', Clem said. 'The place of his youth.'

'No', said Augustine. 'It was himself. He was the one who had died and come to life again.'

Clem was so surprised she was silent. Then she said, 'Was that so for me too, then?'

'I think so, don't you?' said Augustine gently.

She peered at him in the dusk. 'But how do you know that?'

'It's happened to me too', he answered. 'To everyone in this world at least once, don't you think?'

He began coughing and could not stop at once.

'Don't say your cold is worse', said Clem, falling abruptly out of the world of thought and intuition into everyday existence.

Augustine's cold was not heavy, but his cough was bad, and when they got back to Birmingham he went to bed. The next morning he did not look very well, but he went into the town to meet someone important; it was the reason for his returning the day before and he did not want to put it off. Clem, coming downstairs late in the afternoon, found him sitting on the wooden chair in the hall, with his coat on, and his head in his hands.

To her anxious enquiry he answered, 'I think I'm going to be ill. I'm sorry. What a nuisance.'

Clem saw he was ill already. She rang for Benedetto and sent for the doctor. Augustine insisted on going to bed in a spare room; Clem did not like the implication that he thought his illness was going to last some time. But before very long she was terrified that it was going to be all too short. He had bronchitis and developed pneumonia, and she was horrified to see how rapidly it gained on him; he had almost no reserve of strength. The local doctor, whom they scarcely knew, was so anxious that he asked her to send for the family doctor from London; of course that frightened her still more. When Dr. Stirling arrived she demanded, desperately, resentfully, how anyone as energetic as Augustine could be so quickly reduced to feebleness.

'My dear leddy', said Dr. Stirling, fixing her with a beady blue eye. 'What should surprise you is that he keeps so well, living as he does. It's wull power he lives on, for he's nothing of a constitution, never has had, from a child, and his heart was weakened by the rheumatic fever. He wudna tell you that, I daresay, for it irks him to be fussed, and he's aye been ashamed of his weakness.'

Clem found herself crying. She turned away. 'Why didn't he tell me? It's my fault we aren't back in Rome now.'

She felt that if Augustine died it would kill her. Her little Felix's death had been a terrible shock, but this was another thing altogether, this would tear her to pieces, was already tearing her to pieces.

'Don't give way now, ma'am', the doctor said kindly. 'He'll put up all the fight he can, be sure of that.'

But Augustine's fight for life was her agony. She was sure in her heart that he was going to die, that it was all her fault, she did not deserve to have him. She did all she was allowed to do for him, and it was some relief that he liked to have her there, but fear and anguish pressed on her heart, squeezed her in a merciless vice.

Augustine got worse all the time, but he did, as Dr. Stirling had expected, fight every step, and therefore Clem's worst moment came when he asked for a priest. She knew then he thought he might die.

'No, no', she pleaded, filled with irrational horror.

But Benedetto fetched the priest, a stocky, grey-haired Lancashire man in a black suit, and Clem could not refuse to let him into Augustine's room. She had no idea what he was going to do, and she stood there suspiciously till he said, 'Would you mind waiting outside, ma'am, till I've heard his confession?'

Clem went out and stood on the landing. She heard Benedetto murmuring over his Rosary, sitting outside the bedroom door. The lamps were lit, the house was quiet; outside was black winter night, heavy with cloud. Clem heard the clock in the hall ticking, and her heart beating, and suddenly the fearful terror of being alive struck her, the abyss of knowing herself to be. She felt herself nothing but a heart beating, a tiny pulse in a vast universe of darkness.

From a long way off she heard Benedetto call to her, 'Signora, come now.'

She went back into the room and saw a crucifix and two candles burning. 'He is dying', she thought, walking stiffly, feeling herself walking, as if her body moved of itself.

She stood by Dr. Stirling. Benedetto knelt on the floor.

The priest held the Host, like a small round piece of paper, and made the sign of the cross with it over Augustine and put it in his mouth. He only just had the strength to receive it.

Presently the priest began some more Latin prayers, and took some oil and touched his eyes, his ears, his nostrils, his lips, and then the palms of his hands, lying limp and flat, and lastly his feet. Somehow his feet, sticking up, thin and familiar, made Clem cry; silent tears, she made no sound. It seemed stranger than anything she knew to see Augustine touched like this; she thought the priest was sealing him away from the world, away from her. He lay so still, with his eyes almost shut, that he might be already gone, but that she could see him breathing.

The rite completed, the priest went outside the door, and Clem heard their voices, low, in question and answer. She went slowly to the bed and stood looking at Augustine, feeling terribly alone. He looked so quiet, it frightened her.

But then he opened his eyes and she saw him looking at her. He murmured something, but she could not hear it. Quickly she knelt down to be closer, and he turned his head a little towards her.

'Clem, don't be frightened.'

She pressed her shaking lips together, trying desperately not to give words to her anguish, but she realized, soon, that he had seen it in her face. A troubled look came where there had just now been none.

'If only there was something I could do', she said.

'You could pray for us.'

'I can't pray', she muttered, the words slipping out before she could stop them.

Augustine said, 'Ask our Lady, then, ask her to pray.'

His voice was weak, almost a whisper. Dreadful fear shook her. She caught his hand and held it tight, as if she could drag him back from death like that.

Then she felt a hand on her shoulder. It was Dr. Stirling and he beckoned her out of the room with him.

'Please to keep away just now, ma'am', he said bluntly. 'I sympathize with your feelings, but I cannot have him excited now.'

'Keep away?' Clem said, ashamed and angry. 'Do you want him to die when I am not there?'

'There's no call to talk of dying yet', said Dr. Stirling, irascibly. 'I'll send for ye, ma'am, if there's any change. Now let him rest.'

He went back into the bedroom and shut the door against her. Clem moved slowly to the top of the stairs and looked down. She saw the Lancashire priest talking to Benedetto in the hall; he had short thick grey hair, rough as a mat. She wondered if she should speak to him, but at that moment he went off towards the kitchen with the little Italian. All the same, she went downstairs, stiffly, as if she were already old.

She went into Augustine's study. His desk was covered with engineer's plans for a new type of press for the factory. There was no lamp in the room, but light shone in there from the hall, and in the beam of it, pretty as an Arcadian shepherdess, stood the little porcelain Virgin from France that Augustine was so fond of; he called it Madonnina and in the summer always put a rose beside her. There was no rose there now.

'Ask her to pray for us', he had said.

Clem got down on her knees on the floorboards and clasped her hands as she had in childhood, staring up at the little statue.

'Please, Mary, pray for us', she whispered aloud. 'Don't let him die.'

She felt entirely alone in the cold room, could not now believe in any presence beyond her own; there was only winter darkness outside the circle of small flames, human beings, burning in the world of nature, and the one she loved best was dying upstairs, lying on the edge of nothing, soon to be blown out in the inexorable wind of time. She spoke the prayer because he had asked her to, but she said it to nothing more real than a china figure a foot high.

Presently, as it seemed pointless to go on kneeling in the draught, on the hard boards, she stiffly got up and went to sit by the drawing-room fire, to wait for Dr. Stirling.

He came at last, opened the door and stood there, silent.

Clem stood up. She thought Augustine had died and he had come to tell her.

'My dear leddy, your husband's sleeping', he said, with a hint of surprise in his voice. 'I wudna take my oath, but I believe he's past the worst.'

Clem could not believe it at first, and from his voice she knew the doctor himself had been expecting death. But she went upstairs and saw for herself Augustine lying asleep and relaxed, as he had not done for days. His hair looked very black and thick on the pillow, growing with all the strength his body did not have. She gently touched it and began to cry with relief.

Augustine took a long time to get well again, but he did get well. He said the Blessed Virgin knew he was not ready to die yet. Clem said nothing about her prayer from a hopeless heart, but she felt his recovery was indeed a gift from a heavenly providence. Her landmarks through a long and especially cold English winter were his coming back to sleep in their bedroom, his coming downstairs, his staying up to dinner again. Long before that he had started to take an interest in the firm again, and engineers and managers from the factory, and even from Dudley, came to see him while he was still in bed. Clem complained of it.

'Do you think I'm going to turn into another Mr. Bodley?' he said, amused. 'Well, tell me what's going on in the world.'

'I'll tell you what's been going on in Oxford', said Clem. 'If you count that as part of the world.'

She had just had a letter from an Oxford acquaintance who had married a Canon of Christ Church, and was full of news.

'Oh, Oxford is a world in itself', Augustine said. 'But I suppose you could call it a fair picture of the mind of England, the brainworks, if not the common-sense works!'

'Well, just listen to what's been going on in the Sheldonian Theatre', said Clem. 'It's as good as a play.'

Chuckling, she read him the letter. Ward of Balliol, the fat philosopher, who enjoyed nothing better than shocking the cautious, had written a book about his Ideal Church, which, it seemed to his readers, was much more like the Church of Rome than the Church of England, whose sworn minister he was. On a snowy February day he and his book were called to trial in the Sheldonian; Ward, slipping in the snow, was wildly cheered by the undergraduates outside, who followed this up by snow-balling the Vice Chancellor's retinue. Inside, although (perhaps because) he spoke for hours in his own defence, Ward's book was condemned by the elders of the University, which everyone had expected, and he himself deprived of his degrees; that was unexpected, almost unprecedented. The votes had caused enormous excitement, when declared.

'That's very severe', Augustine said, in surprise. 'I don't think they have gone so far with the clergymen at the other extreme, who give up articles of faith. Rome is worse than infidelity, in fact.'

'They nearly got Newman too', Clem said. 'He wasn't there, but Tract 90 was brought up for condemnation.'

She read out how, in the wild uproar of cheers and boos, the proctors had stood up and shouted their veto. They were Newman's friends, especially the Junior, Richard Church. The meeting ended in pandemonium, but Clem's friend said that most people were glad Newman had been spared this public condemnation. All the same, he could not fail to know that the authorities were implacably set against him, and the antics of Ideal Ward did not commend the Movement to the sober.

Augustine thought Ward a comic character, and he was delighted when, a little later, this fierce exponent of asceticism and celibacy announced his engagement. 'It is in the wide variety of its eccentrics that the Church of England gains its peculiar flavour', he said.

But not long after, Ward made his submission to the Catholic and Roman Church, the first of the famous to do so.

'I bet our bishops are crossing their fingers', was Augustine's irreverent comment.

By then the long winter was done, the fitful sun of an English summer brightened through the flowering trees of Edgbaston gardens. Clem had never met Ward, and what he did held no great interest for her, but it put an idea into her mind.

'Is it difficult to become a Catholic?' she asked Augustine.

'Not if you accept the Faith', he said, giving her a quick, questioning glance.

'I don't know whether I do or not', said Clem. 'But I think I want to be one, because you are.'

Augustine laughed and said she had better have a talk with Mr. Kirby. At their first conversation Mr. Kirby, in his blunt northcountry way, remarked, 'We'll go through the penny catechism, ma'am, and see what you *do* know. All right?'

Clem did not mind that; learning doctrine as if it were grammar appealed to her. But she could not make up her mind whether she believed it all or not.

Mrs. Bodley, of course, got wind of what was happening, and in August she invited Clem to tea and made a direct attack. She tried one line after another. The picture of busy Mr. Kirby, with his brisk take-it-or-leave-it manner, as a cunning and unscrupulous angler for her soul merely made Clem laugh. So did the horrified assertions that she would be forced to worship idols. In fact, everything Mrs. Bodley said made her feel more of a Catholic than she ever had before.

She protested at last. 'Don't you think it is better for married people to be of the same religion?'

'Indeed, no, if it means your husband's perverting you', said Mrs. Bodley, peering at her with puzzled pop-eyes, as if she expected to find visible signs of religious dissipation. 'How can you allow it, Mrs. Firle? He must have some peculiar hold over you.'

'Yes, he has!' cried Clem in a burst of irritation. 'It's love, that's his hold over me, and I love what he loves because of it. Is that so very strange?'

Mrs. Bodley was not so easily vanquished. 'Ah, my dear, love is blind', she said, shaking her head so emphatically that her double chin wobbled. 'But when he was so ill last winter, did it not come home to you then how false are those idolatrous ceremonies, what a hollow mockery all that mummery and superstition?'

Clem stared at her, not speaking, vividly remembering the scene when Augustine had received Viaticum and the last anointing.

Convinced she was making headway at last Mrs. Bodley rushed on in triumph. 'Why, my dear, that was your chance to draw him away from all those vain practices to true religion. And instead of that you let him teach you to crush your Christian conscience and give up your will to those cunning priests. My dear, can't you see that now he will not rest till he has made you as corrupt as himself?'

Clem jumped to her feet. 'Stop!' she cried. 'Don't say any more or I shall do something dreadful—hit you, I do believe!' She clawed desperately at her purse, her umbrella, her shawl. Her furious hands fumbled, shaking.

'My dear Mrs. Firle!' cried Mrs. Bodley, astonished, her satin bosom heaving with alarm and excitement. 'What is the matter?'

'Matter!' shouted Clem, furiously. 'Do you expect me to listen to such horrible nonsense about Augustine and like it?' She rushed towards the door in a blind fury, knocking into the furniture on the way, so angry was she and clumsy in her anger. 'I suppose you don't know what you're talking about', she said ungraciously. 'But oh, to speak of him like that to me!'

She blundered out into the hall, wrestled with the front door and ran all the way home, arriving panting on the doorstep to find Augustine, just back from the factory, looking at his letters in the hall. She flung herself, incoherent and trembling, into his arms.

'Oh! I could kill Mrs. Bodley! When can I be a Catholic?'

Augustine laughed helplessly, even while he hugged her with such enthusiasm that her bonnet fell off the back of her head, hanging by the strings round her throat.

'I'm throttling, help!' she cried, her anger turning into laughter.

Augustine released her and kissed her.

'Why have you gone suddenly mad, my precious Clem?'

'Oh dear, I have been so rude to her', Clem said, and began to explain as well as she could what had happened. She meekly accepted it when he said they must go back and apologize to Mrs. Bodley, who was only stupid and meant well.

Augustine did all the apologizing, so gracefully that he had Mrs. Bodley smiling at him before he left, quite as if he were not, after all, so very corrupt. Clem teased him, as they walked back, arm in arm, for such a blatant exercise of charm. In return he made fun of her perversity in deciding to join the Church because Mrs. Bodley warned her against it.

'You are more like your father than you think!' he said. She had told him a great many stories about her father.

Clem was received on the eve of the feast of the Nativity of the Blessed Virgin, making her First Communion on that day. Now she knelt with Augustine at the altar rail and was content. She felt that she had come into a great house full of hidden wonders, and yet, now that she was there, it was her home.

They were already preparing to leave England; Clem was now more afraid of the northern winter than Augustine, and they were gone before the end of September. So they were in Rome when they heard the news of Newman's submission, in the wild wet beginning of October. Creating his book, tracing out the growing of the great tree of redemption in time, he had re-created his own heart, so that at last he was able to take up all that was his and offer it on the altar of sacrifice. Nor, when he did this, kneeling at the feet of Father Dominic Barberi, the Italian farmer's son called in a vision, long years ago, to God's work in England, did he see any shadow of what was to come of it.

# 7

In November the next year, 1846, Clem bore a second child, whom they christened Henry. He was a quiet, brown-haired baby, not so strong as Felix; he reminded Augustine sometimes of his brother, Alexander, which Clem thought hardly a compliment. But she knew the brothers were very much attached to each other.

The same month Newman arrived in Rome to study for the priesthood, a year after his reception. He stayed in the College of Propaganda, where Augustine visited him.

'It's unbelievable how humble Newman is', he said, chuckling, when he came back. 'He really thought he would be treated the same as the boys!'

Clem asked how he got on as a Catholic and Augustine laughed. 'I think he was quite surprised to discover *some* educated and intelligent men in our English colleges!' he said. 'He really knew so little about us—his decision was entirely on faith.'

Later, Newman paid them a Christmas visit. Clem showed him her baby. 'He is John Henry Alexander,' she told him, 'after you and his uncle.'

'You called him after me?' said Newman, evidently as surprised as he was pleased. He scrutinized the baby's face. 'A nice little fellow, he is. He will wonder why you called him after such a dry old fogie. Jemima has quite a family now, but I doubt if I shall see them. I am afraid she feels I have made it impossible to continue on our old terms.'

But he did not talk much of the past, and on the whole Clem thought he seemed happy; not so lively as in the early days of the movement, but more settled and serene. There were certainly trials, for someone of his temperament, in plunging into this new life and new society. The latest was an unlucky sermon he had been persuaded to preach, against his better judgement, at a Roman society funeral. Everybody seemed to have been offended: the English Protestants present, their noble Italian hosts, and even, it was said, the new Pope Pius IX. Newman thought he had only made some remarks about everyone being in need of conversion, but apparently his words were taken as discourteous and unnecessarily violent.

'You have a special gift for being misunderstood', Augustine told him.

Newman smiled. 'Inwardly I writhe with shame when I think of it', he admitted. 'I never shall make a public man.'

They saw him several times during the winter. He lived quietly, read and visited the churches of Rome with Ambrose St. John, who was called by the Romans his guardian angel, 'because he is fair and Saxon-looking', said Newman. They were also trying to decide the future of the whole Littlemore group, who all hoped to find a common vocation. Clem and Augustine left Rome before the question was settled and before Newman said his first Mass, at Corpus Christi.

They did not go back to Rome. Augustine thought the state of Europe too unsettled, and he gave up his apartments. His caution was justified the next year, when revolutions broke out everywhere, in Paris, and in Rome itself, when Pius IX fled to Gaeta. No one felt safe, even in England, though the great Chartist agitation did not issue, as many feared, in open rebellion. Some said one reason for this was the Ten Hours Act, for which Lord Ashley had been campaigning for fourteen years, carried at last and opening up prospects for fairer dealing to the workpeople. Augustine had always been in favour of this measure, and the presswork factory was one of those that celebrated its enactment with free beer and medals struck to commemorate the event, though conditions in Birmingham differed a good deal from those in the cotton mills of the north. All the same, there was great misery among the town poor, and from time to time outbreaks of cholera. One of the worst epidemics coincided with the birth of Clem's third child, a girl they called Charlotte Mary, three years after Henry was born. Birmingham was not so stricken as London, where many thousands died, but the emergency had its unexpected moments. Newman, for instance, hurried off to Bilston to help, but found the danger already passing; heroic occasions always passed him by, Clem thought, perhaps a little to his disappointment. He had a keen admiration for the early martyrs and felt his life was dangerously comfortable compared with theirs.

For Newman also had become a Midlander. The Littlemore group became an Oratory of St. Philip Neri, Newman was appointed Superior and they were settled first at Old Oscott and later in Alcester Street, in Birmingham itself. Another clergyman convert, Frederick Faber the hymnwriter, with his own little band of disciples, joined them, but were soon sent to London to found a second Oratory. Newman remained in Birmingham, and after some initial misunderstandings with the new bishop, Ullathorne, he settled down to a long and faithful friendship with him, perhaps just because they were so different. Ullathorne, a few years Newman's junior, was a small dynamic Yorkshireman who had started life as a cabin boy, become a Benedictine and afterwards spent some eventful years with the convicts in Australia, valiantly battling against appalling conditions and government apathy. Downright, practical, fearless and active, he yet shared with Newman a love of the Fathers, and somehow found time to write books and pamphlets and letters to the papers even while he struggled with his growing industrial diocese, the flocks of starving Irish immigrants, and the enormous debt he had inherited. Augustine, as one of the richer members of his flock, was soon lending financial assistance to the diocese, to the Oratory, to various communities of nuns—he could never say no to nuns. Clem, who had at first been the more conscience-ridden of the two, now persuaded him to put some money in trust for Henry's education, especially when she discovered that Lord Gornal's favourite form of expressing his perennial irritation with his son was to threaten to cut off his allowance.

So now here they were, far from the European civilisation of Rome and its revolutionary dangers, far too from the scholarly decorum of Oxford, further still from wild Cornwall; here they were in this roaring, grinding Midland town, which was growing all the time like some giant red and black fungus in the green heart of England. Industry grew so fast that no one could keep pace with its proliferations, physical or moral. These were railway years, when England was crossed over with iron, and here in Birmingham, between the smoking stations, stood Pugin's hidden, red cathedral, with its lovely arches cheating the eye, for of course it all had to be done by sleight of hand, never enough money to spend; he had to create his Gothic dream out of so little, because the Catholics were so poor. An anachronism, some people said, as they were beginning to say it about Newman. And now, as the century turned, the same thing was said of the religion both professed: the Church belonged to the darkness of the past, and those who joined it were cowards at heart, in flight from a present they could not face. All the same, here they were, living in the middle of it all, the battle and smoke and guilt and adventure of the new age.

In the autumn of 1850 the Pope restored the English Catholic hierarchy. Clem could not understand what it meant at first.

'But Ullathorne is a bishop already', she said.

Augustine explained that now, instead of being mission territory under Propaganda, England would rule itself, with Wiseman as Cardinal Archbishop of Westminster, and ordinary Canon Law in force. After three hundred years the Church was going back to normal.

'What about the Archbishop of Canterbury?' Clem asked.

'It won't make any difference to him', said Augustine. 'He probably won't even notice it has happened.'

A few days later he discovered his mistake. Wiseman wrote an enthusiastic pastoral letter from Rome, which was read in London at the beginning of October. On the fourteenth *The Times* published it with shocked and furious comments; the editors seemed to think Wiseman was coming back with the Spanish Armada to dethrone the Queen and set up an Inquisition. All the papers, even the weekly illustrated ones, took up the situation in a frenzy of patriotic indignation. Guy Fawkes' Day was not far off, dormant fears of Giant Pope came seething to life all over the country and mobs began to burn effigies, not only of the Roman Pontiff, who was no more than a symbol and a name to them, but of the new Cardinal too, so that Catholics began to wonder if Wiseman would be physically safe if he returned. Not only riotous crowds but public assemblies of respectable citizens shouted themselves into an hysteria of patriotic and Protestant fervour, especially after Lord John Russell's letter to the Bishop of Durham, which was published at the beginning of November. One of these took place the very day Wiseman returned, the eleventh, and Clem was sorry to hear that the chairman was that very Lord Ashley, whose work for the lunatics and the poor factory children she had so much admired.

'How can an educated man lend himself to this sort of thing?' she said. 'Does he do it to curry favour with voters?'

'No, no, he's the most sincere man alive', Augustine said. 'But he's a keen evangelical and sees only what he expects to see. Mass is a mummery to him, so he thinks it's a mummery to us. Naturally, if it were, we should be as despicable as he believes us to be.'

'Idiots, we should be', said Clem, not altogether convinced.

She found that her astonishment was shared by other converts. Those who had been born into the Catholic community barred their windows and prepared for the worst, but the converts, who had been brought up in what they had imagined to be the most free, most tolerant and civilized society in the world, simply could not believe that their countrymen were really afraid that Pius IX, who was in such dire political straits himself, intended any kind of invasion of England, or that the brilliant, kindly, enthusiastic Wiseman was seriously setting out in the hope of burning hecatombs of heretics at Westminster. Yet English people behaved just as if they were facing a mortal threat. High and Low Church quarrels were forgotten as the clergy united to vituperate the iniquities of the Roman aggression. Fear of rebellion by the hungry poor was forgotten, and the mobs spent their energies in riotous bonfires, burning enemies they knew nothing about, images of evil lurking somewhere in the ruined temples, the wildernesses of their hearts, the lost dark places forgotten in the scramble to keep alive.

Even in the country, in Cornwall, the bonfires were lit. Clem heard from a friend, 'As well as burning the Pope and the Cardinal they have burnt and blown up a great cross of wood, mocking and jeering at it, and they say that's been done in Exeter too, outside the cathedral doors.'

Crucifix and statue, wherever they were found, were hurled into the flames; mild Tractarians found themselves, to their surprise and horror, treated no better than papists.

Clem thought Augustine took it all too calmly.

'What would England do for a scapegoat without the Pope?' he said.

'I'd rather they hated the Pope than the Blessed Sacrament', said Clem. 'But they mock that too.'

'It's only a bit of bread to them', said Augustine. 'I don't suppose they would insult our Lord himself if they met him as a man.'

But as Clem drew the curtains in the misty November evenings she could not but wonder what might happen. Suppose the mob got out of hand? Augustine, as a known papist, a factory owner and the son of a rich peer, seemed to invite all the hatreds possible to the disinherited working people of England. But he smiled at her fears and went on as usual, driving himself to town, as he liked to do.

One Saturday evening she was in the cathedral when he came in there on his way home from the factory.

'Well met!' he said when he saw her. 'Now I'll have the pleasure of driving you home.'

Not far from where they started they passed through a narrow street by one of the canals that netted the backends of the city; a short cut, Augustine said. A single lock was there, and on the other side of the strip of still, oily water, a bonfire was blazing; and people, reduced to black scarecrows by the brilliance of the flames, crowded round it, shouting with raucous laughter. High on a pole was stuck a stuffed, drooping guy, draped in a scarlet petticoat and crowned with a triple tiara of old hats. Mopping and mowing in front of the fire was a grotesque old man with a blanket round his neck like a chasuble, waving a biscuit with both hands and screeching 'Hocus Pocus' amid the cheers and guffaws of the crowd.

Clem stared at the scene, sharp as a puppet show in the black night. It was one thing to read about such things in the papers, another to see them happening, to feel the ignorant hate directed against the thing of all things to her most holy.

Suddenly, on the same side of the lock as themselves, they saw a knot of urchins and youths, running and whistling and howling, and they were pelting a hurrying man with mud, scooping it up from the ground as they ran. The man wore a religious habit.

'It's one of the Italians', said Augustine.

They could see the young priest's face, strained with fear; he made no attempt to shield himself from attack but held both hands clutched across his breast.

'He's got a pyx there', said Augustine suddenly. 'He's got the Blessed Sacrament.'

He pushed the reins into Clem's hands and jumped down so quickly that his hat fell off and rolled away under the wheels. He ran towards the priest, just as the bonfire crowd, with hoots and shouts, came streaming across the lock, stepping on the beam of the gate. Augustine reached him first, but the excited mob were not going to let a real Romish priest get away as easily as that. They surrounded them both, yelling and laughing. Laughter like that was not reassuring; great hoarse bellows they let out, like maddened animals.

Clem was terrified. She did not know what to do. Even the well-trained horses were restive at the leaping figures and flames ahead. She dared not leave them, but although she knew she could be of no use except in holding them, she longed to jump down and run to Augustine, to share whatever was going to happen to him. She was high enough, on the box, to see him, still holding the priest's arm and shouting back at the mob leaders. Once she heard his voice above the din: 'Shame! Fair play!'

As if, she thought with a desperate sob, as if these poor wretches had ever had fair play themselves. This was fair game, not fair play, to them.

'He's a papist too!' they shouted. 'Duck 'em in the cut! Duck 'em in the cut!'

Clem saw them fall on their victims, pulling and tugging at them till she was terrified they would be pulled to pieces. They dragged off Augustine's big overcoat and began to fight over it, greedy hands clawed at their clothes while others were hauling them towards the water. Clem saw a child using the priest's wooden Rosary beads as a weapon against his mates. All the black figures jerked and danced against the glare of the fire, smokily reflected in the dirty canal, below the looming brick walls of the warehouses, empty of light and sound, the tombs of the machines, and over all opened the huge sky of night, of dark and starless November.

Clem suddenly heard herself sobbing aloud; she was shaking with terror. She saw the priest still clutching the hidden pyx with one hand, and trying to shield his face with the other from the angry blows aimed at him from every side; and she saw Augustine hitting out with both fists, struggling on the slippery bank, and then a wild yell of triumph went up as both of them fell backwards into the greasy water above the narrow lock.

She half rose on the seat, gasping, helplessly staring. The canal was not deep; she saw them floundering, trying to climb out, but the boys threw stones at them, shrieking excitedly, and the men kicked at their hands when they clutched at the lock gate. The screeches of laughter sounded to her like the cries of maniacs.

'They'll kill them; they'll drown them', Clem muttered in her agony.

But then, and it was really not many minutes since they had turned down the street, some policemen, attracted by the flare and noise, came running, swinging their truncheons. The little crowd of ragged enthusiasts melted away into alleys and corners, as rapidly as stray cats when the dogs come, and soon two black and dripping figures were being helped out of the canal. Clem could hear Augustine coughing and laughing, actually laughing, she thought, almost angry with him in her relief. Tears stung her eyes as she climbed down at last and ran stumbling towards him, her knees shaky, her heart pounding. He just put his arm round her and went on talking to the constable.

Presently he turned to the priest and spoke to him in Italian. The poor young man burst into a torrent of gratitude.

'Well, I don't see that I was much use', said Augustine, in English. 'Come on, I'll drive you home.'

Refusing all police offers, he insisted on taking the priest to the house where he was staying, and handed him over, dripping and still gratefully talking, to his companions in religion. The Fathers wanted him to come in, but he would not, and they started for Edgbaston. Augustine began coughing again.

'That damn cut-water has stuck in my gullet', he said cheerfully.

Clem leant close to him. 'My darling, you're so terribly wet', she said anxiously. 'Why didn't you stop with the Fathers?'

'I'd rather get home', he said. 'Phoo! Don't I smell? Wasn't it lucky the peelers came when they did?'

Danger seemed to have put him in high spirits, but Clem felt tired to death. She gave such a shuddering sigh that Augustine hugged her, with one arm, and said she was a poor little Clem, watching was always worse than action, and they were both going to have hot brandy and water and go to bed.

The next day at Mass there was a pastoral from Bishop Ullathorne, and on Monday a public meeting when Wiseman's 'Appeal to the English People' was read, and this so changed the aspect of things that in Birmingham at least not much further was done against Catholics by anyone respectable. Wiseman's appeal was printed in the principal papers, even reluctantly by *The Times*, and was read all over the country. He too, Clem noticed, appealed for fair play; he also made it plain that the jurisdiction of the bishops was spiritual, and exercised over their own Catholic flocks, and he turned the tables on those who had accused him of ambition in claiming Westminster as his See by saying he left the Abbey and palaces to those who owned them, and wanted for himself only the miserable slums and tenements which, to England's shame, surrounded them. His courage and obvious Englishness won the day with the majority; only fanatics continued their campaigns after it.

But what had happened changed the religious scene in England. Till now Catholics had been almost a forgotten people, nobody thought it worth while to enforce the penal laws against them, had even voted for their emancipation, convinced that such a benighted remnant of superstition could not long survive in the present century of enlightenment. But now here suddenly appeared a Church, with a Cardinal Archbishop, with other bishops, some as full of fight as Yorkshire Ullathorne with his letters to the news-papers, here was a Church with territorial dioceses, colleges for training priests, convents full of nuns and a continuing stream of educated converts. 'Rome' had appeared on the map of England again, and Catholics could not now be forgotten, and their Faith ignored.

Augustine caught a chill from his ducking, of course, and he was sent to bed by his doctor. But this time he was not seriously ill. He complained of boredom.

'You shouldn't be so active', said Clem. 'Try a little contemplation.'

'I will, if you sit there and sew', he said.

Clem pretended to scoff at his flattery. 'Have you forgotten I'll be forty next year?'

'And do you know I've got grey hairs?' Augustine said.

'You haven't!' cried Clem, peering with anxious affection at his black tousle.

Augustine laughed. 'Benedetto tweaked them out. He evidently thinks I would look better bald than grey.'

'Bald!' said Clem, giggling. 'You would look funny!'

'Heartless creature', said Augustine. 'You know very well my hair is my only beauty. Clem, shall we fly together? What about Christmas in Sandgate?'

'You're just sentimental about Sandgate', Clem teased him.

'Well, we can take the children to keep us sober.'

At Sandgate, at the year's end, the sea was wide and pale and still, the sky dimly bronze, echoing the sun sinking behind them, low over England. The waves turned over in long shallow folds, softly hissing on the empty shore.

Clem suddenly sighed, as they sat on the brown shingle bank, watching the moving of the sea.

'They didn't know what he was holding', she said.

'What who was holding?'

'The priest, that time by the canal.'

'No', said Augustine slowly. 'But they knew whom *they* were holding.'

'What do you mean, whom they were holding?'

'A man', he said, and was silent.

It was true, Clem thought. The rioters did not know the hidden God, but they did know it was a fellow man they were mocking and ill-treating. Yes, she thought, staring into the silken sea, so calm, so desolate, and God forgives the crucifixion of himself, but men do not forgive each other, though that was what he asked of them.

'I can't blame them, though', she said at last.

'I don't blame them', said Augustine. 'But isn't this a sad, a terrible age? Hunger, slavery in all but name for thousands, rebellions that never give joy to those for whom they are made, knowledge all fixed on outward things and people losing faith everywhere in the providence of God. Sometimes I think it is like the beginning of the end.'

'The end of what?'

'Of the world.'

How opaque the sea was, Clem thought, the water thick like milk, hiding all below. She remembered Newman lamenting, ten years ago in Oxford, 'And now the second millennium draws to its close.'

'Newman used to say things like that', she said.

'Still does', said Augustine, smiling. 'Because he lives on our doorstep you don't listen to what he says! And do you know, the Oratory is coming literally to our doorstep, on the Hagley Road.'

They began to talk about that then, but Clem was surprised, because, as Augustine was such a cheerful person, she did not expect him to be thinking about the end of the world.

'Come on home!' he said at last, jumping up and holding his hand to her. 'It's cold now.'

But Clem sat for a moment looking up at him, and she thought suddenly, Yes, we are going to grow old, we are going to die, our bodies left on the shore of this world like the dried dead gull down there, our own bodies, his and mine. And what then?

Augustine saw the chill of fear in her eyes and took hold of her hand, pulling her up gently. Clem suddenly clung to him.

'It is frightening to be alive', she whispered. 'Sometimes I can't believe—not in anything.'

'I know that feeling', he said, and kissed her mouth.

'That's cheating', she murmured.

'Is it?' he said. 'Lovers expect trust, don't they, not proof?'

'I'm not afraid of losing myself', she said. 'Only of losing you.'

'Shall I make a vow not to die first?' he said, smiling.

But Clem was still lost in the horror of death. She could not smile.

'Do laugh, Clem', Augustine pleaded, putting his finger in her cheek. 'Make your dimple come, I do like it so much. I believe Charlotte's going to have one too; isn't it nice? I am lucky to have two women with dimples in the family!'

He always did make her laugh in the end, and when they went home and he opened a bottle of wine for dinner, she was happy again. But later, as she lay in bed and heard the sea outside, so soft, but always breathing over and over its perpetual sighs, hollow echoes of the heart that beat and beat, even asleep, drawing up time and throwing it away, then she felt how deep was the shadow under the shining surface of the sea, how small their vanishing words, sketched like ripples by the passing winds, their passing lives.

Augustine was asleep. She laid her hand very lightly on him and felt his heart beating. It was so strange to feel that little throb and know that if it stilled all that she knew of him would be gone. But curiously, as she lay there with her hand on his side, she felt quieted; there was no reason that she could discover for the peace that came to her, but still it came, rising like a deep tide out of hidden ocean wells, unseen, far off, the secret springs. She too slept.

# 8

Although official antagonism lessened as soon as the true position of the hierarchy was known, a general bad feeling against Catholics persisted, and in the next summer Newman was persuaded to undertake some public lectures on the situation. They were given in the Birmingham Corn Exchange and began on the last day of June. It was the year of the Great Exhibition.

Ladies were not admitted and Clem, a little annoyed at her exclusion, walked down after the first lecture to meet Augustine and saw Miss Giberne prowling outside, equally frustrated. Maria Rosina, who had first met the Newmans at the time of Mary's death, had been a beautiful, enthusiastic, evangelical girl then, rather bewildered because John Henry did not break out in extempore prayer on every occasion. Frank had fallen wildly in love; the adored image of her had brought him back from trying to convert the Persians to be Plymouth Brothers, the very same summer that his brother had returned from Sicily possessed by the vision of the supernatural Christian society incarnate in England. Miss Giberne refused Frank; Clem sometimes wondered if she would have refused John Henry if it had ever occurred to him to propose marriage. But on the whole she thought Miss Giberne a woman who preferred emotion neat, unhampered by the physical demands and burdens of ordinary love. She went through a series of passionate friendships with other girls and somehow never entirely grew up. Her admiration for Newman never failed, and with many qualms and ecstasies she followed him into the Catholic Church and continued to seek his advice on every occasion. Newman's other friends could not help being a little amused at this enthusiastic feminine echo, but Clem liked Miss Giberne, whose heart, however silly, was generous and warm.

'I could hear them laughing from here', she told Clem now.

'*Laughing*?' said Clem, astonished. 'What is there to laugh at?'

Newman's audience began to come out, still smiling, Augustine among them.

'Miss Giberne said you were laughing', Clem accused him.

Augustine chuckled. 'You would have laughed if you had heard Newman taking off the horror of some poor stranger, ignorant of legal jargon, reading about the British Constitution', he said. '"The Sovereign is omnipotent." What! The Queen usurping the nature of deity? "The King can do no wrong." The English believe their monarch is impeccable! How shocking! How blasphemous! And look at the way they put wreaths on the statues of public men! Idolatrous!'

Clem smiled. 'So he has made fun of all the silly prejudices', she said. 'But will that do any good?'

'I think it's just the thing to do good with English people', said Augustine. 'It will make them feel ashamed of themselves. He wants them to look at the reality, not the lurid pictures they have conjured up out of stories like *Maria Monk*.'

He pressed her arm suddenly. 'Look there, Clem', he said quietly. 'There's Archdeacon Manning—ex-Archdeacon, I should say.'

Clem looked at him with interest; a straight handsome man in his forties, with a narrow, long face and large piercing blue eyes under a high forehead. It was a keen crusading face, intense and dedicated. He reminded her a little of Bertram Scarvell; yet she felt that this was at once a more introspective and less compromising soul than Bertram's.

She knew about Manning of course; he had never been one of Newman's particular disciples, but after Newman's departure he had become very prominent in the Movement. When Newman had resigned St. Mary's Manning had surprised some people by coming especially to Oxford to preach a furiously anti-Roman sermon from the famous pulpit; but since then events had been too much for him. What finally shook his belief in the Catholicity of the Anglican church was the fact that the State had supported against his bishop a clergyman who refused to admit that baptism effected any regeneration in the human soul. The 'Papal Aggression' demonstrations, which had showed the widespread hatred and ignorance of the Catholic religion still left in England, so far from frightening Manning, had acted as a call to battle. This very Easter he had been received into the Church, sorrowfully leaving his best friend, the politician Gladstone, at the Anglican altar.

'Why is he wearing clerical dress?' Clem asked Augustine.

'Wiseman has already ordained him priest.'

'What!' cried Clem. 'And Newman had to wait over a year and a half—and at first did not even expect to be a priest at all.'

'Wiseman's enthusiasm again!' said Augustine, smiling. 'He's desperate for help in London and Manning is full of pastoral energy, an excellent practical man, I hear. However, I believe he's going to Rome before he sets to work.'

'I should hope so', said Clem, rather disapproving.

'What a man, though!' Augustine said. 'He's given up a great career. Don't you think he would have been a bishop, probably Archbishop of Canterbury, if he had stayed in the Church of England?'

Newman came out of the building and they went to congratulate him; Clem thought how different his face was from Manning's, a face made for endurance rather than for action, and yet, in its own way, no less powerful. He was looking very cheerful, pleased because the first lecture had gone off so well.

'No interruptions, as I rather feared there would be', he said.

'You may have some after that wretch Achilli has spoken at the Town Hall', said Augustine. 'He stirs people up wherever he goes with his lurid tales of being tortured and starved by the Inquisition in Rome.'

'Yes', said Newman thoughtfully. 'People prefer to believe the lies of a man like that to the criticisms of my old apostate friend Blanco White, with whom I used to play quartets at Oriel. I think I shall say something about Achilli in my lectures. Dr. Wiseman put all the facts in an article in the *Dublin Review*.'

'Pretty nasty facts', said Augustine, doubtfully. 'Do you think it wise, Father, to bring them up in public?'

'Don't you think he ought to be shown up?' Newman said. 'But I shall ask advice, of course. Hope-Scott knows all about these things. I'll ask him. Why should our Birmingham people be misled by that wretched fellow? The things he says will provoke them to attack priests and even nuns, as they have in other places; the bishop has had endless trouble already with such cases, slanders and interference. If I have a chance to save defenceless religious any of that, ought I not to take it?'

He had to go, and Clem and Augustine walked slowly home along the summer roads.

'What has Achilli done?' Clem asked.

'He's led a busy life seducing girls in sacristies', said Augustine. 'That's why he was imprisoned and unfrocked, of course, and not as a Protestant martyr.'

Clem could not imagine Newman denouncing these sordid sins in public and said so.

Augustine said, 'I don't think he's squeamish, Clem.'

But in July, when the lecture was delivered, even Augustine was a little surprised at the force with which Newman issued his attack. He shirked neither the nature of the offences nor the expression of them, though he wasted no energy on the kind of lurid detail that Achilli himself went in for.

'He went at it like St. Basil himself', said Augustine, delighted that Newman could call a spade a spade in an England which seemed to him to be growing ridiculously prudish. Not even his worst enemy could call Newman coarse or vulgar, but he had grown up before the fashionable reaction in favour of morality, which was tending to make any physical activity unmentionable. Mrs. Bodley was typical of this new middle-class respectability.

'Fancy a minister of religion mentioning such things in a public hall', she said to Clem. 'I declare, I was shocked at what Mr. Bodley told me.'

'I should have thought it was a priest's duty to talk about sins sometimes', said Clem, amused. 'But this was done only because the man has posed as a martyr for conscience sake, and works people into dangerous rages with his imaginary wrongs.'

Mrs. Bodley looked unconvinced. 'It must give your priests nasty minds, listening in confessionals', she said. 'And if it's true about Dr. Achilli, it's probably true about others, if you don't mind my saying so.'

Clem felt it was as much as Mrs. Bodley could do to refrain from suggesting that Dr. Newman had similar opportunities at the Oratory.

Before a month was out Achilli brought a libel action against Newman. He had not expected the man to brazen it out like this, and the prospect of an unsavoury and expensive case, in a blaze of notoriety, was a most unpleasant shock. However, sure of the rectitude of his case, and intending to plead justification, he wrote to Wiseman for the proofs of his list of Achilli's crimes. After an anxious interval it appeared that Wiseman had mislaid them.

'How can he have lost them?' Clem cried, incredulous and indignant.

'He's not been well, you know', Augustine said. He was fond of Wiseman, whom he had known in Rome, and he always defended him. 'And he never has been methodical. But it's a disaster for Newman, because his opponents are pushing things on at speed, hoping he won't have time to collect the necessary evidence.'

'Who's backing Achilli?' Clem demanded. 'A doubtful horse, I should have thought.'

'Oh, he's got backers all right', Augustine said. 'Any stick is good enough to beat Catholics with, especially if you can blacken the name of a famous convert in the process, and make him out a liar and a slanderer. I hear the judge appointed is Lord Campbell, a notorious anti-Catholic.'

'No one will believe that sort of thing of Newman!' cried Clem.

'Will they not? This won't be an Oxford affair', Augustine retorted. 'Achilli will pose as the victim of persecution and the scene of his crime is far away in wicked old Italy where everyone is corrupt anyway, in an Englishman's opinion. If Newman can't collect evidence in time he'll be branded for the rest of his life, in the eyes of the great British public, as a malicious hypocrite, trying to smear a man who has broken away from the infamous system that he himself has adopted, doubtless with dishonourable motives.'

Clem had to admit he was right, when some of the vulgar gossip stirred up by the case came round to her. But it still seemed fantastic that Newman should be the centre of a storm of this kind of scandal, figuring among the 'Dreadful Murders' and 'Horrible Disclosures' on the police pages of the paper. He could hardly believe it himself.

'If the devil had raised a whirlwind, rolled me up in sand and transported me some thousands of miles, it would not be a more strange visitation', he remarked once, with a worried smile. 'Though it would be more imposing!'

When Clem repeated this to Augustine he said seriously, 'I think that's just what it is, a storm raised by the devil! He doesn't want Newman to have any influence in England.'

Clem always found it an effort to believe in the devil. She said, 'How could God allow that?'

'Good heavens, we can never tell what God is up to', said Augustine, making her laugh. 'Look at Job.'

Newman's lawyers told him that if he lost the case he might be imprisoned, for at least a year.

'*O bona crux, diu desiderata!*' he murmured, asking for everyone's prayers.

In December Clem met Miss Giberne in the town. She was looking rather dazed.

'I've just promised Father Newman to go to Italy and bring these poor women over as witnesses', she said.

'What! Alone? You, a single lady? You're surely not going to do that, Miss Giberne? The Father is much too unworldly to realize what he is asking of you. Why, Augustine could go for him.'

'He thinks a lady should go, because they are women', said Miss Giberne. 'He came into the guest room and leaned on the mantelpiece and asked me, point-blank. I couldn't say no!'

'No, really!' Clem said, beginning to laugh in spite of herself. 'He can't be allowed to be as unconventional as that! You can't do it!'

'I expect I can', said Miss Giberne bravely. 'Father Gordon is going to collect them. I shall only be escort. Oh, Mrs. Firle, I would do anything to help the Father in this terrible trial! It is so shocking!'

And off she went at once, into a series of disasters and difficulties, starting with a fire on board ship and ending with a dreadful five weeks' wait in France, maintaining the reluctant and recalcitrant witnesses; for Newman's opponents, alarmed at the promptitude of his friends, were now playing for delay, in the hope that time and expense would rid them of these inconvenient evidences of Achilli's misdemeanours.

During these months of anxiety Newman had to superintend the removal of the Oratory to Edgbaston. There were endless difficulties during the building operations. The church had to be as inconspicuous as possible and the house a simple flat-fronted affair, to frustrate the attentions of fanatics on the look-out for idolatry. At the time of the lectures rumours were rife in Birmingham of dungeon cells being built for the incarceration of recalcitrant 'monks'; Newman laughed at the idea of his walling up the devoted Father St. John or Father Gordon in the cellars, but the continual snooping was a nuisance. Even more of a nuisance was a large building erected by some ill-wishers next door, so close as to cut off the light and most of the air from the Fathers' rooms on that side, and from their tiny strip of garden. However, there the Oratorians were, by April, and no sooner were they settled than Newman had to go off to Ireland and deliver some lectures in Dublin.

This was the beginning of a great scheme for a Catholic university in Ireland, an Irish Louvain, and it seemed likely that Newman would be called upon to play a large part in its foundation. He was just back from Dublin when the trial began at last, in June, nearly a year after the fuss had first started.

Newman had to be in London, to be ready in case he was called as a witness, but his advisers hoped he would not have to appear in person. Clem and Augustine went, however, to see what happened. The court was crowded; everyone wanted to be in on this *cause célèbre*.

A round tidy little man, pushing just ahead as they went in, kept rising eagerly on tiptoe. He said peevishly, 'Where is he? Where is this Oxford pervert?'

It was the common phrase for a change of religious allegiance, but that did not make it a pleasant term to hear applied to a friend.

'Oh, he won't dare show his face', confidently replied the little man's larger companion. 'I shouldn't be surprised if he didn't run away abroad, slip off in disguise, don't you know.'

Augustine whispered to Clem, 'Can you see Newman skulking down to the docks in a false moustache?'

It was certainly a funny picture; it would be so very difficult to disguise Newman. But Clem felt indignant, all the same. She knew that probably at this very moment Newman was kneeling in prayer before the Blessed Sacrament; whenever he had any time to himself in these difficult days, that was where he was always found.

They settled in their places and looked round.

'Is Achilli here?' Clem asked.

'There he is', Augustine said. 'That unctuous fellow in the black wig.'

Clem saw a prognathous jaw, a receding forehead, strong fleshy nose and mouth and deep-sunk dark eyes. She wondered how anyone could trust a face like that. But he seemed

completely confident, bold, even truculent; the honest man
whose character had been blackened by a wily priest. She
thought he looked about fifty, much the same age as Newman, and suddenly the incongruity of this coincidence struck
her. Almost as if he were present, she saw Newman's face
beside this one. She wished he were there, so that people
could see the contrast, and said so.

'You expect too much of people', Augustine observed.
'They see what they want to see. If they believe Newman
is a cunning treacherous fellow, that's what he would look
like to them. You know how shy he feels on public occasions; they would think him hard and stern, the represen-
tative of what they imagine an Inquisitor looks like.'

It was strange, all the same, Clem thought, that these
two should be opposed, in the middle of their lives, the
unchaste renegade and the blameless scholar and convert.
As long ago as 1827 Achilli had been deprived of a lecture-
ship for bad conduct, at the time when Mary's death and
his own breakdown had roused Newman from his unconscious intellectualism, opening his heart to a deeper understanding. And when Newman returned from his apocalyptic
visit to Sicily and flung himself into his great campaign, in
which, for him, the English Church stood for the authority
of the supernatural against the influence of the world, Achilli
was committing offence after offence, some against young
girls. When Newman was at Littlemore, in prayer and fasting and agony of mind, slowly finding out that he must
leave all he loved because the truth he loved even more was
to be found only in communion with the See of St. Peter,
Achilli was making a living out of credulous Protestants in
Malta and elsewhere by vilifying the Faith he had professed
and the authorities who had tried to restrain his conduct.
It was not Achilli's sins which disgusted Clem so much as

his dishonesty, his pretence of martyrdom. So here they were, two men called to be priests, pitted against each other by the law of England.

Lord Justice Campbell had a sharp nose and baggy eyes. Clem felt that all through his feeling went against Newman, even if it were not directly in favour of Achilli. The Italian, faced with a string of women who accused him of seduction, brazened it out pretty well, denying everything and only once or twice losing his temper. Clem thought the evidence overwhelming, even though it did not cover all the charges, and she was astonished when the judge made an extremely biased summing-up, making light of what they had heard, as well as the unfortunate witnesses, and laying emphasis on the omissions. In a fit of pious fervour he thanked God there was no Inquisition in England.

At this a wild uproar of applause broke out, so fierce that it made Clem feel quite sick. There was no doubt as to where public sympathy lay. Judge, jury and audience, they all shouted for the foreign mountebank and against the English scholar who had dared to call him an unreliable witness. She was glad now that Newman was not there to hear that animal roar of triumph, to see how he was made a scapegoat for the irrational hate and fear of popery that he had so clearly and ironically exposed in his lectures the year before.

It was some comfort, next morning, to find that *The Times* was also disgusted with the verdict, chiefly because it would lend colour to the complaints of papists who maintained they were never given a fair hearing.

Judgement would be given in November: more suspense for Newman, who still expected to go to prison. In spite of these personal trials he went off to Oscott for the first provincial synod of Westminster, and there preached on the second spring of the Faith in England, a raw but hopeful spring after the long winter of persecution and dereliction. Augustine heard all about this great occasion from a priest who had been present.

'Wiseman broke down and cried like a child', he told Clem.

'That's just what he is, a big child', Clem said, with a smile. 'And he does love ecclesiastical functions, he says so himself.'

'He did just the right thing in the crisis', said Augustine. 'But he's no organizer, I'm afraid. He loves people, but he can't manage them.'

'I'm glad Newman had such a triumph', Clem said.

'He was so overcome Manning had to help him escape', Augustine said. 'Trust Manning to keep his head!'

They went away for a holiday at Sandgate with the children, returning in the autumn to find Newman very busy with the new Oratory and the plans for the Irish University. He was working much too hard—and still with the threat of prison hanging over him. In October he saw a doctor who told him he would have a premature old age and an early death unless he drastically curtailed his activities. Clem got this information out of him one rainy afternoon just before he was to go to London for the judgement.

'I feel the truth of what he says, that my brain and nerves cannot bear the strain', he said thoughtfully. 'Every book I have written has been a sort of operation, and this one on the University the most painful of all.'

'Are you going to take his advice, and rest?' Clem asked, suspiciously.

Newman said, with a mischievous look, 'That medical affidavit may come in useful if there's a question of sending me to prison!'

'They could not be so unjust', said Augustine indignantly.

Newman looked out of the window, streaming with rain, at the dull, suburban, provincial road. 'All my life I've been speaking about suffering for the truth', he said, with a sort of sigh. 'Now it has come upon me, but in what a curious way! Well! May it be accepted for my sins. I shall pack my portmanteau for prison.'

And pack it he did, and got permission to say Mass in jail, if necessary, so that Clem already began to imagine him behind bars, eating off a tin plate and being exercised along with thieves and burglars. She wondered whatever would be said at the Oxford dinner tables. The ex-Vicar of St. Mary's doing time? An Oriel fellow picking oakum? Yet it was not inconceivable that Newman would be given a prison sentence, and although he might joke about medical evidence in his favour, Clem could not help fearing that such an experience might really make him ill.

But at the last minute, when he was actually in court, his lawyers persuaded him, much against his will, to apply for a new trial. It meant more waiting, more uncertainty, to him almost worse than being sent off to jail at once. The case was not decided till the end of the next January. A re-trial was not allowed; it would have been too humiliating for Lord Justice Campbell, but the sentence was probably milder than his would have been: a hundred-pound fine and imprisonment till it was paid, which meant not at all, since Newman's friends paid all his expenses.

It was some redress, but Newman was still treated as a delinquent; Mr. Justice Coleridge administered a severe reprimand, and told the court how shockingly the characters of converts deteriorated after joining the Church of Rome. It was all reported in *The Times*. Augustine was extremely indignant.

'What right had he to lecture you like that in public?' he said to Newman when they met him again.

But Newman seemed cheerful, unruffled by the incident. 'Poor Coleridge, I suppose he meant to impress me', he said. 'He spoke very low, from agitation, I think.'

'That doesn't show in print', Augustine pointed out.

'His speech was full of mistakes, of course, and inconsistencies', said Newman. 'I wasn't allowed to reply.'

'Can't you write a reply now?'

'I don't think that would be quite in order', said Newman. 'He thought he was doing his duty. I must be thankful the case has turned out as it has; heaven knows what I should have done without your help, the help of all my friends.'

Augustine, who did not want to be thanked again for his share in bearing the expenses, persisted. 'But it is so unfair that you should be held up as a deteriorating character, and Achilli get off scot-free!'

Newman laughed. 'But I don't think he will be listened to with quite such attention, do you?' he said. 'As for me, I have not been the butt of slander and scorn for twenty years for nothing. Even skinned eels must get used to their state!'

Clem thought this was more what he wanted to feel than what he did feel; she did not believe he had ever got used to being called a liar and a coward and a traitor, whose motives for desertion were discussed by people who had never known him, and assigned to weakness, fear, lust for power, effeminate love of ceremonial or an atavistic passion for self-abasement, but never to honest conviction. But there was certainly a great change in his way of bearing this evil reputation since the days at Littlemore; now, sure of his way, and inwardly at peace with himself, it did not weigh so heavily on his spirits; it was a trial still, but no longer a torture. Nor did it now affect what always mattered most to him: his work in the Church. Whatever was said against him by outsiders, he had the support and friendship of his fellow Catholics, and he now could go straight ahead in the task for which he felt most fitted, creating the intellectual background for the young men of this new age of scientific invention and metaphysical scepticism, a university training for the sons of the faithful, legally emancipated but mentally undeveloped.

So he went back to the Oratory full of hope.

A few weeks later Father Gordon died, the priest who had done so much in Italy to find the witnesses for him. Newman felt his loss keenly, and his grief brought on a reaction from the long tension of the legal proceedings.

Standing at the front door of the Oratory house one February day, he remarked pensively, 'This year and a half of troubles reminds me of a week of rain we had after a glorious summer, in '26, when I was doing duty at Ulcombe, in Kent.'

'Why should it, Father?' Clem asked, puzzled by the way his mind always worked over past events, as if life itself were a series of mysteries, whose meaning could be extracted only by long brooding. And perhaps it was, she thought, looking at his face, just now tired and sad, a face where thought became feeling and feeling thought.

'It was fine again afterwards', he said. 'But the season had changed, the ground was thoroughly chilled. Autumn had set in and the week of rain divided the two seasons as by a river. And so I think I have now passed into my autumn.'

Augustine would not have it, called him gloomy and made him smile again, but Clem was silent, and watched as they drove away, that tall thin figure standing still in the winter afternoon, thinking back to the long past time when he was young, before Mary died, and the weather changed.

'Why should he say that now?' Augustine complained. 'Now all goes well with him.'

'But somehow he always knows', Clem said, and shivered a little, feeling how cold the wind was, what a cold place Birmingham could be, and comfortless.

# 9

Now Clem was not young any more; life was not an adventure, but ordinary business. And Augustine was not young either; the position he had taken over in industry now began to take him over. He discovered that action was not, after all, simple, and things happened which he had not intended, but for which he was partly responsible. Because of his father's wealth and his mother's rank he had been brought up more or less in the aristocratic tradition, that a master was responsible for the welfare of his servants, but he found another tradition among the men of Birmingham and Dudley, of competitive independence, every man responsible for himself alone. His anomalous position in the firm, which seemed at first to give him greater freedom, in fact made action increasingly difficult as his colleagues took his measure and began manœuvres against what they considered mere interference.

'Everyone can blame me, but I can blame no one', he said bitterly, after a particularly galling defeat. 'If only Father would back me up!'

But Lord Gornal, far from backing him up, was getting jealous of his influence. For years he had taken only a casual interest in the firm's affairs, but now he began to poke and pry, and listened to reports from men only too ready to misrepresent his son's activities.

Augustine blamed the new Lady Gornal for the rapid deterioration in his relations with his father. His mother had died very soon after the mid-century had passed and a month or two later Lord Gornal had married his mistress. 'One can't complain of that;' was Augustine's comment, 'if only she were not such a bitch!'

Dora was only a few years older than her stepsons, to whom she took an immediate dislike, perhaps partly because she brought with her a son popularly supposed to be a bastard of Lord Gornal's; she may have considered the legitimate heirs a danger to this handsome boy's advancement. Good looks and a strong will had taken Dora far, but she had not the generosity for which people forgive social climbers their ambitions. Clem did not meet her for a few years after the marriage, and then she came with Lord Gornal on a visit to the factory and the Dudley Works. They refused Clem's invitation and stayed at an hotel, but they condescended to drive out to dine in Edgbaston.

In one way Lord Gornal's marriage was a success; Dora looked after him, judiciously flattered and managed him. He looked very well for a man over seventy who had never stinted himself of anything. Clem had always found his hearty manner endearing, but she realized by now that it covered a weak judgement. He was never quite sure of himself, and this made him bluster and blunder his way through situations he did not even try to understand.

Henry, who was seven now, was kept out of bed to meet his grandfather. Lord Gornal puffed and wheezed and stared, and made audible comments on his appearance.

'What a miserable little fellow!' he said. 'Why, he's no better than you were, Augustine. Nothing to say for yourself, my boy?'

Henry looked so alarmed that Augustine took him on his knee.

'There's nothing wrong with him', he said. 'And his arithmetic is much better than mine!'

'What are you cossetting him like that for?' Lord Gornal demanded irritably. 'Making a baby out of a great boy!'

Henry's pale face turned crimson and he hid it in his father's coat.

'Don't be so dictatorial, Father', said Augustine, with his usual spirit. 'I shall hug my boy if I feel like it.'

Lord Gornal snorted. 'Well, I prefer the girl', he said. Little Charlotte, rosy-cheeked and impudent, was intimidated by no one.

Lady Gornal insisted on being taken round the house and made adverse comments on all Clem's arrangements. 'I wonder you put up with this', or 'I wonder you have not done that', till Clem found it hard to go on smiling at her. Later she overheard Dora remarking to her husband, 'The house is full of images!' He merely muttered something irritable about foreign ways.

He spent dinner making it quite clear that Augustine knew nothing about business and that his authority in the firm was not as great as that of various other men whose opinions were mentioned with approval. It was no use trying to argue a point; he refused to listen. The visit, which Clem had hoped would establish a better relationship between Augustine and his father, in fact diminished confidence.

Alexander Firle sometimes came to stay with them. Clem soon realized he was ill; he had a consumption which was slowly wearing him out. She asked Augustine why he did not spend the winters abroad and he replied, 'Because he would be too lonely.'

'What do you mean?' She knew Alexander had long been estranged from his wife; they lived at opposite ends of their big London house.

Then Augustine explained that for years his brother had been in love with a woman called Catherine Craven, who lived in London with her mother, a clergyman's widow.

'Are they lovers?' Clem asked, puzzled by his manner of telling it.

'No', he said. 'It nearly happened when they first met, but they made up their minds to part. Catherine is a strong-minded young woman. Later, they met again by accident, in a museum, which is typical of them, and they allowed themselves to be friends after that. They are an odd pair. Catherine is clever, she helps him ferret out things in the British museum, tracks down old music and so on. She's by way of being a free-thinker, but Alexander says they don't talk about religion. I can't think why they love each other, but they do.'

At first Clem had not liked Alexander much; she thought him negative and imagined Augustine only felt protective towards him, an elder, but much weaker brother. But when she knew him better she began to understand the affection between them. Alexander was bad at dealing with people; their rapid changes of mood and flow of opinions frightened him into blinking silence. But to her surprise she found he held a real and respected position among fellow researchers in his favourite subjects; he might be vague about meal times and social duties, but he was not at all vague about intellectual things. He and Augustine supplemented each other, for Augustine, so good at practical affairs, was impatient and careless when it came to abstract thinking. Clem rather envied the close bond between them. 'I believe I could have felt like that about Mary Newman, if she had been my sister', she thought once.

Even after all these years Mary, her first real friend, remained a person to her; death had taken away the sight but not the knowledge of her. Sometimes, especially at Epiphany, when she had died, Newman would mention Mary; in a way this loved little sister who had died so young was less lost to him than the rest of his family. They had not altogether cast him off, but they kept at a distance, physically and emotionally. Frank was using his brains teaching in provincial universities and casting off the articles of the Creed one by one; he was said to be a Unitarian now. Jemima did not invite Newman to Derby, to see her growing family, and Harriett, who had died last year, had died estranged from him.

Not only his sisters and brothers (Charles was still having to be supported, a harmless eccentric, who once referred to his patient elder brother as "an old cat") but all his old friends had become remote, perhaps not intentionally, but he felt it as a desertion. Keble, Pusey, Church and the rest of them who had stayed in the Anglican church, had they forgotten him? Or did they think he no longer cared for them? He had the friendship of St. John and the other Oratorians, but they were all younger men and, dear as they were, could not replace his contemporaries. Clem had before now heard hinting sneers that Newman could not care for his equals, and preferred devoted disciples, but it was not his fault that his conversion had divided him from the old circle, nor could anyone call Bishop Ullathorne, his greatest friend among the Catholics, an inferior or sycophant. Not that Father St. John was that; his devotion to Newman did not prevent him from being so busy with his own work that sometimes there was little time for conversation beyond the practical needs of the day.

Now, in his fifties, and the fifties of the century, Newman was struggling to get his idea of a Catholic university translated into fact, and a struggle it was, beset with complex and unforeseen difficulties. He put up a tremendous fight, for six years travelling to and from Ireland, lecturing, writing, organizing; threading his way through a maze of financial problems, national antipathies, ecclesiastical misunderstandings and the nerveless indifference to intellectual things that is a characteristic defect of English nature, and, in a different way, of Irish nature too. What defeated him in the end was the lack of authoritative backing, both in England and Ireland. He was invited to initiate a great work and given neither men nor means to do it; faith might move mountains, but not the faithful. Newman did not stand on his dignity; he did everything he could himself. It was noted with some surprise that the Rector had been seen ladling out soup to his poor little University.

Augustine was very angry at this wasting of Newman's talents.

'Do the bishops think men like that grow on trees?' he complained. 'As for the rich Catholics, they don't realize how stupid they are; learning to write was enough for them; why not for their sons?'

'Why not send them to Oxford?' Clem said. 'After all, they don't have to take the anti-Transubstantiation oath now.'

'Because it's considered dangerous to submit young Catholics to a secular education and the sceptical tendencies said to be predominant nowadays', said Augustine. 'And yet they leave the only alternative, Newman's University, to sink or swim. Look at this bishop business.'

Wiseman, who was always interested in intellectual ventures, had told Newman that in order to give him proper authority as Rector, he would be made a bishop, with only a titular See, of course, and that this was a decided thing. Ullathorne, delighted, spread the news, and Newman received letters of congratulation and even a pectoral cross to wear when he was consecrated. Everybody knew about it. And then nothing happened at all, not even an explanation.

Newman would do nothing about it; he took this strange silence in silence, but his friends did not. It was the beginning of a new series of domestic discussions among English Catholics. One of Clem's greatest surprises, on coming into the Church, was that people who agreed so absolutely on their Faith could disagree so fiercely on almost everything else. She had never met so many individualists, both clerical and lay. On the whole she found this reassuring. The Faith was divine; the faithful, very human.

Too human, Augustine said, when he discovered something of what Newman was suffering, during this long Irish battle, from the division of feeling and policy between the Birmingham and London Oratories. Faber was a good man, a zealous priest; Wiseman had always respected Newman, and yet now they acted together without reference to him, though he was the Founder, and he had been appointed Superior in Rome. He went to Rome himself about it; but it was the others who were listened to there. The Oratories were separated, which he had himself advocated, but the way it was done made him very unhappy. He did not talk about it much, but he was never good at hiding his feelings. The Oratory in the capital became famous, figured in *Punch* as the repository of foreign religion; Faber wrote hundreds of hymns, widely praised and sung in that hymn-loving time. The Oratory in Birmingham was hardly known to exist; there were people who said Newman had put himself on the shelf. Nobody could quite forget him, but nobody knew what he was doing—nothing important, anyway. Other converts wrote books, brought in families and friends; Newman's remained aloof. People did not know about the endless crossings to Ireland, the hundreds of letters written, the everyday humiliations and disappointments; if they had known, they would not have cared. There was nothing dramatic in such a life.

At last Newman was forced to resign his Rectorship, feeling that all his labours had accomplished very little, and that time was going by and nothing was being done to train the minds of the young to meet the growing threat of scepticism, the rationalist attack on religion and the distractions of mere materialism. Older people, secure in their faith, were apt to think blind trust enough; Newman had always believed that love without knowledge was as dangerous as knowledge without love. And in this age of invention and discovery people were dividing the two, and devoting themselves to one or the other, some worshipping reason and some faith, and each group accusing the other of obscuring the light. Perhaps more clearly than anyone Newman saw this dichotomy and its devastating consequences, some still far in the future; he saw it and utterly rejected it.

'And he himself is one answer to it', said Augustine, who had often discussed the question with Newman. 'An answer nobody listens to. People are just lazy; they prefer Either-Or to Both-And.'

He was glad when Newman was offered another task, to undertake the supervision of a new English translation of the Bible; Douay, even as revised by Challoner in the eighteenth century, was, after nearly three hundred years, growing somewhat archaic. Full of enthusiasm, Newman began to lay his plans and write to experts.

Towards the end of the decade Clem and Augustine suffered a sudden and tragic invasion of their happy provincial life: Alexander, who had come to stay, had a bad hæmorrhage, and he was pronounced by the doctors unlikely to live many weeks longer.

Augustine refused to believe it; he called in London specialists, he sent ardent appeals for prayers to all the convents and monasteries he knew, he would not give up hope. But Alexander himself accepted the verdict without fuss. He only said wistfully, 'Could Catherine come?'

Of course they invited Catherine Craven, and in a few days she arrived, a tall straight woman with a square, thoughtful face and thick brown hair coiled in a net, *en chignon*. Her hazel eyes were direct and observant; her mouth firm but not tight. She was younger than Clem, a year or two under forty still.

Catherine was calm; she took over some of the nursing duties, which she discharged with quiet efficiency. 'I thought of volunteering for the Crimea with Miss Nightingale', she told Clem. 'But I felt I could not leave my mother, who has delicate health, and I had not really had the necessary experience.'

Clem was non-plussed by her. She said to Augustine, 'Does Catherine really love him?'

'People love each other in different ways', he reminded her. 'They don't all behave like you and me!'

It evidently made Alexander happy to have Catherine there. He never complained; Clem felt Augustine suffered more than he did as he grew slowly weaker and weaker. Augustine was fifty this year, hard to believe because of his energy and his lively habits of speech, but there was grey in his thick hair and his face was hardening, taking on the toughened look of middle age. In some ways he looked older than his brother, whose vague blue eyes, myopic and dreamy, sometimes looked almost like an infant's eyes, unfocused, innocent. His fairer hair had only faded, not turned grey.

Suddenly and without warning one windy evening, Lord Gornal arrived on the doorstep and stamped into the house in a furious temper.

'What's all this about Alexander?' he demanded. 'Is it true you have invited his mistress here with him?'

He was somewhat taken aback when a cool voice answered him, 'I am not your son's mistress, Lord Gornal, but I am his friend.'

Lord Gornal snorted helplessly for a moment and then, unable to deal with the self-possessed woman who faced him, turned on Augustine.

'What's the explanation of this, eh? Eh?'

'Father, he's ill; he's terribly ill', Augustine said, taking his father's arm. 'Dying, they say.'

'Dying? Nonsense!' said Lord Gornal. 'Alexander has been playing that game all his life.' He shook off Augustine's hand impatiently. 'Where is he?'

'What do you want of him?' Augustine demanded. 'He's much too ill to be shouted at.'

'How dare you speak to me like that, sir!' roared his father. 'I've something to say to you too, Augustine. I know all about what you have been doing behind my back at the works.'

'I've done nothing behind your back', said Augustine, exasperated. 'For heaven's sake sit down and stop raging about like a madman.'

It was not his usual tact and his father responded with an outburst of passion that surprised Clem, who had heard of what Augustine called fireworks displays, but never witnessed one.

'That's the last straw! I've stood enough from you two boys, miserable weaklings, both of you, making a convenience of your father. Yes! that's all you take me for, a convenience! To keep you in comfort, and your women too, it seems, that's what you think I'm for. No consideration at all. I've had enough, I tell you! You'll not get another penny, either of you, not a penny. Let Alexander try making money out of his ridiculous note-taking and see where it gets him! I daresay this brazen young woman won't be so anxious to stand by his bedside then.'

'Father!' Augustine protested. 'Do stop insulting everybody. You must realize Alexander is very ill indeed.'

'Damn Alexander! Don't put me off!' shouted his father, with perverse irrelevance. 'It's you I've come to see, not that silly ninny who runs off to bed whenever he hears me coming. I'll not have you ordering this and that behind my back. Who do you think you are? A philanthropist? Lord Ashley's agent, perhaps?'

'Are you talking about the factory?' Augustine asked, making an attempt to introduce some reality into the situation. 'About the revised working schedule and pay for the women? The rest of the Board agreed to try it out.'

'Oh, did they? Macpherson didn't agree, did he?'

'But you have transferred him to London', said Augustine. 'It's not his business any longer.'

Lord Gornal merely blustered. 'I know all about your plotting and planning, my boy. Don't you try arguing with me.'

'Very well', said Augustine sharply. 'I had better give up my place on the Board then, and at the works too, if you wish it. It's no good my staying in the firm if I've lost your confidence.'

'Give up your position!' jeered Lord Gornal. 'And how do you propose to live, eh? Do you expect me to go on supporting you?'

Augustine lost his temper. 'I don't expect anything from you', he said. 'Your money means nothing to me in comparison with my freedom. I've wasted years of my life working for you, for the firm, and got nothing out of it but worry and a grudged allowance I can't even call my own.'

'Working for me!' cried his father, enraged. 'Interference! Worming your way in, trying to step into my shoes, you call that work? I'm not dead yet, my boy, and I don't propose to die to put you in my place.'

'You shall have my resignation in writing in the morning', said Augustine, in a cold fury. 'Now, please go away and leave us alone.'

Lord Gornal stood staring at him, his mouth dropped open, quivering with astonishment.

'Are you turning me out of your house?' he said at last, uncertainly.

'Do you want to stay in it?' Augustine retorted. 'You have just told me that all my work in the firm is nothing but scheming for power to push you out—don't tell me that after such an accusation you now purpose to sit down and eat dinner with me?'

His father stood there, silent and blinking. 'We will discuss it again', he said at last, flatly. 'Perhaps I have been too hasty.'

Clem, a little nervously, because she was not sure of Augustine's reaction, said gently, 'Of course you can stay if you wish, Lord Gornal.'

Lord Gornal grunted and wheezed and blew his nose; he looked at her doubtfully and then sideways at Augustine, who deliberately turned away. 'I'll call again to-morrow', he said at last, and without further words stumped out of the house and climbed into the waiting cab.

Catherine, who had characteristically remained a silent and impartial spectator of the scene, now went quietly upstairs to Alexander.

Augustine flung himself into an armchair.

Clem turned to him. 'Were you angry with me for saying that?' she asked anxiously.

'No, no', he answered wearily.

Clem came and squeezed into the chair with him. 'I think you are a little cross', she whispered. 'I just felt sorry for him, suddenly. He's such a stupid old thing, sometimes.'

'Yes', said Augustine. 'And I just wanted to finish it, that's all. I'm tired of being suspected and spied on and reported all the time. I can't stand it. I'm getting old, I suppose.'

Clem leant her face against his. 'What would you do, really, if you had to leave and he did cut off supplies?'

'God knows', he said. 'I'm not much good at anything, am I? I used to think I could manage people, but I can't even manage Father, let alone Curtis and Macpherson and the rest of them.'

Clem said, 'Well, let's start our own factory and run it right.'

Augustine only smiled and they were silent a long time. Clem knew he was exhausted by the unexpected battle, coming on top of his anxiety about his brother, the strain of waiting for the death he felt he could not bear. And it was bitter to have given the best of his strength for years to the business, just because he felt it his duty, and now to find he had produced nothing but dissensions and was not wanted.

'Clem, perhaps I'm beat', he said presently, stroking her hand.

'You know you're not', she said gently.

'I know *you're* not!' he replied, with a smile. 'All right: let to-morrow come.'

But he sighed after he had said it.

As he had feared, the row, like most family rows, came to no definite conclusion. Lord Gornal did not apologize; he simply behaved on the assumption that he had not meant what he said. He began to talk about young Aubrey, Dora's son, whom he had now legally adopted. Aubrey was just down from Oxford and would Augustine have him to stay and show him the ropes, in Dudley and in the factory? He was quite annoyed with Augustine for driving a bargain; he would do all this only if he was paid a definite salary. In the end it was agreed, but both of them felt ill-treated all the same.

Lord Gornal went upstairs to visit Alexander before he left. When he saw his son, shrunken and exhausted by his long illness, he became silent, frightened. He had hardly looked at him before he began edging towards the door again.

'Father', said Alexander, nervously gripping the counterpane with his thin pale fingers. 'Don't let people in the firm put you against Augustine. They only want what they can get, and he has worked so hard.'

'Augustine seems able to look after his own interests', said Lord Gornal, irritably. 'You know nothing about it, never have.'

Alexander shrank from his tone and shut his eyes. Clem, who knew what agonies of fear he had suffered as a child because of his father, saw that even now he did not know how to face him. It was his great weakness to be so crippled with fear.

Lord Gornal, alarmed by his silent pallid face, mumbled something about his getting better soon and hurried away downstairs, Clem following to see him off. As she went, she heard Catherine's clear, composed voice, answering some inaudible lament from Alexander.

'There would have been no point in saying any more. He never listens to you. Don't worry about it now.'

A week or two later Alexander quietly died. They had got so used to his being there, dying but not dying, that the moment of death came as a shock, after all. But in an hour or two that great change was made; he was gone. No one came from London to the funeral; Flora, his wife, wrote that she was not well enough for the journey. She was never ill, but they did not want her. Alexander was buried as quietly as he had died, and Catherine packed to go home, silent, showing no sign of her feelings.

Clem sat on the bed, watching her quiet, neat movements. 'You are going back to your mother?' she said at last.

'Yes', said Catherine. 'I think I shall start a school for girls. I thought of it before, but I felt Alexander needed all the time I could give him.'

Clem said, 'Would you have married him, if you could?'

Catherine looked up from her packing in obvious surprise.

'Of course', she said. 'He was the only person I ever felt at one with. At first I wanted to go and live abroad with him; I would not have minded the scandal. But I found that it would have cut him off from his God, and that would have made him more unhappy than ever. As well, there was his daughter and my mother, and later, his illness. It was best as it was.'

Clem hesitated, knowing Catherine was a clergyman's daughter. 'But didn't you share his Faith at all?' she said, at last.

'I am not the sort of person to believe in anything that can't be proved', said Catherine, looking away and busily packing.

'But surely now . . .'

For the first time she saw a quiver pass over Catherine's face. But with a firm effort she controlled herself and said quietly, 'I have my memories.'

Clem respected her courage, but when she went to say the Rosary with Augustine and the children, she felt sorry that Catherine, under the mistaken idea that life can be explained entirely by scientific analysis, had shut herself out of this circle of consolation.

Henry lit the candles by the little statue of the Virgin Mother; the soft light gleamed on some grubby snowdrops Charlotte had found in the garden and on the boy's face, pensive and grave. He was eleven now.

'Mother,' he said, turning to her, 'do you know, one of the Oratory Fathers showed me a French newspaper which says that our Lady has appeared to a little girl, in a cave, I think it said.'

'How lovely', said Clem mechanically. 'Who's beginning to-day?'

'It's Papa's turn', said Charlotte, as Augustine came in and knelt down beside her. Clem saw he had been crying, mourning his brother.

It was the circle of the Sorrowful Mysteries they said that day, following the fate of love in the world where worship is all for power and glory.

# 10

'All this about *The Rambler* is enough to drive one to drink', said Augustine furiously, one Sunday afternoon in May, over a year after his brother's death.

Josephine, Alexander's daughter, who was paying them a long visit, looked at her uncle in alarm. A timid, plain young woman, shy and musical like her father, she had infuriated her fashionable mother by announcing that she wished to be a nun. Augustine had persuaded Flora to let the girl come and stay, promising that no Mother Superior should be given the chance to walk off with her. Josephine, happy in the comfortable provincial household, did not fuss about her vocation; the only indication of her feelings was a little pile of books by her bedside on Carmelites and Poor Clares.

Josephine looked as if she expected her uncle to take to the bottle at once; Clem, amused, poured out his tea and surmised that he had been talking to Newman.

'Yes, I have', he said. 'What do they mean by getting him to take over the paper and then asking him to resign after the first number? It's Ullathorne, too. I can't understand it of him.'

'You can't expect bishops, even the best, to like being jeered at by the clever young fellows in *The Rambler*', said Clem.

'That was before Newman took over', said Augustine. 'That was why he took over. Goodness knows, he didn't want the labour of running a review, and just after this fiasco of the Scripture translation.'

For it had been found that a new translation was also projected in America; it was Newman, of course, and not the Americans, who was persuaded to give up.

'He was enthusiastic when I saw him', said Clem. 'It would be quite his thing, you know. He did well with the *British Critic*, years ago. Is he very upset about it?'

'Oh, you know what he is! He would never question anything his bishop asked him to do, even if it were not Ullathorne. He laughs at himself and says he is like an old man who has rolled up his sleeves to help in a fire, but can take the hint when a fireman comes up to him and says, "My good old boy, you're doing your best, but don't you see you're drowning your friends with your ill-directed attempts?"'

Charlotte bounced in her chair, laughing.

'My good old boy!' she squeaked out.

'Now don't you be cheeky about the Father, or I shan't take you to see him again', said Clem, well knowing that her nine-year-old daughter would miss her visits to the Oratory, where she had made her First Communion, and where Henry was now at the newly opened school.

'It's worse for us than for him', said Augustine gloomily. 'Without him Acton and the rest will just be considered wild young men, the review will be censured, and we shall be left with nothing but Ward in the *Dublin*, out-poping the Pope. If the bishops *want* Catholics to be intellectual idiots beside Protestants and Freethinkers, this is the way to go about it, persecuting Newman and crushing every effort he makes to get the laity educated.'

'I'm sure Ullathorne doesn't want us to be idiots or Newman to be persecuted', said Clem decidedly. 'Probably he's afraid Newman's own reputation might be damaged by associating with the *Rambler* lot. Some of them are much too liberal. I don't care about politics but it's no good being liberal about the Creed.'

'Newman would have seen to that', said Augustine. 'Damn! Damn! Damn it all!'

This conclusion shocked his pious niece, to Clem's amusement. Augustine had always said just what he felt, but nowadays he was unusually irritable when things went against the grain. His difficulties in the firm had been increased by the advent of Aubrey, the adopted bastard, a young man of easy charm who deferred to him in public, but behind his back had thrown in his lot with his enemies. Luckily for Augustine's temper Aubrey spent most of his time in London, but that meant interminable rows with the office there, and with Lord Gornal himself, who became more unreasonable and gullible as the years destroyed whatever judgement he once had. Naturally this division among the heads of the firm did not help the business; Firle and Sons were not doing as well as they should in these booming times, and there were those who were delighted to blame this partial failure on Augustine's interest in new methods and machinery, and his efforts to improve the conditions of the working people.

On top of these private worries there were repercussions of the Pope's troubles in Italy. The Papacy was losing all its hereditary possessions; by the next year, 1860, they were practically all gone but Rome itself. It was not the material loss which principally mattered to the Pope and to the Church, but the loss of independence. How could the Vicar of Christ, it was argued, become the mere subject of an earthly government? In 1848, the governments of Europe, in their fear of revolution, had supported the Pope; now, they not only did not help him, but actively cheered on his enemies. The freethinking Garibaldi was a hero to the

English, who imagined that Pius IX was merely clinging to power for power's sake. Consequently among Catholics there was excited an intense loyalty to the Holy See, and a party came into prominence that began to talk as if the necessity of the Temporal Power were a dogma of the Faith. Manning, who was now Provost of the Westminster Chapter and right-hand man to Wiseman in his illness and premature old age, was one of the leaders of this Ultramontane party in England, and Ward, the hard-hitting lay theologian, another; their supporters were even more violent and intolerant on the subject than they were.

In that year Clem and Augustine went to a dinner party in London, where everyone present was a Catholic; not many were known to Clem, who hardly stirred from her home except for occasional holidays in Sandgate. At first the talk was all of events in Italy, but presently it came nearer home and Newman's name was mentioned.

'Oh, he is tarred with the *Rambler* brush, you can't rely on him', someone said positively. 'He would like the Pope to be as powerless as the Archbishop of Canterbury.'

'Isn't he regarded as unsound, Father?' a lady demanded of a priest who sat in the place of honour. He was a sleek man in his forties, neat and well-brushed, with pink hands and a smooth face; Clem was quite surprised that he was not at least a Monsignor. She was not sure of his name; when they were introduced it had sounded like Summary, but she felt that could hardly be right.

He said, 'There's that business of his article on consulting the laity in matters of faith. It was delated to Rome, I hear, and no explanation has been forthcoming from Father Newman.'

'Has Newman had a chance to answer the charge?' Augustine asked, in surprise.

'Naturally one would *expect* some answer', said the priest, suavely. 'But perhaps Dr. Newman prefers not to have an enquiry made into his opinions. For all his reputation, he is not a trained theologian.'

An old man, who spoke with a slight hiss, owing to missing teeth, remarked in high-bred tones, 'I've always thought Newman very much over-rated. After all, who *was* he? And what has he *done* since his famous conversion? He's in with a disloyal set and whenever we hear of him there's trouble. Eh? What say, Father Simmering?'

Simmering? thought Clem dubiously.

'I'd say he has dangerously liberal opinions', said the priest. 'I suppose that was why he was not made a bishop; they discovered in time.'

'I hear he was planning to re-write the Bible', remarked an old lady. 'Just like a Protestant.'

'He's a Protestant at heart still', said another lady, whose prominent teeth flashed nearly as brightly as her pearl necklace as she spoke. 'I've heard he's preached a sermon in favour of Garibaldi.'

'I'm sure he has not!' Augustine said emphatically. He had stopped eating and was crumbling his bread in nervous irritation. Clem looked across at him, anxiously hoping he would not lose his temper.

'Protestant or not, he's certainly a trouble-maker', said a distinguished gentleman, a convert and a friend of Ward's. 'He is always making up to the old Catholic families, and you know what minimizers they are about the Pope's rights. Wouldn't you say Newman was a trouble-maker, Father Summerly?'

Summerly, that's it, Clem decided.

This was too much for Augustine, but he spoke quietly enough.

'What kind of trouble-maker, Mr. Davenant? The devil's? Or God's?'

Mr. Davenant fixed his monocle in his eye and stared across the table.

'Heh? What do you mean by that cryptic remark, Mr. Firle?'

'I mean, trouble is made in this world by two kinds of people', said Augustine, 'There are those whose own evil stirs up the evil in others, and those whose very integrity provokes the response of evil against them.'

This was a little too much for Mr. Davenant, who looked bewildered and murmured, 'I don't think I quite take your meaning, sir.'

'Did not our Lord himself provoke a great deal of trouble?' Augustine demanded. 'Would you call him a trouble-maker?'

Mr. Davenant was shocked.

'Mr. Firle, I do not consider that a suitable comment for the dinner table.'

'Indeed?' said Augustine. 'But you do consider slander and detraction perfectly suitable?'

The hostess quickly intervened.

'I'm sure we all respect Dr. Newman', she said. 'We know you are one of his most loyal friends, Mr. Firle.'

It was evident from their expressions that most of the guests had not known it. Augustine, by electing to bury himself twice over, in trade and in the Midlands, was not well-known in London society now.

The incipient Monsignor turned to Augustine with a winning smile.

'We are all waiting for some great work from Dr. Newman's able pen', he said. 'It is a pity that his high reputation rests almost entirely on his Protestant works.'

Clem knew that this backhanded compliment infuriated Augustine almost more than anything else. His voice was edgy as he said coldly, 'Then I suppose you have not read his work on the Idea of a University?'

'I'm sure Father Shimmery knows all about that', said the anxious hostess. 'He and Dr. Manning are so interested in education.' And she hastily began to talk about the Provost, who in the ten years since his conversion had accomplished much useful work. He knew how to deal with public men and government departments.

Augustine said no more, but in the cab going home he let fly his pent-up feelings.

'Fools! Idiots!' he said furiously. 'Why bring Manning into it? He's doing all right in his line; why not give Newman a chance in his? Can't they see what's going to happen if we don't train the intelligence? We shall lose the clever men of the next generation, and that means we shall lose the ordinary men of the generation after. It's no good sticking our heads in the sand and saying *Credo, credo*. Real questions demand real answers. Even bad questions need answers. And when we're given the very man for the job, what do we do? Sneer at him for toadying the old Catholic families and in the same breath denounce him as a liberal. Throw suspicion on his motives, his faith, his loyalty, and why? Just because he has the perception to see the real conflict that's coming, between faith, the faith in Christ, and atheism, and the courage to say battles can't be won by standing still and cheering the flag.'

'My darling old thing, don't look so wild', said Clem, affectionately. 'You know I agree with every word you say.'

Augustine laughed and subsided. But he said, 'I only wish Newman did not know what the fools say about him, but I'm afraid he does.'

What they had heard in London was nothing to the case built up by the gossips against Newman in the next few

years. He knew it well enough, and although he said nothing about it in public, his friends knew how much he suffered from it, not only because it was personally painful to
lose the trust of so many of his fellow-Catholics, but because
that mistrust made it impossible for him to do the work he
felt he was called to do. The need for it became plainer to
him with every year that passed, years that were making
him an old man, soon perhaps to be past work, soon, it
might be, to die.

Friends who continued to trust him solaced his feelings,
and in spite of the repeated failures, never his fault, of all
his particular projects, he went quietly on with his work at
the Oratory, adding to his church, preaching, writing innu-
merable letters, and teaching the boys to act Latin plays,
which he adapted for them. Henry, who had been so shy
before, suddenly blossomed out as one of the best actors;
his success was good for him and Clem was delighted. He
was happy at school and did well at his lessons. Newman
did not teach, but he was a familiar figure to the boys, who
did not seem greatly in awe of him.

'Do you know, Mamma,' Henry said once, 'at night one
of the boys knocks on the floor and shouts out, "Good
night, Jack!"'

'I hope the Father doesn't hear that piece of cheek!' said
Clem, amused.

'I don't believe he'd mind', said Henry. 'Do you know,
he can make jokes in Latin?'

Clem was glad he could make jokes in any language, but
humour rarely deserted him. But he had aged recently; he
had always been thin, now he looked frail; he was not very
well, yet his ailments never amounted to a real illness. Father
St. John and the other Oratorians looked after him with
the utmost solicitude; he took comfort in these good friends,

who never failed him. The Oratorians had bought a small country property at Rednal and built a little flat-fronted villa on the side of the hill, under high overhanging woods. It was a homey place, with an old dog in residence, and an even older pony grazing on the lawn. Sometimes the boys from the school were taken there for an outing. One summer day Augustine drove his family out to see Newman, who was having a short rest there. It was so warm they sat outside and watched the children, taking turns riding old Charlie, the pony. Henry was already sixteen and his voice breaking, but he was slender and looked a mere boy still.

Augustine, who was feeling indignant about some gossip he had heard, the usual stuff about Newman's secret disloyalty, began talking about it, but Newman tried to stop him.

'It is no good talking about such things', he said. 'I know I am not guilty of anything serious, and there's nothing I have written I would not retract at the bidding of authority. So I must leave my vindication in God's hands; he will accomplish it in his own good time.'

Clem could not help wondering if he would live to see it. He looked so fragile, sitting there in the sun; it shone on his thick, rather untidy cap of hair, gone almost white on top, and showed the deep lines on his face. There was a look that hurt her on that expressive face, no tightness, no hardness, even no reserve, his mouth was never drawn in, but all the same, pain had left its image there, the suffering not of the body but of the heart, no less real because it was not seen. Sadly she thought, 'It's killing him by inches, all this suspicion within the household of the Faith.'

She broke out aloud, 'It's intolerable that it should be Catholics who are so unfair to you! How can they be so cruel?'

'Don't, don't!' Newman said, smiling at her, but his voice was not very steady. 'I don't pretend not to feel it, so it is better to be silent.'

Augustine said belligerently, 'I don't see why you should not defend yourself.'

'A man can defend himself only when he is accused', said Newman. 'There's no fighting enemies who won't come out into the open, who call themselves your friends but whose actions speak otherwise. I don't hide what I think and do; why do they? I always have preferred the evil that speaks to the evil that rankles and plots.'

'So do I!' cried Augustine, and Clem knew he was thinking of young Aubrey and Mr. Curtis and Macpherson and the rest, who schemed against him behind his back while deferring to him in public.

'The truth is, they dare not attack you openly', she said to Newman. 'They are afraid of you, when it comes to the point.'

Newman smiled. 'Afraid of an old grey grasshopper?' he said, fondling the dog's soft head. She pushed her muzzle affectionately against his knee.

The warm sun shone down on them, the trees, heavy and green, stood up the hill behind. Everything was quiet and still but the echoes of trouble in their minds.

Newman sighed and gazed down the slope at the children: Henry leading the pony, Charlotte astride with her little black boots stuck out.

'I don't mind it so much for myself', he said. 'After all, I have dear St. John, and all my friends, here and elsewhere. But this haunts me, that I have not yet fulfilled my mission and have work to do.'

Vividly Clem remembered the room at Rose Bank, years ago, and Newman, thirty years younger, full of the work, which, so it seemed to him, he had come back almost from the grave to do. He had had to change his ground since then, from the shifting sands where human opinion had mixed itself with divine revelation, to the Rock of Peter, where the storms beat hardest and yet could not prevail; but his mission had remained essentially the same, to reveal the supernatural reality of Christ's work to men as they were now, their eyes more and more turned away from eternity into time, their minds fixed on knowledge, their wills on what earth can give. It was the same holy flame, but set on the proper candlestick to give light to the whole great house of the modern world, where rooms unknown before were opening all round, shadowy caverns, palaces or prisons, no one yet could tell. And yet this fire that burned in him, to make truth known, must smoulder under the wet weeds of petty suspicion, while the spiritual war went on without him, and the enemy advanced to capture the castle of reason and reduce Christ's people to the feeble weapons of habit and sentiment.

Newman rubbed the old dog's head and sighed and said, 'But perhaps I am too old to do anything now. I am certainly very cowardly. I shrink from sacrifices.'

'I don't believe that', said Clem. 'You would still make any sacrifice for your work if you were given the chance.'

'It seems to me a pretty big sacrifice to give up your rightful place without making any kind of public noise about it', said Augustine warmly.

As usual, when they praised him, Newman began to laugh. 'You are too kind to me', he said. 'You talk as if I were some important person, fee-fa-fum stuff! But you know very well I don't live an heroic life! Look at me, these last few years, going bathing at the seaside, quite an expense, too, trying to get rid of my colds by papering my room and putting matting down, and now I have even got a shower bath, an excellent one. I thought perhaps I ought to keep up my strength in case I should still be any good for some work, if it came, but really I don't know ... I woke up in bed once, when it was all done, and I said to myself, "What is the good of all this? What am I living for?" I felt I was just cumbering the ground, and maybe that is the truth.'

Augustine sat up in his chair and said fiercely, 'I won't have you saying that! I think your gifts have been wasted, but we don't value you for what you do, as if you were a machine!'

'Thank you', said Newman, looking at him with affection. 'Have I been croaking? Sometimes I feel inclined to think that as a Protestant I felt my religion dreary, but not my life, and now as a Catholic my life is dreary but not my religion!' His laugh ended a little like a sigh. 'Well! I must not complain, for don't all God's servants have to put up with that? I know Job and Moses and Habakkakb felt as I feel.'

Augustine, amused at this choice of predecessors, remarked, 'Not to mention most Christian saints!'

'Yes, and how I wonder at the *old* saints now', Newman said gravely. 'When we're young, natural enthusiasm takes us a long way, but when we're old the same grace goes less far, because it has to encounter more opposition. Old men are in soul as stiff, as lean, as bloodless as their bodies, except so far as grace penetrates and softens them. And it requires a flooding of grace to do this. Our own St. Philip now, think of him.' He gazed meditatively at the green summer country falling away before them. 'When I was young I thought that with all my heart I gave up the world for God. I used to pray not to be given wealth and fame and so on, but now I think those prayers were prompted chiefly by natural rashness, and some generosity, perhaps. I was bold because I was ignorant. I know more about the world now, and what it means to give it up; perhaps that can't be known till you wish to make friends with it and it will not make friends with you! I wish St. Philip would teach me better how to be despised, and to despise being despised, as he used to say. I often ask him to. And not to let the shadow on me affect the Oratory, which belongs to him.'

They sat silent, Clem thinking that perhaps Newman's soul was not as stiff and bloodless as he thought it was, and then he said softly, as if he were thinking aloud, 'Well! All this turns one more to God. *Deus meus et omnia.*'

Charlotte came toiling, panting up the slope and flung herself on the grass beside the old dog, who thumped a lazy greeting with her tail. Charlotte was thirteen, but in some ways very much a child still.

'Oh, Father! Why don't you come and ride the pony too?' she said with breathless affection.

'Poor old Charlie and I are both too old for the exercise, my dear child', he answered, smiling.

Charlotte cocked her head at him. 'Which is the oldest, you or Charlie?'

Newman laughed. 'I am!' he said. 'We don't know the venerable Charlie's age, but I am so old, Charlotte, I can remember the night we had news of the battle of Trafalgar, and all the windows were full of candles burning for the victory.'

'Were they? But that's history! Before Papa was born! How old were you then?'

'Oh, little', he answered. 'A little tiny boy, I suppose about four years old, lying in my crib.'

Charlotte gazed thoughtfully up at him, pulling the dog's ears gently.

'I wish I were as old as you!' she said at last, earnestly, and was offended when they all laughed.

'But I know what she meant', Clem said to Augustine later, as they were driving home in the green gloom of the midsummer evening. Charlotte was leaning comfortably against her, fast asleep. 'She meant she would like to be like him, and put it down to age instead of goodness.'

'He is never bitter, is he?' Augustine said. 'He counts so many ventures as failures, and he's too sensitive not to suffer by all this misrepresentation, more than most men would, perhaps. Yet he never attacks the other party, never even makes pronouncements of his own, though he knows a lot of us would support him. Whatever they say about him, he doesn't retaliate, and however sad it makes him, he is not bitter. What a victory over himself! Because he's a fighter, if ever there was one, it isn't natural to him to sit down and refuse to take action; the only just cause he won't defend is his own!'

And after a moment he added, 'I only wish I could get anywhere near such freedom from bitterness.'

'My lovey, I don't think you are doing so badly', said Clem, with affection. 'You are always telling me what a good engineer Macpherson is and how Mr. Curtis is such an excellent manager.'

That made Augustine laugh. 'They annoy me, all the same', he said.

Henry had been leaning back, gazing at the black trees lacing their leaves overhead, floating in the soft blue chasm of night coming. Now he sat up and said, 'Papa, should you mind if I did not go into the firm?'

'There's no need for you to', Augustine said. 'I wouldn't have myself if I hadn't been a rash young idiot who imagined he was going to transform the poor old concern for the better. What do you want to do, Henry?'

'I want to be a priest', said the boy.

Not long after this they went to London for Josephine's wedding. For Josephine, now nearly thirty, instead of joining the Carmelites had fallen in love with a country doctor, ten years her senior. A convert, he had a practice in East Anglia, which his father had run before him; he met Josephine while visiting his sister in London. Flora had at first opposed such a dull choice of husband, but as there was no real hope of her plain daughter now making a good match, she finally gave her consent. Only the family were invited; Josephine wrote asking Charlotte to be her bridesmaid. 'Charlie's relations are so Protestant they won't even come to the church', she said.

'Charlie! Just like the dear pony at Rednal!' said Charlotte sentimentally, prepared to love Dr. Cley on sight.

Aunt Scarvell, like the Cley family, held aloof from the papist ceremony, but she condescended to attend the reception afterwards. Until now she had refused any invitation from Lord Gornal, in order to show her extreme disapproval of his second marriage; but evidently curiosity had finally overcome pride, for here she was, a very old lady now, still straight-backed and uncompromising, her hawk nose projecting like a beak from her brown, withered face, her thin lips drawn in tight, partly from loss of teeth, mostly from lifelong obstinacy. She and Lord Gornal sparred with each other, he, with beetling white brows and heavy jowl, leaning goutily on his stick and grumbling to himself when there was no one else at hand to grouse with. Both he and Aunt Scarvell showed signs of beginning a scene with Augustine, so he and Clem kept out of the way, not wanting to provoke more storms at poor Josephine's wedding party.

Charlotte was the only guest who really enjoyed herself. She ran about with sandwiches and cake so energetically that she banged her hand on a door and broke the clasp of her bracelet; she brought it, crying dismally, to her mother. Augustine, who was neat-fingered, managed to mend it for her and Clem was just putting it on again when a voice boomed above them.

'My dear Clem! My dear Augustine! How pleasant to see you again after all these years!'

Clem looked up and saw a tall, stately, grey-haired man, wearing the gaiters of an Anglican bishop as elegantly as if they were court dress. For quite a moment she did not recognize him and it was Augustine who said, 'Hallo, Bertram. I didn't know you were coming.'

'Didn't attend the service, of course', Bertram said, firmly shaking his hand. 'Well! Well! And so you are quite the business man, I hear, these days. It is not at all the career we expected of you, but no doubt it's just as well to see where the money comes from, eh? Ha, ha! And where it goes to! Well! This is the age of the machine, so I imagine you are doing pretty well for yourself.'

'You seem to have got on even better in your profession', retorted Augustine.

Clem gazed at Bertram, fascinated. He was not fat, but solid and pink. She looked in vain for the keen ascetic Bertram of her youth. His cheeks sagged a little, his lower lip was slightly pendulous, but he was handsome still, barely sixty, she supposed, a splendid ecclesiastical figure. She caught Augustine's eye and hurriedly looked away. She could think of nothing to say and yet felt it would be ridiculous not to speak.

'What's happened to George Pierce?' she asked, at random.

'Oh, didn't you know? The poor fellow died in one of those cholera epidemics. He never got beyond that first curacy he held and as his vicar grew older I'm afraid he overworked, and so when the disease came it just carried him off, carried him off. Sad thing. Luckily he never married, so there were no dependants to think of. Poor old George, a good steady fellow, but no initiative, you know. He was not forward-looking. He had very narrow views, never got any further than those Oxford days.'

Clem was reminded of that long-ago time when she had heard so much of who was in advance of whom; evidently people were still hurrying on—where to, nowadays, she wondered? Not to Rome, evidently. She heard Augustine say soberly, 'That was a good life he lived, and a death worth dying, in the service of God and his people.'

'Quite, quite', said Bertram, obviously not much interested. George was a creature of the past to him, who had known his fate for years. 'Well, how's the family? Just been talking to your boy. Tells me he wants to be a priest.'

How rash of Henry, Clem thought, apprehensively.

'That won't be allowed, will it?' Bertram went on.

'Why not?' said Augustine.

'Well, I suppose he'll be Lord Gornal in due time—hardly suitable', said Bertram. 'However, I daresay it will wear off when he leaves school and gets away from all those priests.'

Augustine said demurely, 'Henry will probably see even more priests when he goes to Oscott.'

'Oxford?' said Bertram. 'Which college?'

He was obviously a little deaf.

'Oscott is our diocesan seminary for training priests', said Augustine.

'Ah', said Bertram, non-committally. Clem had an idea he had not realized there was such a place and thought that all Catholic priests were trained in Rome. 'By the way, the boy's at Newman's little school, isn't he? How is the poor old fellow? I hear he is quite breaking up.'

'Breaking up! Why, he's not much older than you are, Bertram', Clem could not resist saying.

Bertram's eyes wandered to her and then away again. She wondered if he remembered that painful and ridiculous scene twenty years ago.

'Your people have put him on the shelf, haven't they?' he said. 'I hear he's been trying to get in touch with his old Oxford friends again.'

'He met Copeland, one of his old curates, by chance in a London street and invited him to the Oratory', said Augustine. 'I think Copeland must have passed round the word, for I believe Keble and others have written. Perhaps they didn't realize before that he would have liked to keep in touch, for no one could be more generous than Keble.'

'But doesn't that prove he's unhappy where he is?' said Bertram. 'Poor Newman, it did not turn out at all as he expected, did it? I daresay he wishes himself back with us, now.'

'Didn't you read his letter in the papers rejecting that assumption?' Augustine demanded.

'Oh yes, in *public* I quite see he cannot admit disappointment', said Bertram. 'Too proud, for one thing, to confess he was wrong.'

'He was not too proud to confess that before', said Augustine crossly.

'Bertram, can't you see how he can be content with his Faith and still miss his old friends?' Clem said. 'We don't make people's opinions our criterion of liking them, do we?'

Bertram shook his head. 'It was a terrible mistake', he said. 'And you won't convince me he doesn't regret it, bitterly. How much more good he could have done if he had remained in the church of his baptism!'

'He wasn't looking for results, he was looking for truth', Clem said, beginning to feel annoyed by what she considered Bertram's impenetrable smugness.

'It's a sad thing', he persisted. 'But what a lesson!'

'A lesson? What in?' Augustine demanded.

'My dear fellow, we must face it, Newman just did not have the courage to meet the challenge of our day', said Bertram, and Clem knew at once what his sermons must be like nowadays. 'New ideas, new knowledge, social progress: they are a challenge, and we have to think out our faith anew to meet them. But he, who was so gifted, I do not deny that, he turned tail and ran for the false security of an infallible authority, an inflexible dogmatism. Wasn't it simply giving up the fight?'

Augustine and Clem both stared at him helplessly, and Bertram, left holding the field, pronounced impressively, 'It is left to us to reconcile scientific progress and faith.'

'Suppose they can't be reconciled?' said Augustine. Clem, who knew he was the last person to oppose scientific knowledge in its right place, guessed that he put his protest like that because Bertram's assumptions annoyed him; Bertram evidently took his remark as a sign of incurable frivolity and laughed, shrugging his shoulders.

'You Romans!' he said. 'I believe you think you can convert modern men with fairy tales of the Virgin Mary's miracles.'

'Why not?' said Augustine. 'But don't run away with the idea that Newman has given up thinking; he hasn't.'

'But he's not allowed to speak, is he?' said Bertram, triumphantly. 'Ah, my dear fellow, you can't put the clock back. Newman fled from the present into the past, but he has found living in an anachronism less comfortable than he expected. Poor fellow, poor fellow! He has become an object lesson to us all. Ah, here's Mildred. Let me introduce my wife.'

Mildred, bishop's daughter and now bishop's wife, was a middle-aged, middle-sized woman, gracious, earnest, quietly managing. After a few remarks and a compliment on Charlotte's dress, she manœuvred Bertram away.

Augustine chuckled and said it reminded him of a passage in *Loss and Gain*, Newman's novel, in which he poked gentle fun at the rule of good clergy wives.

'They've got four sons', said Charlotte. 'There's one over there.'

Clem looked at this son of Bertram's, a pretty, fair boy, eating meringues by himself in a corner, and thought of Lucy, years ago, weeping because she had not succeeded in producing a Scarvell son. And now this Mildred had presented Bertram with four.

'Do you know', Charlotte went on, 'his daughter Clara has gone into a sisterhood, Josephine told me. And he didn't like it at all. Now she's called Sister Clare and wears a veil, a sort of nun, I suppose.'

'Ah', said Augustine, smiling. 'Perhaps that's why he's so sure the Catholic Faith is an anachronism!'

'Fancy Clara an Anglican nun!' Clem murmured, remembering the pretty, headstrong child she had tried to teach years ago.

'Mamma, why does he wear gaiters?' Charlotte asked. 'And why doesn't he believe in miracles?'

But she did not stay to be answered, running off to tease Josephine's Dr. Cley, to whom she had taken a great liking; she had told him about his beloved equine namesake and they made a tremendous joke out of calling each other Charlie and whinnying when they met. Dr. Cley was a thickset genial man with a round ruddy face, spectacles and curly hair; he called his bride 'Jo' and did not seem at all in awe of her disapproving relations. Soon they set off on the long journey to Norfolk, the busy country-town practice and something like a twenty-mile drive every Sunday to get to Mass.

Augustine and Clem went back to Birmingham, ugly, grimy and familiar home to them now. Clem found it hard to believe she had ever been in love with Bertram.

'Have we changed as much as he has?' she wondered.

'I expect so', said Augustine. 'Only instead of going pink and smooth I've turned into old boot leather.'

Clem laughed. 'What about me?'

'You've just got more and more comfortable', he said.

'Fat, I suppose you mean', said Clem. 'I still have a waist, all the same.' Then she suddenly sighed. 'Augustine, life is peculiar, isn't it? In a way it seems to get smaller as it goes on, or we get smaller, narrower, duller.'

Augustine considered this, lying in bed with his hands behind his head.

'Well, do we? Or do we just notice it more?' he said. 'See ourselves more from outside, as we go on. Perhaps the whole point of living is just to get outside ourselves.'

'How dismal that sounds', said Clem, brushing her hair vigorously.

'Does it?' said Augustine. 'But to get right outside, into the light, and see everything in that, even ourselves? I think it might be a tremendous relief.'

Clem put down her brush and climbed into bed. 'But sometimes I feel I'm just getting stuck inside', she objected. 'Slower and stiffer, inside as well as out. One becomes such a habit, somehow.'

'Well, you're a habit I don't propose to break', he said cheerfully, so that she began to laugh and complained, 'Why won't you let me be serious?'

'Because I do like you to laugh, so much', said Augustine, lying there and looking at her.

But for some reason as he looked at her she suddenly felt frightened. His face, close to hers, was so very tired; even his eyes, once so keen and alert, looked blurred and cloudy. And so she clung to him closely, her ordinary habitual affection overflowing suddenly with love and tenderness.

## 11

That same summer Augustine and Clem went off for a holiday alone in France. Henry was on a tour with friends and Charlotte staying in Norfolk, greatly enjoying herself driving Dr. Cley's trap. Augustine, usually an energetic traveller, this time seemed to prefer sitting in the sun to looking at pictures and places. Yet when they went home, at the end of August, Clem did not think he looked very well, and Newman, when they called on him in Hagley Road, said the same thing.

'It was too short a trip', he said. 'Why not go abroad for the whole winter, as you used to do, and let those fellows who plague you in the firm see how they get on without you?'

'It's more effort to go than to stay', said Augustine, with unusual apathy. 'Not that it matters either way. I am doing no good in the firm; I never have done much.'

'I am sure your workpeople don't think so', said Newman warmly. 'Why, old Mrs. Fogarty's daughter works in your factory, and she says it's improved "out of all conscience" since you went there.' He quoted this opinion seriously; Mrs. Fogarty was probably some old woman who came in to clean the school, but Newman knew all those connected with his household, their troubles and losses and families, said Masses for them, helped them and talked to them, so that without knowing much about industry and trade he knew the people involved in it, both masters and men.

But Augustine would not be cheered by Mrs. Fogarty's daughter. 'The places they live in! And England calls itself Christian!' he said. 'It's making a mockery of Christ, and no wonder, when the people reject their masters they also reject him, whom we have called Master and not obeyed. Do you know, I dreamt last night I was in the ironworks and it was very dark and no one was there. I shouted out, "Where's everyone gone?" and a voice came from the air behind me and groaned out, "There is no one left." It seemed to be raining dust and I thought it was the dust of their bones, burying all the place in darkness.'

Clem gazed at him. 'That's why you woke in such a sweat! Why didn't you tell me?'

'I couldn't', he answered. 'It was too real to me.' He looked at Newman. 'Can dreams come true, do you think?'

Newman, pondering the dream, did not answer his question. 'Whenever we look into the world we see death, and darkness, and desolation', he said. 'Look at the Crimea, at America, and now the massacre of the unfortunate Poles. Satan offers power on earth, but all it comes to in the end is dust. It is the same in our hearts, as far as they do not belong to the divine heart.'

'What seems much worse is that good things end in dust too', said Augustine despondently. 'What is the use of trying?'

Newman looked at him in silence for a moment. Then he said, 'Your work may be lost to sight, but *you* are not lost. You are a link in a chain, a bond of connection between persons. God has not created you for nothing; he does nothing in vain. He knows what he is about.'

'He may, but I don't!' Augustine said, with a wry smile.

'God has created you to do him some definite service', said Newman, with absolute conviction. 'You may never know your mission in this life, but you will be told it in the next. Whatever, wherever you are, if you trust him and keep his commandments, you can never be thrown away. You will be doing his work in your own place, without knowing it.'

'Do you really believe that?' Augustine demanded abruptly. 'Because I know you too feel that all your work has been brought to nothing.'

Newman was silent again, evidently examining his conscience, for at last he looked up and said candidly, 'Yes, I think I can say I do mean that from my heart, notwithstanding my weakness of nature, which is apt to complain of being left out in the cold! I don't give up my ideas, either, even if I am not able to act on them. I take this long penance of slander and unpopularity as the price I pay for the victory of my principles in the end, soon after my life, perhaps.'

'Bravo!' cried Clem, delighted with his fighting spirit, and glad to see Augustine's face less heavy with depression.

Newman smiled at her. 'Well, I ought to get back to my job', he said. 'I have started on a tremendous work in the library, dusting and arranging books to an heroic degree, and it's not done yet. Come and see me again soon.'

'Dusting books! He ought to be writing them!' Augustine said, as they walked down the dark passage towards the cloister and the church. 'He's right, I suppose. But sometimes I think I shall hear our Lord say on Judgement Day, "You did not give me a just wage; you did not care, when I stopped work, what happened to me; you worked me to death." '

'Don't', Clem said, tears coming into her eyes at the pain in his tone. 'He knows you have tried.'

They went through the cloister and into the church; not one of Pugin's Gothic churches but built on the old Roman plan, reminding them of so many they had known in the Eternal City itself, though not so large or so fine. As they knelt, side by side, Clem was suddenly overwhelmed by the mystery of their destiny: two immortal creatures, but so small, so weak, held in the grip of time, knowing so little of all there was to know, and yet enough to follow the clue of love through the maze of bright images, of hope and of desire, through the shadows of grief, even of death. Here they were with God, even though they could not see him.

Lord Gornal had found out that Henry wanted to be a priest, through Bertram Scarvell, Clem suspected, and it was the excuse for the biggest row he had indulged in for years. As he was now over eighty he had all the advantages: if he shouted himself to the point of collapse Augustine would certainly be blamed for it. After one attempt at discussion Augustine refused the repeated summons to London; whereupon he was inundated with lawyers' letters and even with lawyers' visits. When it became clear to Lord Gornal that Augustine intended to allow his son to choose his own career, he embarked on a lengthy campaign of financial coercion. Augustine's control over his income had always been precarious; now it began to look as if he would be reduced to the Scarvell money he had inherited from his mother. It was not much, but, undaunted, he worked out how they could live on it and told his father to do as he pleased. Lord Gornal then threatened that if Henry became a priest he would inherit nothing but the title. Henry was most indignant. 'I don't even want his title, let alone his money', he said, 'unless the bishop wants it.'

Bishop Ullathorne was always hard up for money; once he had even been put in gaol for debt, though this was due to a misunderstanding which was soon cleared up. But he supported Augustine, with sympathy, when he was consulted. And when Lord Gornal produced the comparatively mild proposal that Henry should go to Oxford before deciding his future irretrievably, Ullathorne did not definitely oppose it, although it was not the current policy to allow young Catholics to go to Oxford.

'I daresay Henry will benefit by an Oxford training and be of more use to you in the end', said Augustine. 'And he is quite up to it, thanks to Dr. Newman's school.'

Newman himself had gently refused to give an opinion. 'People are always accusing me of preparing boys for Oxford', he said. 'Of course I can't go against the bishops' policy, but I sympathize with the fathers who come to ask what they are to do with their sons—are they to keep company with the gamekeeper and learn idle habits? They can't all go into the army. It's the policy to fear loss of faith at Oxford, but why should it be more a danger there than anywhere else? Faith should be a tough principle, not an exotic plant. Of course a Catholic university would be the ideal thing, but look what happened to that! Something ought to be done, and done soon, but till it is I cannot advise you about Henry's future. It is not my place.'

'Of course it ought to be his place', was Augustine's private comment. 'If they won't back his University, they ought to give him the mission in Oxford.'

But Newman was not considered, in London, a fit person to undertake any educational work. Some people even wanted his school closed.

Henry went up to Oxford, Lord Gornal subsided into a suspicious grumble, and Augustine retained the salary so grudgingly allowed him.

Winter was now clamped down over Birmingham; grey skies and cold, raw days followed each other inexorably.

One afternoon Clem was shivering over the fire and wishing the drawing-room were not so big, when the maid announced, 'Mr. Curtis from the factory to see you, madam, very urgent.'

Mr. Curtis came in at once. Clem had not seen him for some years; he had changed from gingery, pinkish young middle-age to elderly portliness, his small eyes lost in a large heavy face.

'Mrs. Firle, ma'am, please don't be alarmed.'

Clem was immediately so frightened she felt faint and caught the back of a chair to steady herself.

'What's happened? Please tell me.'

'I just took the liberty of coming ahead, ma'am', said Mr. Curtis. 'Mr. Firle's been taken ill and he's coming now, with Dr. Williams, and I thought you should have warning.'

Clem heard carriage wheels as he was speaking. She thanked him hurriedly and ran into the hall. Augustine was just climbing out of the carriage, assisted by the doctor and the coachman. He was wrapped in a rug which fell off as he got down. He came up the steps slowly, one at a time, and smiled when he saw Clem.

Dr. Williams insisted that he should lie down on the sofa in the drawing-room, and not go upstairs yet. Clem followed the doctor into the hall.

'Dr. Williams, what is it?'

'It's his heart, ma'am, a sudden attack', said the doctor. 'Now, you must not worry unduly. I will let him have something to help him another time. Meanwhile, rest, you know. Don't let him do too much.'

He hurried off and Clem, with a sinking heart, went back into the drawing-room and sat down on a footstool by the sofa, so as to look at Augustine properly. But he would not look at her; he was riffling irritably through a newspaper.

'What did that ass Curtis want to come and frighten you for?' he said crossly.

'I rather think he was frightened himself', Clem said.

'And now I suppose Williams has been going on about it?'

'He was putting me off, the usual doctors' stuff for ignorant women', said Clem. 'Aren't you going to tell me yourself?'

'There's nothing to tell. He says it's my heart, so I suppose it is. It's never been a really reliable organ, has it?' He flapped the paper about, irritably.

'Augustine, love, don't put me off', Clem said, desperately. 'Do stop pretending to look at that paper and tell me, was it really bad?'

He dropped the paper then and turned his head to look at her directly. At once she saw the echoes of pain and fear in his eyes.

'Very bad', he said at last, almost in a whisper.

She caught his hand and held it.

'I thought it was the end', he said after a moment. 'It nearly was.'

Clem's throat ached; tears rose in her eyes.

'You haven't had it before?'

'Not like that', he answered.

A tear dropped from her eyes on their clasped hands.

'Now, cheer up, Clem', Augustine said, at that. 'Now that I know, I can take care, can't I?'

'Oh, it is so unfair!' she cried. 'It's because you have been so harried and bothered by your father and all that bunch at the factory.'

'It's probably only my feeble constitution', said Augustine. 'The silly thing is that I'd just got used to being pretty well, much better than when I was young. Well, it's no good grumbling. Poor Clemmy, don't cry so. People live for years and years with bad hearts; it will give me a splendid excuse to be even more tiresome than I have been lately.'

Clem was not a pessimist by nature, but she was always surprised by Augustine's resilience. No sooner was he knocked down by fate than he would jump up again fighting. In the next few weeks, in spite of her anxiety, he began to make her hope he would long outwit the physics of his heart; after all, he had lived much of his life under the threat of death, though not, till now, this sudden death that might take him at any moment. Far from making him more irascible, this new danger seemed to her to restore all his old good temper; she sometimes wondered why.

In this spring, of 1864, they were sharing, with all the interest of old friends, in a sudden storm of controversy which had blown up for Newman. It all started at Christmas with a careless remark in *Macmillan's Magazine*, by Charles Kingsley, a clergyman then at the height of his popularity as a preacher of social justice and a writer of historical novels which were very widely read. Augustine saw Newman's copy of the *Magazine*, with a cross marked against the offensive words: 'Truth for its own sake has never been a virtue with the Roman clergy. Father Newman informs us that it need not be and on the whole ought not to be;—that cunning is the weapon which heaven has given to the saints wherewith to withstand the brute male force of the wicked world which marries and is given in marriage.'

'Can he really believe that *Newman* preaches lying?' Clem said, indignantly. 'And how mean to drag in that sneer against celibacy!'

'Of course Newman has written to ask where he got this peculiar idea from, and all Kingsley has produced is some Anglican sermon, in which, needless to say, he doesn't say anything of the sort.'

'I hope he'll apologize, then, in public', said Clem.

But the apology, when it came, was almost more offensive than the original slander. Kingsley expressed a cold regret that he had mistaken the meaning of Newman's words.

'Meaning of my words!' Newman said, exasperated. 'I never said any such words.'

He wrote a pamphlet on the exchange which his friends found very funny. Somewhat to their surprise, it drew from the Editor of *The Spectator*, who was reputed to be something of a freethinker, a fair summing-up of the episode, giving the right of the case, on balance, to Newman. This article appeared the day before his birthday, in February, and could not but please him, used as he was to being condemned as a matter of course.

Kingsley was even more surprised than Newman, and seriously annoyed to find that everyone was not, after all, on his side. Papists were always the villains of his piece and here was one daring to make fun of him, and actually backed up by a responsible newspaper. Catherine Craven, who knew a friend of Kingsley's, wrote to Clem that he was reported to have said, 'I trust to make him and his admirers sorry they did not leave me alone. I have a score of twenty years and more to pay, and this is an instalment of it.'

When his pamphlet came out, Augustine bought it and read it to Clem. Kingsley's hatred of Rome and all its works they had expected, but they were not prepared for his scorn and disgust of Newman himself. In his angry picture Newman appeared as a cunning and evasive schemer, plotting even as an Anglican to snare the unsuspecting English in the nets of Rome; Rome, of course, being synonymous with superstition, oppression of conscience, and an unnatural cult of virginity.

'I suppose he's fixed all his hatred of the Church on New-man', said Clem doubtfully.

'I don't know about that', said Augustine. 'Here he says, quite truly, that Catholics are not bound to believe all the miracles and legends of the saints, and goes on passionately to attack Newman because he has said he certainly believes some of them.' He read out Kingsley's words. '"He has worked his mind into that morbid state in which nonsense is the only food for which it hungers. Like the sophists of old he has used reason to destroy reason. I had thought that, like them, he had preserved his own reason in order to be able to destroy that of others. But I was unjust to him, as he says. While he tried to destroy others' reason he was, at least, fair enough to destroy his own."'

'*Newman* destroy reason?' Clem said. 'He must be mad.'

'Blind with prejudice', said Augustine. 'I don't believe he has really read Newman's books, only picked at them to find excuses for his righteous indignation. Listen how he goes on: "Too many prefer the charge of insincerity to insipience—Dr. Newman seems not to be of that number." Must he be either insincere or insipient? And here he is, posing as honest John Bull. "If he will indulge in subtle paradoxes, if he will take a perverse pleasure in saying something shocking to plain English notions, he must take the consequences." I suppose that means he must expect to be ranted at in this rude way if he complains of misrepresentation.'

'Of course Newman must answer this', said Clem. 'He can't let such a parody pass for truth. Why, I think it's more of a libel on Newman than Newman's ever was on Achilli. After all, Newman only gave the facts about Achilli, but Kingsley has published a tissue of lies, and all in an attack on lying!'

'It will be difficult to answer', said Augustine thought-fully. 'See how Kingsley has destroyed his credit in advance. Either he is a cunning sophist trying to catch you in his web of false reason, or he is a deluded madman whose beliefs are the result of a craving for the miraculous. So whatever Newman says can be used in evidence against him. Kings-ley keeps harping on the theme, "He says this, but what does he *mean*?" So that the ordinary person will be suspicious of every word.'

'It's very unfair!' cried Clem. 'Kingsley has an enor-mous popular audience who can hardly know much about Newman. Indeed, what does England in general know about him now? Look at what Bertram was saying. The man in the street knows even less than Bertram. Newman must be just a renegade to them; an Englishman who has gone foreign, a don who's sold his soul to the Pope, goodness knows what for—the mere pleasure of corrupt-ing youth, I suppose. Whatever he says, they'll shout him down.'

She could not help remembering the trial and the crowd's howl of applause when Newman and not Achilli was condemned.

'I hope Newman will make a fight for it, all the same', said Augustine. 'He's a good fighter when he's roused. But I don't see how he will set about it.'

Newman did not hesitate long. Soon after Easter he set to work on his answer, which was to be issued at once, by Longman's, in weekly parts, so that Thursdays suddenly became exciting days to his friends. In the first two instal-ments Newman, with masterly clarity and humour, showed up Kingsley's method of disputation, his misuse of evi-dence, and his attempt to destroy his opponent's credit with insinuations of equivocation.

'It's very clever, almost too clever', said Augustine. 'I'm afraid the great British public will prefer old roaring Charlie.'

'What next?' Clem wondered.

'I believe he's embarked on a full-scale history of his religious opinions', said Augustine. 'He thinks it's the only way to prove his good faith and show, *pace* Kingsley, that it was reason which led him into the Church.'

A few days later he came back from the Oratory silent and thoughtful.

'Did you see Newman?' Clem asked, taking up one of Henry's socks from the basket, to darn it.

'I did see him for a moment, but he didn't see me', said Augustine slowly. 'He was standing at his desk writing. Father St. John says he's hard at it every day, checking old letters and journals and even sending off pages to be corrected by old Oxford Anglican friends when there's time—you see, he *does* care for the truth. Time is the difficulty, he's writing against time to get the stuff off to the publishers every week.'

He stopped, and was silent so long Clem looked up enquiringly.

Augustine said, 'He was crying, Clem.'

She put down the sock; tears blurred her own eyes.

'It's a shame', she said. 'It must be an agony to go over all that again now.'

'I don't believe he would forgo it, all the same', Augustine said. 'It's his chance, given unasked, to tell his own story, that he's heard so often travestied. But you know what he's like, he throws himself into whatever he writes, without reserve. You remember the trial and how he was all packed up to go to prison? It's like that now. He keeps saying, "I'm in for it!"'

Clem smiled. 'I only hope it won't be received with jeers of derision', she said.

*Apologia*

'I don't think so', said Augustine. 'He writes too well.'

All the last part of April and through May Newman was hard at it, the parts of his defence, his *Apologia*, growing longer as his subject grew more complex. He stood at his desk for hours at a time, sometimes into the night. They met him once on a Sunday, for a brief moment. He came into one of the public rooms near the front door to greet them, rubbing his fingers.

'They are stiff, cramped', he said. 'They have been walking nearly twenty miles a day.'

'Don't kill yourself, Father', Augustine said. 'It would not be worth it, even to prove to England that you are not a liar!'

Newman smiled. His face was pale, but energy seemed to flame through him. Clem was reminded of his return from Sicily thirty years ago, with the fire of his mission transforming his very appearance. Suddenly she wondered why. What was the same in the two situations, on the face of it so dissimilar? And why should Newman be so deeply concerned with this re-creation of his own past, almost as he had been when he re-created the past of the Church, on the eve of his reception?

'I am not going through with this only for that, my dear Firle', he said. 'I think when you have my last part you will see where all this tends. Kingsley was not only attacking me, but the Church through me, and there are a few words I want to say on the subject of belief and authority. I think I know what makes people fear it, and what can be more terrible, in an age of increasing uncertainties, than to fear the very Rock God has set down in time for our salvation?'

'I knew your Apology would be an Offensive!' Augustine said, laughing. 'But I still say, don't write yourself to death!'

'What would it matter, if I had said my say?' Newman retorted. 'And people are listening!'

It was true, and that in spite of the fact that Garibaldi's visit was the great news of the day, crowding nearly everything else out of the papers. But all the principal reviews, which had at first watched the contest with amusement, reflected soon the fascination of hundreds of readers as the remarkable narrative grew under their eyes. Newman wrote of himself, and yet nothing could be further from the outpourings of egomania; always it was the truth of his quest that absorbed him, not only its rational but its psychological truth. Particularly at the end, as he had told Augustine, this great passion of his life shone out clearer and clearer; when all the complications of his passage into the Catholic Church were out of the way, he launched into a splendid demonstration of all the ideas most dear to him; the tragic and terrible human condition, the startling intervention of God, the mystery of the Body which kept the truth of that divine revelation through time, and the perpetual struggle of men, as individual persons, to hold their balance between the claims of obedience and freedom, faith and reason, heaven and the world.

'This is splendid!' Augustine cried in triumph. 'He has got in everything, even the relationship between science and faith, and what the infallibility of the Church *doesn't* mean. Now Ward and his friends will have to stop baying at him, surely!'

'I like his tribute to the Englishness of Dr. Ullathorne', said Clem. 'That is very nicely worked in. I wonder what Kingsley thinks?'

'It doesn't matter what he thinks any more', said Augustine jubilantly. 'Newman has won everybody else!'

It really did seem like that. The reading public could hardly believe their eyes. The Newman of Oxford days, who was thought to have turned into a superstitious old woman, regretting the past and miserable in the present, suddenly appeared before them in his true form, numinous with all his half-forgotten power. It was a resurrection; he was like Lazarus leaping out of his tomb at the Lord's command, to astonish and dismay the Pharisees and Sadducees of his day.

Just as he had not hidden from his friends the pain it caused him to be so misrepresented and traduced, so now he did not hide his happiness when his good faith was generally admitted and people long estranged came back to him. Most prized of all was the tribute of his fellow priests, who let him know, in a public address at the provincial synod, their gratitude and admiration for a defence which explicitly included their honour with his own.

'He was gasping for words', a priest who was present told Augustine. 'Yet he never used an awkward one. I never before heard a man's heart so plainly coming out in his words. His tears were visible, and most of us confessed to crying when we came out.'

They rejoiced in his triumph, and all the more because it seemed to have put new life into him. He could hardly have called himself an old grey grasshopper now, although, when the last appendices, answering Kingsley's specific charges, appeared at the end of June, he said he felt like a man who had fallen overboard and found the distance grow greater and greater as he swam towards the land.

'At last I am ashore and have crawled upon the beach and there I lie.'

But everyone else saw in him a new vigour and confidence. He was like a man long a prisoner of war who has suddenly been given a sword and told to fight his way out, and now here he was, a victor, congratulated on all sides.

The best of all rewards came to him when it was suggested that he should found an Oratory at Oxford, to form a rallying ground for young Catholics going to the University. So quickly did things move that in August ground was actually bought there. Newman was full of joy at the prospect of being useful at last in the sphere he knew so well. He laughed now at the setbacks that had so much saddened him.

'The Irish University was such a failure', he said. 'The Achilli matter such a scrape, the school is such a fidget!'

Henry went up to Oxford in October, full of delight in the thought that soon 'The Father' would be coming there. Augustine went with him; he returned looking very sober.

'Clem,' he said, 'I've had a nasty jolt. I don't know whether to tell Newman or not. I doubt if I can bear to.'

'Oh, don't say something is going to go wrong *again*?'

'I believe the devil lies in wait to prevent Newman doing what he ought to do!' said Augustine. He flung himself down on the sofa without taking off his coat; he had even forgotten his hat, which fell off backwards on the floor. 'It's Ward and Manning and their friends in Rome—Talbot, for instance; they're pulling strings to stop him going to Oxford. I learned it all from someone who did not know I was a friend of Newman's.'

'To *stop* him? But why?'

'Because they, infallible little gods, think Newman is a siren who will lure the Catholic laity to damnation', said Augustine. 'Of course it's perfectly true that if he's in Oxford all we rich fathers will rush to send our boys there, where infallible Ward and the rest think they will all immediately lose their faith.'

'Much less likely if Newman were there', said Clem. 'They would probably be converting the sceptics before long!'

Rome + Manning
worried
New Newman
would
win Oxford

'Of course', said Augustine. 'If only people weren't so afraid of minds being used! I bet there are more lost to the faith through *not* thinking about it. Oh, Clem, but the plotting and planning that goes on, the horrid to-and-fro gossip! "Newman must be crushed." This fellow actually said that. Oh my God, how we Christians can make purgatories for each other!'

'But the Cardinal? Surely he won't side against Newman?'

'He's a sick man, poor old Wiseman', Augustine said. 'And he doesn't know how to manage people, anyway. I believe Manning is managing him, and of course Manning believes Ward is right when he says Newman is a liberal at heart, or a champion of the rebellious laity, or whatever is his worst crime at present.'

'It's ridiculous when you think that to freethinkers he is a reactionary and an anachronism', said Clem.

'That reminds me', said Augustine. 'I met someone who knows Frank Newman, his younger brother.'

'The beautiful youth with the double first who went off to make Plymouth Brethren of the Persians', said Clem, smiling.

'He's moved a long way from there', said Augustine with a laugh. 'The history of *his* religious opinions would make fascinating reading! More and more about less and less, I imagine. He has any number of pet causes he's fanatical about, but he throws away articles of the Creed one after another, as if they were shoes that pinched.'

'What about Frank, anyway?'

'This fellow met Frank in Oxford the other day, and Frank asked him, as a prominent university character, if he thought John Henry had given the true reasons for his leaving the Anglican Church. And this little potentate actually said, "Of course he could not tell the real reasons in public." '

'Oh *no!*' cried Clem, jumping in her chair. 'He can't have read the *Apologia*.'

'Oh yes he had, and so had Frank', said Augustine. 'And both of them were so sure *they* knew Newman's motives they never dreamed of believing what he said.'

'But why should Frank judge him so harshly?' Clem said, bewildered. 'And why does *he* think Newman left the Church of England?'

'As far as I can make out from his obstinate friend, they both think he wanted priestly power, but without a pope over him, and came over to Rome when the Anglicans made it clear he was going to get no power at all among them', said Augustine. 'I don't know whether they think he gets much fun lording it over a parish in Birmingham.'

'Is Frank just jealous?' Clem wondered.

'I think they're poles apart in temperament', said Augustine. 'Frank is clever and has strong feelings, but no imagination at all. I suppose John Henry was rather an unassailable elder brother, too.'

'But he was so good to Frank, helped him so much', said Clem.

'That may make it harder for Frank to see him straight', said Augustine.

'It seems sad they are all at loggerheads now, when they used to be such a happy family', said Clem. 'I suppose Newman may have been rather austere, even priggish, when he was young, but he soon left that behind. What's happened to the odd Charles, I wonder?'

'Oh, he's still knocking about in an aimless way', said Augustine. 'Newman and Frank support him, you know; Frank's not lacking in responsibility in that way. It's Jemima I can't understand. Fancy not allowing him to see her children! And children always get on so well with him.'

'Probably that's why', said Clem. 'She feels it her duty to protect them from his insidious charm. Oh, poor Father! How things do seem to conspire against him!'

Augustine hit the sofa suddenly with his fist.

'He will not be allowed to go to Oxford', he said.

And in this, he was, unfortunately, correct.

A rescript from Propaganda and a consequent decision of the English bishops meant active discouragement of an Oxford education for lay Catholics, and it became impossible to go on with the plans for an Oratory there after this, since its sole object was to care for Catholic undergraduates.

Newman was not even consulted.

# 12

In February of the next year Cardinal Wiseman died, and it was Manning who succeeded him as Archbishop of Westminster. It happened that not very long afterwards Clem met him, for the first time. They were in London and Augustine was drawn by a friend into some charitable negotiations, and taken along to see the new Archbishop about it, Clem going too merely out of curiosity. Although it was now May, it was a cold day, and there was a fire burning in the room where Manning received them. Evidently it was not warm enough for him, for he soon called out, 'Newman! Make up the fire, will you?'

Clem looked round, astonished, almost expecting the Father of the Oratorians to appear with a scuttle of coal, but she realized in a moment that Manning was addressing his butler. He must have noticed her look, for he laughed and said, 'It's an odd coincidence, isn't it? People always make jokes about Newman's name. He was with the Cardinal, you know.'

Clem, knowing that Manning had been involved in the backstairs intrigue which had prevented Newman going to Oxford, had somehow imagined that he would be a worldly, superficial character, but as he eagerly talked with Augustine's friend on his project for orphans, she began to change her mind. She saw he had a passionate interest in the lives of the poor, and a great understanding of their difficulties. She remembered suddenly stories of his work in Lavington long ago, his Anglican country parish; some people, who implied that he liked to curry favour with the great, she now felt to be quite wrong. Looking at his keen face, with its great piercing eyes and narrow, rather thin mouth, she was conscious of a spirit of dedication, complete and intense; he was the kind of man who could wholly identify himself with his function, for good or ill.

The building of a cathedral was mentioned. Manning swept the idea aside.

'What does it matter about a church of bricks?' he said. 'It is the church of souls that matters, and I am not going to spend money on stone while my poor people of West-minster are without the necessities of life.'

It was impossible not to admire him; at the same time there was a hardness about his self-dedication that a little intimidated Clem. She felt that it would be easy for such a man, sure of the rectitude of his aims, undeniably selfless, to believe that his course was bound to be the right course, his will necessarily in conformity with God's will.

When they went away Augustine said, 'Well! Somehow I feel St. Thomas of Canterbury may have been rather like that!'

Clem said, 'Perhaps he will be a very good Archbishop; he looks a natural ruler.'

'Poor old Newman, though!' said Augustine. 'Those two will never understand each other. Wasn't it funny about the butler? A sort of skeleton at the feast for Manning! All the same, I can't help feeling that unconsciously he would like to have our Newman laying the fire for him! It may be bad for him to be an Archbishop, even if he is good at it.'

It was July before they saw Newman again. Charlotte was with them when they next knocked at the door in Hagley Road and they were all surprised when Newman himself opened it. The half-dozen Oratorian fathers were overloaded with work, school, orphanage, prison visiting and so on, and Newman often undertook the home jobs, doing the accounts and acting as librarian and sometimes as sacristan.

'Are you the porter too, now, Father?' Augustine teased him.

Newman smiled. 'I happened to be passing', he said. 'I'm so glad you've called. Come and see my new treasure.'

He took them into one of the tall narrow public rooms and there on the table was a violin.

'Dear Rogers and Church have given it to me', he said, picking it up tenderly. 'Isn't it beautiful? I had to choose between three from the warehouse; I was quite nervous at not choosing well after all this time. But it is the best fiddle I have ever had, and I began to play when I was ten.'

'What did you do with the old one?' Clem asked.

'I gave it up years ago', Newman said. 'I felt perhaps I should not give the time to it, but now I believe I was wrong, for I always write more when I can play the fiddle. There must be some electric current passing from the strings through the fingers into the brain and down the spinal marrow. Perhaps thought is music.'

Clem suddenly remembered the ancient tradition of song in heaven, the music of the angelic host.

'Do play it, Father', Charlotte said.

'Oh, it would be a penance for you!' Newman said, laughing. 'I am so out of practice. Though I did get down to it on Saturday and had a good bout of Beethoven's quartets. It really made me cry out with delight, they are so exquisite. Beethoven is like a great bird singing.'

'Well, but how shall we admire your fiddle if we don't hear it?' Augustine cajoled him.

So they persuaded him and he sat down and tuned the violin with loving care.

'I shan't play you Beethoven!' he said, with a smile. 'An old air, perhaps, something easy.'

And holding the fiddle against his chest in the old-fashioned way, he played the Londonderry Air.

The summer light fell through the tall window into the deep room, so that the old man in black, with his white hair shining, and the fiddle clasped to him, his strong fingers stopping the strings with firm precision, looked suddenly like a figure in a painting, a mystery of contemplation.

Listening to the plaintive old tune Clem thought how different a single violin sounded from violins in consort, in chamber music or in an orchestra. The wood sang, the roughness of the gut could be heard; it was very close, it was primitive; it was not a violin at all but a fiddle, the voice of ancient dance, wedding and funeral, a noise to touch the springs below thought. And, as it had happened long ago in Brighton, she was surprised because Newman was a fiddler.

As later, they walked away from the Oratory, between the walls of the leafy gardens of Edgbaston, Augustine suddenly said, 'No wonder they don't understand him!'

'Who, Papa?' Charlotte demanded.

'Ward and Manning', said Augustine. 'Ward is the true intellectual, only at home among abstractions, and Manning is a man of action, the sort who calls drawing a distinction "hair-splitting". Curious, really, that those two should be so closely allied, or is it typical of our age, which honours brain and hand but somehow can make nothing of heart but soft sentiment? And Newman is a poet.'

'I thought you said *The Dream of Gerontius* wasn't such very good poetry', said Charlotte. Her father's comment had rankled, for she treasured Newman's poem, published that year and was jubilant because he had given her a copy and written in it for her: 'To Charlotte, who gave me a very pretty penwiper for my birthday, I wish that she may have happiness and no blots in her life!'

'It is more like a scenario for an opera than a poem', said Augustine. 'He has more dramatic than lyric power, in my opinion. He hasn't the verbal and metrical music of Tennyson, for instance, but he has what the old British bards must have had, insight, prophetic intuition, call it what you like. I say he is a seer, and no wonder that in our practical and prosaic age, as well in the Church as out of it, no one quite knows what to make of him.'

'I don't believe he thinks of himself as a seer', said Clem, amused at the idea of Newman in vatic robes.

'No, he probably thinks he's just odd man out', said Augustine. 'But I can imagine how unnerving it is for Manning, who thinks he knows just what's what, to find a retired don suddenly metamorphosing into Merlin!'

'Did the fiddle make you think of that?' Clem asked him.

Augustine smiled. 'Yes, the holy old wizard!'

That October Augustine visited the Dudley ironworks, for the first time in months, and Clem went too, to keep an eye on him, because he used to forget to do what the doctor had told him. He had had another attack this year, frightening Clem terribly, but had got over it well enough.

They went by train. Looking out of the window at the strange smoking landscape, Augustine said, 'Do you remember how angry you were with me, once, for having any part in this place?'

'I remember being very surprised', said Clem, 'because I thought of you then as a witty idle fellow, a worldly dilettante!'

'You didn't guess I was already turning into a money-grubbing manufacturer', said Augustine, with a smile. But then he stared again at the desolate region outside, where the rain poured down on the black ground, and gave a long sigh. 'The waste land', he said at last. 'I can't forget my dream, the works abandoned and death falling out of the sky like dust. How powerless we are! Even what we suppose are good and useful actions may lead to things that are not good at all, even to disasters.'

Ahead in the gloom the flare of a furnace lit the dull cloudy air.

'Don't be discouraged too much', Clem said gently. 'Everything takes time; someone has to make a beginning.'

'Yes', he said, staring out at a group of tall chimneys, their black plumes streaming away into the raining clouds. 'But there isn't much time.' Quickly, before she could answer the implications of that, he turned towards her and said, 'You women are wisest; you care about people, not causes and cases.'

Clem laughed. 'Don't you believe it', she said. 'Didn't Eve think it would be delightful to be a goddess? Perfectionism may be just as devastating on a personal scale!'

The train arrived in Dudley and the world of iron swallowed them up.

Augustine soon discovered that his long absence had been almost like a death; the concern had adjusted itself to being without him. He was no longer the awkward but important part of it he had been for so many years; he simply had no place there at all. Everyone was polite but uninterested. The only people who seemed really pleased to see him were the ones that did not 'matter', old clerks in the office, foremen who had been a long time with the firm, and so on. In spite of his cold reception, he seemed very cheerful when they left, rather to Clem's surprise.

'I'm glad I came', he told her. 'Somehow I don't feel my failure there so personally any more, though I'm sorry things haven't got done that ought to be done. I believe it's pride makes one take one's failures so hard, identifying oneself with one's work. What a pity to find that out so late!'

'Somehow I think most people don't find it out at all', said Clem. 'It certainly wouldn't have occurred to me.'

'Bless your comforting heart!' said Augustine. 'I shall kiss you for that, and the old gentleman in the corner will write to *The Times* about what goes on in railway carriages between stations.'

A few days after their return, on a cold wet Monday, Clem was down in the city alone, looking at pianos, and wondering if they could afford a better one for Charlotte, who liked playing and was more musical than either of her parents. She wrote down prices and particulars, put her notebook in her purse, and went out to meet Augustine, as they had arranged, so that they could go home together. He had been down at the factory, where he still had more influence than at the ironworks.

It was raw outside in the damp air; winter was coming, she pushed her hands deep in her muff. The streets were full of people and horses and clatter; a lamplighter was going round lighting the lamps, a chain of pale gleams in the gloom, haloed in the sooty mist that was coming down with the night. Clem always found something mysterious about this moment in a great city; the sense of thousands of living beings meeting and passing seemed to grow stronger as the houses and signs of day turned into shadow; artificial lights were like the limelight of a theatre, they pin-pointed detail so that its significance stood out from the complex rush of existence.

So she walked slowly, half in a dream, and came to a corner, and on the corner opposite she saw Augustine waiting to cross. He saw her too, and waved a sheaf of papers, smiling.

The next moment a dray, half loaded with sacks, came careering round the bend; the horses had bolted, the driver was standing up, shouting and lashing them with his whip. The swinging rattling dray mounted the pavement. Augustine jumped back, but the wall was too near. The wheel of the cart hit him, knocked him down, pushed him along in the gutter till the wild fury of the horses dragged it right over him, and the back wheel after it.

The cart thundered away down the street. Everybody screamed and shouted. Clem ran straight across the road. She could see nothing but Augustine lying there on his back in the dirt. She flung herself on her knees beside him and raised his head. She saw he was conscious; his eyes, wide open, looked at her. For a moment the shock was greater than the pain, but then she saw pain come, and she groaned because it hurt him so much. She moved him a little, so that she could hold him better, but not knowing how badly he was injured she dared not do much. People were all round her, pushing, arguing, crying, but she was hardly aware of them.

'Clem!' Augustine gasped, holding her wrist so tight that it would have hurt had she been able to notice it. 'Clem! Sorry.'

It was all he could say. It seemed to her that the pain he suffered was suffocating her; it sucked them both into a roaring darkness which swallowed up the city and the world: there was nothing but this agony and it lasted for ever.

And then terror entered it for her, because she felt him going away; his eyes, staring at her, looked blind, his fingers were dropping from her arm. She saw he was trying to speak, to say one thing more to her, but it was too hard, nothing came but gasps, the involuntary noises of a human creature broken and dying in pain beyond his control.

That was all, that was the end, and then he was still and dead, and Clem was left, groaning and weeping in the wet and the dirt, sweat going cold on her skin, holding only a body that was his, not him any more.

People came and took her away, she was taken home in a cab, she hardly knew what was happening. She found herself in her own room and looked down and saw blood on her dress, his blood. She sat down on her bed and sat there a long time before she could move.

Yet the shock did not prostrate her as the death of her child had done, twenty years ago. At first she was borne up by the feeling that somehow Augustine was still with her. She did not quite lose the sense of his presence all through the next few days, when she had to tell Charlotte and comfort her, and write to Henry. When the inquest took place, it was the same. And when at last the coffin stood before the altar at the Oratory, she could even feel a kind of peace.

She saw Newman and felt his sympathy. He tried to comfort her.

'But it does seem so pointless!' she broke out. 'You know how ill he has often been, and then the heart attacks. Why did he have to die like that, so violently? Why did God let it happen? What good could it do? And—and suffering such fearful pain at the last ... not for long, I suppose, but it seemed an eternity.'

'It is terrible for you', Newman said gently. 'It is hard to say *Fiat* when such things come. But our Lady had to say on Calvary with pain—it was like a sword in her heart— what she said in joy at Nazareth: Be it done to me according to thy word.'

'If I could only feel there was some reason in it!' Clem said. 'But it seems just senseless, meaningless, a stupid cruel accident.'

'There are no real accidents', said Newman. 'We cannot know what God means by allowing it, but we know it must be for good in the end. My dear child, he was God's good servant and God loves him. It will not be so long, perhaps, before we are all together in that blessed presence. We must pray that it may be so.'

It was Newman who sang the Mass for Augustine the next morning, though he often refused to take the funerals of his friends, for fear of breaking down in public. But when he did, his sympathy and faith were a great help to the mourners, as they were now to Clem.

She felt Augustine still very close. She went home and sat quietly at his desk, looking over papers and letters, and found one, unopened and addressed to herself. It gave her a curious feeling to open it.

'My dearest Clem, best dear Clem', she read, and began to cry. It was some time before she could read the rest. Augustine had evidently written it after his first bad heart attack and then, characteristically, had pushed it into a drawer where it was soon buried in other correspondence. It was not a long letter, and only told her what she knew already, except for one passage, which struck her very much.

'Clem, you know I don't want to leave you and the children, and I have been afraid and resentful too, and so I have been cross and difficult I know, my dear, I am sorry. But I want you to know I have come to see how wrong and ungrateful such an attitude is, since I have been given so much more happiness than I deserve, and given so little back in return. So I have tried to make an offering of my death, whenever and however it may come, and now I say

every morning, "Let it be to-day if You want it so." Since
I began doing this, dear Clem, it has made all the difference. In a way I feel I have done my dying already and
every day is a sort of holiday, an extra present. Will this
perhaps help you not to be too sad when it comes? I'm
afraid you will be lonely, but please don't be sad. How lucky
we have been, and pray for me, Clem, and somehow we
shall not really be far from each other.'

Although this letter made her cry, Clem was very glad to
have it. She read part of it to Charlotte and Henry, and
later to Newman, whom now she felt as almost the nearest
person to her—and certainly her oldest and most understanding friend.

'See what a good Christian he was', said Newman. 'What
more could he have done? This will be a great comfort to
you.'

It was a comfort to her, and so were the prayers and
Masses said for Augustine in the dark days of November;
but the weeks went by, winter came coldly on, and she
began to know what it was to live without him. The house
was a hollow shell, the whole city empty and dull because
he was not in it. Letters would still come, addressed to him;
people, ignorant of his sudden death, would inquire after
him; all his things were there, his clothes, his shoes and
hats and sticks, but he was not. She could not get used to
his absence; waking alone in the morning was every day a
shock and a renewal of grief.

But, as she was wearily aware, everyone said how well
she was taking it. Certainly she dealt with practical affairs
firmly and promptly; it was a relief to have something to
do. It was a relief, too, when she found she had to sell the
house, though Lord Gornal, in a fit of remorseful generosity, had undertaken to pay Henry's bills at Oxford. Clem

bought a small villa off the Hagley Road and she and Charlotte set about arranging it cheerfully enough.

But she could no longer live in her old content; she felt like someone turned out of her home; the earth was no more a familiar hearth but a strange place, vast, cold, a wilderness, and she was alone in it.

# III

# TWO VISIONS

# 1879: Rome

Thirteen years after Augustine's death Clem, now nearing seventy, was in Rome for the winter. She was staying with Italian friends, the daughter of that princess who had once puzzled her by saying that Augustine had vowed never to marry. She had not suspected then that his reason was only his precarious health, and that he might not have asked her if marrying her had not appeared in the nature of a rescue from the impossible situation she had made for herself in Bertram's household. Now that the first anguish of her loss was past, she liked to remember the beginning of their knowing each other, and Rome was full of memories. Yet Rome was another place from the city of her youth, the whole world was becoming a different place. Physically it was larger and less dangerous; a lull had descended after all the revolutions. In some other indefinable way it was smaller; the spirit in men was shrinking.

Clem had come to Rome to visit Henry. In his last year at Oxford his grandfather had had a stroke and Henry had become Lord Gornal. He took a double first in Greats and went straight to Bishop Ullathorne to offer himself for the priesthood, thereby giving up his share in the Firle inheritance, which had been left him on condition of his never becoming a priest. A scholar and an idealist, he found it easy to put the material temptation aside, but it caused a minor sensation in the gossip columns of the newspapers.

He was sent to study in the English College in Rome, and
after his ordination he was not allowed to return to the life
of a priest working in Birmingham, but kept on for further
study and to teach. His especial interest was in Scripture
and Hebrew, and he was at present rejoicing in the acces-
sion of the new Pope, Leo XIII, who seemed likely to
encourage the expansion of these studies, after the long years
of ultra-conservatism in the last reign.

Charlotte and her husband, Richard Fellows, brought
Clem to Rome, but they went back to their London home
and their children for Christmas. Charlotte was nearly thirty
and the photographs of her children adorned the mantelpiece
of Clem's bedroom. In spite of invitations from Charlotte,
Clem refused to move from her little villa in Edgbaston;
Charlotte teased her that the principal attraction of Birmingham was Father Newman.

'Of course it is', said Clem. 'He's my oldest friend. It's
over fifty years since we first met.'

She did not add that she had no great desire to live in
their house. Richard Fellows had been at Oxford with Henry
and at one time seemed determined to prove the bishops
right by losing his faith in the process of acquiring a modern education. However, he still went to Mass on Sundays.
He was what Clem called 'a literary man', he wrote articles
and essays for reviews, knew everybody and was very charming and talkative. Luckily Charlotte had been left a sub-
stantial sum by her grandfather, with whom she had always
been a favourite; without this her life might have been much
less comfortable and amusing.

The great news among the English in Rome at the beginning of the New Year was that the Holy Father intended to
make Newman a Cardinal. Clem was very surprised to hear
it. Three years ago Manning had been made a Cardinal by

Pius IX, but he was the head of the English hierarchy and had been an Archbishop for ten years, a great public figure, taking his part in the affairs of the kingdom, especially in the cause of the poor, both working people and the outcasts of society. But in spite of the fame of the *Apologia*, Newman remained only a priest in the obscurity of provincial Birmingham; even the Oratory of which he was the founder remained small, and without much noticeable influence. His name was well-known and his books were read, but he never succeeded in overcoming the suspicions of the Ultramontane party, for whom Ward was chief spokesman and Manning the keen guiding spirit. As far as Manning was concerned, his attitude at the time of the [First] Vatican Council, now nearly ten years ago, was absolute confirmation of his fundamental 'disloyalty'. Yet when the final definition of Papal Infallibility came it had been in a form more according to the opinions of Newman and the other Moderates than to Manning's extremism; in fact, it was this type of extremism which had made so many think definition at the time inopportune. As it turned out, the council could hardly have been more opportune; it had meant the end of all absurd exaggerations and irresponsible imputations of heresy. All the same, men like Manning could not easily acclimatize themselves to this moderation, and Clem could not imagine what he must feel at the notion of Newman, of all people, being raised to the same rank as himself. It was the Duke of Norfolk, too, who had moved in the affair, and that meant the English Catholic laity, another bitter pill for Manning.

Rumour was quite definite now that Leo had offered the hat to the old Oratorian, for whom he openly professed to have a cult, and confirmation was expected from Manning, who had started for Rome, when *The Times* played its usual part, creating a furore by publishing a statement that the cardinalate had been offered to Newman but that he had refused it.

Clem's Italian friends were shocked and astonished.

'Does your Newman feel he is above an honour from the Pope?'

Clem was sure he did not; she did not suppose him desirous of distinction, but he would hardly refuse an honour which would give his dearest projects the stamp of authority. And a couple of days later *The Times* published a report of a meeting of the lay Catholic Union, presided over by the Duke of Norfolk, which publicly acclaimed the honour in such emphatic terms that her suspicions were at once aroused. She went round to the English College to call on Henry. She found him very indignant.

'Now, Mother, look at all this! Someone is having a cruel game with our dear old Father.'

'Has he really refused?' Clem said. 'And who told *The Times* he had, if he hadn't?'

'Well, who knew about it? Who but Manning?'

'You mean he has persuaded Newman to refuse?'

'No, I don't. I have a letter from a Birmingham friend here who says old Ullathorne is in a real Yorkshire rage about it. Apparently, when the thing was first mooted Newman was very worried by the thought of having to live in Rome, but did not like to make conditions. So Ullathorne advised him to put down the reasons for his hesitation, while he himself wrote a covering letter to Manning to make it all clear. You can't imagine he failed to make it clear—not Ullathorne!'

'But Henry, then it looks as if Manning had chosen to ignore Ullathorne's explanation and take Newman's answer at its face value.'

'And the worst of it is, Newman can't do anything,' said Henry, 'because he hasn't yet had the official offer. Meanwhile the secular press in England is crowing with delight because it thinks Newman is scorning the Holy See. Listen to *Punch* on the subject.

> '"A cardinal's hat! Fancy Newman in *that*
> For a crown o'er his grey temples spread!
> 'Tis the good and the great head would
>     honour the hat
> Not the hat that would honour the head!"'

Clem laughed. 'I think that is rather nice!' she said.

'I daresay you do, Mamma, but you know it will mean all the old suspicion revived against the Father, that he's disloyal, and that sort of rubbish, that has always hurt him so much.'

'Well, we shall see when Manning comes.'

And when Manning came Clem felt she had perhaps maligned him, for he at once went to the Pope, cleared up the misunderstanding and sent a telegram to Birmingham. In a few days it was known everywhere that Newman was indeed to be made a Cardinal, but was to be allowed to go on living at the Oratory in England. At seventy-eight, less could hardly have been done for him.

Manning was staying at the English College and Clem caught a glimpse of him as he passed, a fine upright figure in his Cardinalatial scarlet, his great eyes looking out of his stern face with almost hypnotic intensity. His face haunted her long afterwards; she always forgot how strange he was.

'We must have been wrong, Henry', she said.

'I don't know', said Henry, frowning. 'It was a queer business. It wasn't all nothing, you know.'

'But he has put everything right now, and straight away.'

'Yes, when it's become plain that there's been a mistake, and what people feel about it. But suppose Ullathorne had not been involved? Suppose Newman had taken it as silently as he took the affair of the bishopric, or the Oxford business? He would have been really in the corner then, wouldn't he? The Holy Father offended and all.'

'I don't believe such a conscientious person as Manning could have done such a thing deliberately', said Clem. 'He may think Newman dangerous, but he has never censured him in public; in fact I believe he has on occasion restrained his more vociferous supporters.'

Henry considered. 'You may be right that it was not deliberate. But somehow he must have shelved Ullathorne's explanations and remembered only Newman's hesitations, and taken it as a refusal. Perhaps the wish was father to the thought. But doesn't that show how peculiar his mind can be? He is much too sure he is always right; someone told me he believes the Holy Ghost specially guides him, and you know people who think that often go mad.'

'Henry! You don't think he's going insane?'

'No', said Henry. 'But I do think he's a bit of a fanatic. It's always a danger to a powerful mind and will, even when directed to good ends, as his undoubtedly is.'

'His mind and will are no more powerful than Newman's', Clem objected.

'Well, there you are!' Henry said, smiling. 'However strongly Newman has felt about the rightness of his ideas, he has always doubted himself.'

'And now he is to be a Cardinal!' said Clem. 'I feel a little like *Punch*, I must say. Dear me, how odd to be friends with a Cardinal! I shan't know how to address him.'

Early in April she had a letter from Father Neville of the Oratory, describing some of the excitements the news had caused in England, and in particular a visit Newman had made to London to receive an address from the Irish members of Parliament, who had not forgotten his long struggles to found a Catholic university in their country.

'The Father was quite nervous beforehand', Father Neville wrote. 'He said to me, "It has all come too late. I am unused to public speeches. I am old and broken. I fear I shall break down."'

Henry, to whom she read this, remarked sadly, 'Late indeed, but not too late, I hope.'

Clem went on reading. '"On the day itself he hardly had any breakfast and when he got out of the train his stoop was very marked, he seemed to walk with difficulty, and even dropped his hat and gloves on the platform." Father Neville says he made him drink some brandy, but felt quite anxious as he saw him off. "But when he came back in the evening he walked with a firm step and erect figure. 'All is right', he announced. 'I did it splendidly.'"'

Henry laughed. 'I bet he did, too!'

'He always did find public occasions a strain', said Clem. 'Especially ones which are liable to make him cry.'

Henry smiled. 'I suppose he belongs to the Byronic era, when gentlemen were so sensitive to emotion', he said.

Clem was surprised. 'Why, aren't you now?' she said. 'Is there some cult of hardness coming in?'

'My dear little Mam', said Henry, laughing. 'You are long, long behind the times! And please remain so.'

'Well!' said Clem. 'I never thought to hear Newman called Byronic! I'm sure he would be astonished!'

'But he grew up at that time, didn't he?' Henry persisted. 'Byron must have died about the same time that he met Hurrell Froude—and Beethoven too, whose music he admires so much. Look at the way they used to go off for months to tour abroad, and called each other *Carissime*, and wept on all the appropriate occasions. We don't do that now!'

It had never occurred to Clem that this was not the only possible way to behave, but Henry evidently thought it was the manners of a past age, touching in a way, but slightly comic.

'So Newman and I are Gothic ruins, are we?' she said, smiling. 'Poor relics of the age of enthusiasm!' But still she felt it was very odd that people should not think it natural to express their affections, or to cry upon a pathetic occasion.

Newman arrived towards the end of April and at once went down with such a heavy cold that directly after his first audience with the Pope he was sent to bed by the doctor.

'He *would* get one of his colds now', said Henry, exasperated. 'Just when we want to show him off!'

The doctor kept Newman indoors till the day fixed for the ceremony of receiving the *biglietto*, but allowed him then to go to Cardinal Howard's residence, which had been lent for the occasion. Clem went, of course, escorted by Henry; practically all the English in Rome were there, and Americans too, and Roman nobility, all full of curiosity about the famous Englishman whom nobody ever saw, even, it appeared, in his own country. It was a splendid assembly, and Clem wondered how her old friend would manage an occasion like this; to receive an honour was a new experience for him, and knowing how shy he was she felt some misgiving as to what all these people would think of him, so very English, so very retiring and now so old.

Newman came in; his sudden cold had left him looking weak and remarkably pale, his face was thin and bleached; but he stood very straight, and seemed alert and calm. His hair, gone very soft and silvery now, shone when he turned his head.

'What a beautiful old man!' exclaimed Clem's Italian friends to each other. 'What a presence! Yes, he is pale, but so beautiful!'

The *biglietto* which pronounced him Cardinal was brought and read and then he had to make a speech in reply. He spoke a sentence of thanks in Italian and then apologized for going on in English. His voice was perfectly clear and steady, and he did not cough.

Clem thought it typical of him that he made this short address a kind of manifesto of his personal faith. He said he had always attacked liberalism in religion, the notion that all religions are to be tolerated only because all are no more than matters of opinion. Liberal principles, though good enough in themselves, without the sanction of faith in a supernatural revelation would lead, in practice, to a future in which governments would no longer uphold Christian morals. The religion of Christ would be regarded as 'a private luxury which a man must pay for and which he must not obtrude on others or indulge in to their annoyance'.

'It must not be supposed for a moment that I am afraid of this', he said, with all the old fire of conviction. 'I lament it deeply, because I foresee that it may be the ruin of many souls; but I have no fear at all that it can really do aught of serious harm to the Word of God, the Holy Church, to our Almighty King, the Lion of the tribe of Judah, Faithful and True, or to his Vicar.'

He stood there, thinking into the future and wondering about it. Clem found it wonderful, suddenly, to see him here in Rome, at the seat of the apostles, saying with honour what he had said so long in an atmosphere of suspicion and misunderstanding. It now seemed almost incredible that he should have been suspected of that very scepticism which he had spent his life in combating; and, as time went on, how inept and blundering the weapons of the extremists began to appear beside the delicate probing tools he used, trying to drain away the poison of destructive rationalism from a healthy use of reason, while they seemed to do little but wave the stick of mere authority on every occasion.

He speculated now on the way in which God would rescue his inheritance from the evil he had outlined, of progressive unbelief, and concluded that the Church could only go on with her own special duties in confidence and peace, 'stand still and see the Salvation of God'.

And, almost as if to prove that he had felt the same all his life, he ended with the quotation he had long ago chosen at Littlemore for *The Lives of the Saints.*

*'Mansueti hereditabunt terram*
*Et delectabuntur in multitudine pacis.'*

Later she called on him.

'You come between Cardinals', he said, smiling as he greeted her. 'One says he can read English and knows the *Apologia*! It is very polite!'

'Father, aren't you very happy?' Clem said, entirely forgetting the question of the new title.

'Yes, I am happy', he answered seriously. 'The cloud is lifted from me for ever! Now perhaps I may be able to do a little more, because my voice will carry more authority. So much needs to be done!'

Clem began to admire his robes and Newman said, 'They were all given to me. People have been so kind.'

'I like your motto', said Clem. '"Heart speaks to heart." '

'*Cor ad cor loquitur*', he said. 'Yes, isn't that what all speaking should be? Reason without love is inhuman. Love looks for the person to speak to.'

'What about Mr. Kingsley?' said Clem mischievously.

'But I never felt anything against him', he said. 'I had to show up his nonsense of course. Do you think I showed malice to him?' He looked quite worried at the thought.

'No, of course not', said Clem. 'He was much more angry with you.'

'I said Mass for him when he died', said Newman. 'That hard year.'

He sighed, and Clem knew he was thinking of the death of Ambrose St. John, some three years before. Ambrose had been his disciple and friend ever since Littlemore; it was the last and greatest loss, forty years after the death of Hurrell Froude, the friend and companion of his youth. It was the penalty to be paid for his deeply affectionate friendships, to suffer so much when one by one his friends left him, and he, who had expected death for so many years, was left alive.

'Did you like the Holy Father?' Clem said, changing the subject.

'He received me most affectionately', said Newman. 'He kept hold of my hand and asked me all sorts of questions about the Oratory. When I told him of our sad losses he put his hand on my head and said, "Don't cry!" You know, I always do cry on such occasions, it is very tiresome.' Then he added, 'He is not many years younger than I am. What a strange destiny to be called at the end of his life to the supreme charge! Yet how much he has already done!'

'That could happen to you too, now', said Clem, astonishing herself at the idea of Newman as a possible pope.

Newman laughed and then began to cough. She found herself wondering, as she left, whether this extraordinary apotheosis might not bring on him a final collapse. She heard later that his lungs were affected; the doctors were anxious and adamant. He was not allowed to do any of the things he wanted to do, to talk to the other Cardinals, and the Holy Father himself, about his favourite educational projects, or to visit on his way back the German theologian Dollinger, whom he greatly respected, and whom he hoped to persuade to submit to the decrees of the Vatican Council. Nor was he even allowed, as he went through France, to visit Sister Maria Pia, once Miss Maria Giberne and such a great help to him in the Achilli affair, now an old nun in a Visitation convent.

Clem thought it typical of the pattern of his life that even in his moment of triumph he had to be disappointed of his hopes of usefulness. But now he only said, 'We must submit ourselves to the will of God. What is our religion if we can't?'

It took him so long to get home that Clem was back before him. On the first day of July all the Catholics of Birmingham turned out, going in crowds to the station to welcome him and sending a smart carriage and pair to meet their old friend the new Cardinal. Much to everyone's surprise and delight, on the way to the Oratory he put on his red cassock and cloak and cap, and so was able to descend in all his splendour for the benefit of those who had gathered to greet him there. It was pouring with rain and he went straight to the church. After some prayers and a short ceremony he sat down on the throne they had put in the middle of the sanctuary and looked at them all, and they looked at him, so old and fine and frail, an ivory face above the brilliant red robes, a face that seemed to them all hardly to belong to the earth.

He leant his head on his hand and said, 'It is such a happiness to get *home*.'

# 1890: *Ex Umbris et Imaginibus*

Clem, an old woman not far off eighty, lay in bed, not very ill, and not very well either. 'Old age is itself a disease', she and Newman quoted to each other when they met. They did not meet often because Charlotte had at last persuaded Clem to give up her Birmingham villa and come and live with her, not in London now, but on the edge of Oxford, where Richard pursued his desultory literary occupations in an atmosphere of Morris curtains and Burne-Jones pictures. A great many people came and went, talking all the time, and Clem found this new world a little confusing after her long years in smoky and prosaic Birmingham. Listening to all this talk it seemed to her that to most of these people God had become no more than a habit of mind; he was the top of the social pyramid, even less visible than Queen Victoria, since he never came out of retirement, even for a Jubilee. Everything went along on the assumption of his existence, but most people never looked at him.

'It's a hollow world', she said to herself as she mended her grandchildren's pinafores, for she still had good eyesight and liked to be doing something useful. 'The clever people already think anything supernatural is unlikely, if not nonsense, and what clever people think to-day, ordinary people will think to-morrow. But why don't the new generations see God as real?'

Perhaps it was a failure in her own generation; they had believed, and had raised great churches and done great social works, but had their good works perhaps been more real to them than the God in whose name they were done? Not to some, she knew; never to Newman, but Newman, although people listened to him, had always been a voice crying in the wilderness, crying that knowledge would not lead to the love of God, that only in the love of God could knowledge be safely pursued by men. And power too, even to do good things, was dangerous, divorced from obedience to God. Clem found the expression of her feelings in her missal: 'Let not man prevail.'

'People are blind with the fascination of knowledge and power over nature', she said to Richard once, after some friends of his had talked themselves out and gone away. 'All kinds of nature, human as well. But what about death? God has the ultimate power, not us.'

Richard was only amused. 'I'm really interested in Beauty, not power', he said.

Clem privately thought there was no such thing as Beauty, only beautiful things, and that those who made a cult of them were no better than fetish-worshippers. But she did not say so to Richard, who, she felt, did not think it worth while to argue with an old woman of eighty, who was only his mother-in-law. She retired to her room and her thoughts.

Her room was not isolated, the nurseries were not far off, and it amused her to listen, unsuspected, to the chatter and quarrels of Charlotte's half-dozen children. She probably heard more secrets than anyone in the house, but she did not tell them.

Now it was August; was it lazy to lie in bed on an August day? Propped up on a pile of pillows she could look out of the open window away over the soft green Thames country, as she had looked so often long ago, and could sometimes hear, when the air was still, the far-off chimes of the Oxford bells, always ringing in new ears the same haunting fall. Someone had left the dressing-table mirror tipped forward and she caught sight of herself suddenly, a little shrivelled brown thing with a face like a nut, crowned with a small lace cap.

'Is that me?' Clem thought, inwardly repudiating the image.

There was a time when she had realized she was no longer young, long since, when her first child had died and death began to threaten love. 'And that is a profound moment', she said to herself. 'A getting outside, as Augustine used to say.' But after that, although everything changed, the body began to wither and fail, she felt very much the same in her inmost being. 'After all', she thought, staring with half a smile at her own reflection, 'we are immortal souls, only less of us is soul than we imagine.'

Charlotte came into the room with a letter in her hand.

'Mamma, you will be pleased to hear the dear old Cardinal is much better.'

'Better?' said Clem, surprised, because she had heard he was dying.

'Yes, quite suddenly he came into his room looking just as he did in the old days, firm and upright—"soldier-like", Father Neville says; they could hardly believe it. Even his face looked different; they had such an impression of power and calm.'

Clem said, 'Then he will die soon. People are like candles, they flare up before the flame goes.'

Charlotte laughed. 'That's a nice cheerful thing to say!' she remarked. 'Poor old man, I often wish he had died ten years ago, after he was made a Cardinal. This has been a pathetic aftermath. One of Richard's acquaintances in the journalistic world, apropos of some "Men of Today" series, was laughing at his inclusion in it and calling him "Man of Yesterday".'

'Don't they respect him any more?' Clem said, not pleased.

'Oh yes', said Charlotte. 'But he does seem to belong to a bygone age, dear old man.'

She was called away and Clem was left alone, thinking about her old friend, nearly ninety years old now.

Newman had not been taken away from his home as she had, but nearly everything else had been taken away from him.

First of all went the violin, given to Mary Church, the Dean's daughter, when her twin sister married. His fingers could not manage it any more, though till he was eighty people sometimes heard the sound of it behind his door, long after the days when he would take it out to Rednal to 'make a noise without remonstrance from trees, grass, roses and cabbages'.

His hands failed him slowly; writing away all his life, now they would not do what he wanted. He struggled for a long time to keep up his correspondence, but the act of forming the letters was so laborious he lost his train of thought. This sometimes happened too when he was talking, especially with younger men, who would muddle him with their quick turns of mind; he hated this feeling of mental fumbling, especially as he was always so anxious that thinking should go on. It happened to him once when he was visited by Ward's son: Ward was dead now; so many people had died. But in other ways the visit was a success.

'So you know what Wilfred Ward told me?' he said to Clem afterwards. 'He said his father actually wished to send him to school here, so as to absorb some of my influence. Now wasn't that good in Ward? And how very unexpected!

First of all Wilfred only made some remark as to his father's respect and affection in spite of our differences: well, you know, one cannot feel a person's affection is very deep when he spends his energy trying to prevent one's every undertaking! But to think of sending his own son here, that *is* something.'

'There was something likeable about Ward, for all his vagaries', said Clem.

Newman smiled. 'There was, indeed. You know he once said he had the mind of an angel in the body of a rhinoceros? Just like him! And it was true, in an odd way.'

Clem thought of a story which Wilfred Ward had told her. Towards the end of his life his father had dreamed he was at a dinner party, sitting next to a veiled lady whose conversation so charmed him that he cried, 'I haven't heard talk like that since I knew John Henry Newman at Oxford!'

Whereupon the lady threw back her veil.

'I am John Henry Newman!' she said.

Clem had laughed and laughed and yet she felt the inward truth of Ward's dream. For him Newman had always represented what he himself had feared and shirked, the mystery of something deeper than reason, though not antagonistic to it: intuition, the creative imagination. But Clem did not relate the dream to Newman; she felt he might not like to be identified with Ward's veiled lady.

Newman was saying, 'Ward was at least open in all he did.'

'Not like our Cardinal Archbishop', Clem remarked.

For Manning was still alive and still inexorably opposed to the idea of Catholics going to the universities. Obviously no change of policy would come till after his death; it was unlikely that Newman would ever know whether his principles had won the day or not. Manning had always retained a courteous public relationship with Newman, but Clem felt that it was done out of policy; it was hard to think otherwise when he had so consistently opposed, in private, Newman's every enterprise. Yet he had once been surprised and offended when Newman had said, in a private letter to him, that in dealing with him he never knew whether he was on his head or his heels.

'I have never altogether understood Manning', Newman said now. 'I don't think he wished me ill, but he has an iron will and was resolved to have his own way. Well! He is doing great work, especially for the Catholic schools. People will bless what he has done in time to come.'

He had expressed this appreciation of Manning's work several times in public, and last year too, on the occasion of his successful intervention in the Dock Strike. Most people never knew there were any differences between the two Cardinals. Manning wrote his thanks for this letter, and yet Henry had told Clem that this very year Manning had told a young friend, with vehemence too, that he could point out any number of heretical doctrines in Newman's books.

He could not admit that he had not been right.

Not only his hands failed Newman at last, but his eyes too. He could not see by candle-light any more and so had to wait for the few hours of brightest daylight to pursue the last tasks he set for himself. Then even the daylight began to fade away. He could no longer read his daily Office, so much loved, ever since dear Hurrell had sent him, from the grave, his Roman Breviary. When people condoled with him on this loss he would cheerfully say that the Rosary more than made up for it. The large beads would be always in his hand, material for meditation on the great mysteries. But then came the time when he could not even manage the beads any more, and that must go too. Last of all, the

Mass. He was too shaky, too blind, to say Mass any more since last Christmas. Every day he said by heart a 'dry' Mass, going through the action of the holy sacrifice in the hope that one day he might be well enough to offer it once more. But the day did not come.

Ten years of dying, Clem thought, but she did not agree with Charlotte, that it would have been better had he died in the glory of his Roman triumph. It would have been more dramatic, but Newman, like most men of creative imagination, was not himself dramatic. It seemed to her that from this long, tranquil endurance of common human extremities, God had drawn a beautiful coda to the last movement of his servant's life, when the theme he had given Newman to play was returned to him, more perfect, even, in weakness than in the day of his strength.

All through his life he had been called to give up what was dearest to him, and sometimes it had been very hard to see why, when the thing itself was good and necessary and could be done by no one else. It had been an invisible struggle, and the wounds always unseen. To accept defeat after defeat had always hurt, had sometimes been an agony; not to fight back in the wrong way always a difficulty to a courageous and sensitive spirit; and yet he had endured it, and come through without bitterness. Now, all the great conflicts were over, he was a man of yesterday, as the journalist had carelessly said, and yet there were still things left to be sacrificed, light to see, hands to work and to bless, music, so like thought to him, and the company of friends, all dying before him, one after another. Once when someone wished him *many* happy returns of his birthday, he had said, 'You don't wish me to outlive you all?'

But his well-wisher cried, 'Yes, to ninety or a hundred years, like St. John!'

'Oh, how cruel!' Newman had said. But now he had to accept what he called the special cross of his great patron, the beloved disciple.

Yet when Clem thought of him, she knew he was not sad. Early on Good Friday morning, five o'clock or earlier, people had seen him in his favourite place, kneeling before the altar of repose, where Christ in his Sacrament was hidden among the flowers till the time of his going out, till the memorial of the death that resurrected the world. As long as he could, Newman would remain watching, awake in Gethsemane. And perhaps he was praying then, as he had before: 'Remain with me till death in this dark valley, when the darkness will end. In this decay of nature, give me more grace.'

The grace he knew, but the decay he knew too; he never shirked the humiliations of nature and even at this great age his eye, dimmed to the world outside, was keen enough to detect inward weakness. Humility had become almost a habit with him, Clem thought.

Something came into her mind which had happened three years ago, when Bishop Ullathorne had at last succeeded in giving up the cares of the diocese he had served so long. Illness and old age were wearing him down, but he was still full of fight and hard at work writing memoirs of old friends and touching up his own autobiography. Clem had met him one August day, very like to-day.

'I've just been visiting Cardinal Newman', he said to her. He seemed subdued and meditative and she asked him if anything was the matter.

'No, indeed', he replied. 'You know he's just been to London again to see if anything can be done about his eyes. Of course it can't; it's just old age.'

It was one of Ullathorne's endearing habits to drop his aitches; many were the funny stories this had given rise to.

But sometimes, as now, Clem found his simplicity more moving than funny.

'I'm sorry', she said.

'So am I', he said. 'Well, we had a long cheery talk, but as I was rising to leave he suddenly said, very low and humbly, "My dear Lord, will you do me a great favour?" "What is it?" I asked. He glided down on his knees, bent down his venerable head and said, "Give me your blessing." What could I do? I could not refuse without giving him great embarrassment. So I laid my hand on his head and said, "My dear Lord Cardinal, notwithstanding all laws to the contrary, I pray God to bless you and that his Holy Spirit may be full in your heart." As I walked to the door, refusing to put on his biretta as he went with me, he said, "I have been indoors all my life, whilst you have battled for the Church in the world." '

Ullathorne paused and then said softly, 'I felt annihilated in his presence.'

About a year later one of the Dominican nuns at Stone had told Clem about a visit paid to them by both the old men.

'The Cardinal had been to London. He said it was like a glimpse of the great Babylon and made him think of the words, "Love not the world nor the things of the world." But then he added at once, "Perhaps I am too severe and think that way only because I am an old man." '

Clem had laughed at that. 'How like him!' she said. 'First the prophetic judgment, and then the gentle doubt of himself!'

'After he had blessed us we gave them some tea', the Sister told her. 'Our dear old bishop, as we still think of him, insisted on pouring out the Cardinal's tea, and even holding the cup for him to drink; he's so blind and weak now and can't move about much without help.'

Yet it was Ullathorne who died first, game to the last, muttering while the prayers for the dying were being read, 'The devil's an ass!'

Appropriately, he died on St. Benedict's day, and when someone said to him that St. Benedict might well come to fetch him to heaven that day, he began to remark on the angels with the Patriarch.

'Do you *see* St. Benedict and the angels?' they asked him, in surprise.

'Yes, I see them', said the old man from Yorkshire, quite distinctly.

Newman said, 'The best die, and here I remain, really of very little use.'

He still felt the only point of his existence was to be of use. The last time Clem saw him, the year before this, in November, he had just come back from a remarkably energetic expedition into the town, visiting a factory to try to settle some trouble between Catholic working girls and their Quaker employers. These good men were indignant when the local priest told them that the Catholics should not be required to attend the daily prayers and exposition of Scripture which preceded work. They thought him a bigot.

'Cardinal Newman would not take such a view', they said.

So Newman insisted on going down to the factory himself, and he succeeded in convincing the Quakers that their good intentions would be better served by letting the Catholics say their own prayers in a room apart.

'If I can do work such as this I am happy and content to live on', he said to Clem, almost gaily, delighted with his peace-making.

Clem said, 'Don't you remember what Augustine said once, that we don't value you only for what you do?'

'Did he? What good friends I have had', he said. 'You know what always reminds me of him? "He that could have transgressed and did not transgress, could have done evil things and did not do them ..." Someone once told me that was a poor tribute, but I don't think so. In all this world's temptations, to hold fast to the right, what could be finer? And in these days it is a hard task to find out the truth, let alone keep it. Yes, the first and second generation after us will have a dreadful time of it. Satan is almost unloosed. May we all be safely housed before that day!'

Before she went, she asked for his blessing.

'I don't know when I shall see you again, Father.' She forgot his title, she nearly always did.

'May it be soon, and in heaven', he said, and his old smile came, lighting up his face so that she saw no more the hollows and deep lines, the sunken heavy-lidded half-blind eyes and mouth drawn in, an old man's poor tooth-less jaw. His sudden and beautiful smile was like the sun coming out from behind a cloud, the thick cloud of time, a sign that beyond all the weaknesses and humiliations of the dying flesh, someone was there immortal, always himself, yet who would be a new creature in the eternal world.

'And then we shall see our dear Lord at last', he said.

Clem lay now alone, with her Rosary in her hand, and thought of that recent sudden revival, surprising his younger friends; the last of many returns to life. Always dying, always being raised up: wasn't that a Christian's life in this world? But his more than most.

What a long life, almost as long as the century, he had lived through, and all of it against the stream, against the general trends of the times, not from any mere preference for the past because it was familiar, but because he looked out from the apocalypse of the Incarnation. Of what use, then, to build a paradise for the future on the shifting sands of human nature? Men would always fail their own ideals and failure would only be the worse if they ceased to expect it. In one sense, Clem felt, Newman had always been where he was now, at the point of death, seeing history as the illustration of divine judgement; perhaps that was why he had made such a deep impression on those who had heard him, even if they thought and felt quite differently.

The door opened and Henry came in, Henry now over forty, on holiday from his work in Rome and the East, for Scripture studies claimed him more and more. She knew he had come from Birmingham.

'What's the news, my darling?'

Henry sat down and took her hand. 'Mamma, our dear Cardinal is dying.'

Although she knew it already she felt a pain in her heart.

'Charlotte said he was better.'

'Yes, just for a moment. And he got up the next morning— yesterday—but had to go to bed again. He received the Last Sacraments and most of to-day he has been unconscious. He may be gone already; it won't be long now.'

Clem found she was crying a little.

'Henry, I feel very lonely to think he is going. I wish I was good enough to go too.'

'My dear little Mam, and leave us all?' Henry said, in his affectionate way.

'I love you all', Clem said. 'But still, I do miss your dear father so much.'

They sat for a while saying nothing, but holding hands.

'Mamma, I saw Bernard at the Oratory School.'

Bernard was his nephew, Charlotte's son.

'And how is naughty Bernard? The way his mouth turns up so reminds me of Augustine.'

'He told me he wants to be a priest', said Henry, smiling. 'The Cardinal was so pleased when I spoke of it. He knew who Bernard was, he ran into him one day in the passage—Bernard did, I mean. Apparently whenever Newman met him he used to say, "Ah, you're the boy in a hurry." '

Clem smiled. 'I hope Bernard will keep his vocation', she said. 'There will be such a need of priests as never before.'

'Why, Mother?' Henry asked, looking at her.

'Because of all this failing of faith', she answered. 'When I was young it was a startling thing for a man to say he did not believe in God; it was almost unheard of. Now all the clever men go on that way. When ordinary people pick it up then everything will have to be begun again from the beginning. It will be like living in the old Roman Empire, and perhaps Bernard will have to say his Mass in the catacombs again.'

'I think you are looking on the dark side of things, Mamma', said Henry. 'Very unlike you!'

'I don't call it the dark side, I call it the bright side', said Clem. 'Didn't our Lord tell us to rejoice at the terrible signs of the world ending, because it means he is soon coming to make all things new?' And then, mindful of her old friend's example, she added with a smile, 'But perhaps I see the end too close, because I am near my own end.'

'Not yet, dear Mamma', said Henry.

'Tell me more about our Cardinal', she said.

'There's nothing to tell', Henry said. 'Nobody could die with less fuss. I saw him for a moment lying there, so still, not aware of us at all. He had an old silk handkerchief round his neck and I asked Father Neville why. He told me Newman had kept it more than thirty years, and why do you think he loved it so? Because it was given to him at the door by a poor person at a time when he himself was poor and felt he was set aside and useless.'

'Yes, he would keep any token of love', Clem said. 'You know, when he turned part of his bedroom into a chapel, after he was a Cardinal, he left all the little pictures pinned up, of his friends, dead and alive, and said his Mass in the middle of them.'

After a while Henry kissed her and went away to see Charlotte, and Clem looked out of the window again, at the long hills of afternoon, yellow and hazy with the sun, beginning now his slow retreat.

She remembered Newman once gazing intently at the picture of a dead friend and at last slowly saying, 'And now he has gone beyond that curtain.'

He was never one to make light of the mystery of death, the finality of it.

Presently as she lay there she heard a small quick tap and in came seven-year-old May, with a bunch of field flowers in her hand. Her round face glowed, her fair hair hung all in a tangle.

'Granny, I picked these for you.'

'How pretty they are!' Clem said. 'Thank you, May, very much. Put them in the glass here by me.'

'But suppose you want a drink, Granny?'

'I think they want it more than I do, don't they?'

May pushed the flowers, already drooping, into the toothglass.

'Granny, Uncle Henry says our Cardinal is going to see Jesus to-day. I wish I could too.'

'We have to wait till we're called', Clem said, smiling. 'He's had to wait a very, very long time.'

'Because he was naughty?'

Clem laughed. 'We don't know why we live the lives we live', she said. 'God is the only person who knows.'

'God does have a lot of secrets, doesn't he?' said May, jealously.

'Do you remember the Cardinal, May?'

'Of course I do!' said May indignantly. 'He said Mother made him penwipers when she was a little girl. And he said he remembered candles burning in the windows on Trafalgar Day. Granny, was that a story?'

'No, he really did. He is nearly ninety years old, you know.'

'I don't think I want to be as old as that', said May, standing by the window, swinging the tassel of the blind cord to and fro, unaware of time and what it would do to her.

'It seems long when you look forward, but not when you look back', said Clem. 'What happens to you remains and changes with you.'

'But the past can't change, can it?' May said, swinging on the bedpost, her fair hair falling back. She had no past, the whole world was her past.

'The curious thing is that it does', said Clem.

'Not in history books', said May.

'No, in people.'

May stood still, not understanding, gazing at her little brown grandmother sitting up in bed like a bird in a nest. She was suddenly restless.

'May I go now?'

'Yes, go, my Mayflower.'

The little girl laughed and ran out of the room and out of the house, into the huge space of summer air.

Clem remained inside, in the echoing shell of eighty years, looking out of the window into a world where the sun was slowly beginning to go down.

People came and went, there was tea and talking and reading, and then she was alone again, and still the sun was going down, now far down behind the trees, and light was failing in the vast caves of the sky, earth turned green and cool, birds among the shadowy leaves sang.

'And now, what is it like to die?' Clem said, gazing out on that vanishing world.

She could hear the children in the nursery, not asleep, whispering and laughing, turning and curling in their little beds, restless because it was so light and the birds outside sang so loud.

What a long century it had been, and the world had turned over, turned from a pattern of fields to a pattern of streets, the dirty, noisy, everlasting streets of the Midland towns, growing over the ground, covering the earth with bricks and stones, the houses of the machines. She heard the hooters and saw the furnaces glaring, and the smoke streaming away in funereal plumes over the desolate land. And here were people trying to live in these hard places, and people too trying to keep hold of the great new powers clever minds had released, but they were so strong some were bound to be crushed, wounded, pushed aside in the forward rush, and what would happen in the end?

'No one can tell', she murmured. 'Good and bad grow together till the end. But perhaps people have forgotten there will be an end, and perhaps it will come sooner than they think.'

She was falling into a dream, perhaps she was wandering the abandoned ground of Augustine's dream, where the dust fell and darkness came down, but where she went there were always people, people struggling and hurrying, lost in the crowd, looking for the way out, the way home, and going the wrong way, as often as not, the way everyone else went, without looking. They were like the poor mob of outcasts by the canal long ago, mocking the image of the one they did not understand; they were like the people who stood round the place of the skull and cried, 'Let him come down from the Cross and we will believe.'

But the one who must be believed before he is known remained on the Cross.

'Where I am,' he said, 'there shall my servants be.'

Some shared in the suffering of his body, some in the crucifixion of the spirit, for his heart also was broken.

Now the birds and the children were quieter, sleep was coming into their quick eyes, weighing down the small thin tongues, folding up wings and hands into the womb of darkness again, and the world turned over into shadow and dream, away from the sun.

What would happen to this nestful of children, going out into the trodden ways of the world? When God was dethroned how long would man remain in control of the divided kingdoms? But whether in ease or disaster, it would be for them, as for all men at all times, a long fight with the dark. And that, even if the sun shone.

Now the sun was going down into the deep cave where silence reigns, and dream, the region of shadow, the reverse of the bright image of reason, and how far down in those cold seas the seed of fire must plunge! But in the great town thundering in the cloudy Midlands there was a secret place, the heart of the pale red cathedral set there in a pattern of stone that did not belong to this time, nor to any time, though it echoed time past, and it was a witness of eternity among the smoking stations of the hurrying thousands, coming and to come. And there was another secret place in rather a dark house, where a very old man lay on his bed, still breathing, but not looking any more at this world where the shadows were coming down. Now he spoke no more, whose voice had made people turn round and listen and wonder where they were.

Or did he now, in the great light beyond the reach of time, its heavy seas, so bitter and so cold, did he now first begin to speak?